A PUG LIKE PERCY

Percy the pug is homeless, abandoned by his owner at an animal rescue centre on a cold winter's night. So when he finds a loving new home with Gail, his deepest wish is that this time, it's forever. Gail, meanwhile, hopes that Percy will be the little miracle that her family so desperately needs. Her young daughter Jenny is in and out of hospital, and she's only just holding things together with her husband Simon. With the family at breaking point, and Christmas just around the corner, is Percy the furry friend they've all been waiting for?

SPECI ADERS

THE ULVERSCROFT FOUNDATION
(registered UK charity number 264873)
was established in 1972 to provide funds for
research, diagnosis and treatment of eye diseases.
Examples of major projects funded by
the Ulverscroft Foundation are:-

- The Children's Eye Unit at Moorfields Eye Hospital, London
- The Ulverscroft Children's Eye Unit at Great Ormond Street Hospital for Sick Children
- Funding research into eye diseases and treatment at the Department of Ophthalmology, University of Leicester
- The Ulverscroft Vision Research Group, Institute of Child Health
- Twin operating theatres at the Western Ophthalmic Hospital, London
- The Chair of Ophthalmology at the Royal Australian College of Ophthalmologists

You can help further the work of the Foundation
by making a donation or leaving a legacy.
Every contribution is gratefully received. If you
would like to help support the Foundation or
require further information, please contact:

THE ULVERSCROFT FOUNDATION
The Green, Bradgate Road, Anstey
Leicester LE7 7FU, England
Tel: (0116) 236 4325

website: www.foundation.ulverscroft.com

Fiona Harrison has been a freelance journalist for several years, writing for a wealth of publications including the *Sunday Mirror*, *Daily Express*, *Prima*, Woman and *Grazia*. Originally from Cornwall by way of Bath, she now lives in Berkshire with her husband. When she is not writing, she can usually be found devouring other people's novels.

FIONA HARRISON

A PUG LIKE PERCY

Complete and Unabridged

ULVERSCROFT
Leicester

First published in Great Britain in 2016 by
HQ
an imprint of HarperCollins*Publishers* Ltd
London

First Large Print Edition
published 2018
by arrangement with
HarperCollins*Publishers* Ltd
London

A catalogue record for this book is available from the British Library.

ISBN 978–1–4448–3551–9

Published by
F. A. Thorpe (Publishing)
Anstey, Leicestershire

Set by Words & Graphics Ltd.
Anstey, Leicestershire
Printed and bound in Great Britain by
T. J. International Ltd., Padstow, Cornwall

This book is printed on acid-free paper

*For Chris, the only human version
of Percy I know*

1

My eyelids felt heavy, and the pull of sleep prevented me from opening them, despite the early morning autumn sunshine streaming through the windows. Instead, I snuggled deeper into the blue cashmere blanket my owner Javier had bought for me. I screwed my eyes tight, happy to enjoy a few more minutes in bed with the blanket I loved, and wriggled around until I was comfortable. Yet no matter how hard I tried to return to the land of nod, something felt wrong.

Blinking my eyes open with renewed determination, I scrambled onto all four of my paws and looked around. With a start I realised the room I found myself in was completely unfamiliar. Where was the sofa I liked to nap on? The television I liked to watch *Tom and Jerry* on? The glass coffee table I always ran into, and the thick multicoloured rug I liked to roll around on? Why was I not at home?

My heart pounded with fear as I glanced over each of my shoulders to find I was alone in a small room, containing my bed and an old basket of toys, while on the other side stood an old easy chair. My food and water bowls were near the door and an old sheepskin rug lay on the floor. Hearing the sound of feet scuffling outside the room, I turned my head and peered through a large Perspex window that looked out onto a busy corridor and saw it was teeming with excited dogs and humans in green uniforms.

All too quickly, the memories flooded back as fast as a speeding greyhound and my entire body trembled as I realised I was as far away from home as it was possible to be. I remembered only too vividly that I had been dumped in a dog shelter by Javier but had no idea why. Was it because I had been bad? Did Javier no longer love me? Was I mean to another dog? Or worse, had I committed the ultimate dog sin and bitten a human for no apparent reason?

Filled with despair, I slumped back onto my bed, flung my paws over my eyes and tried to understand why Javier had left me here to rot like so many other good dogs before me. I knew the tails of the forgotten, which was what we in the dog community called dog shelters like this one, was for hounds that were unwanted. It was the home for waifs, strays and the unlovable. Was that me now? Was I unlovable? I had adored my owner Javier, and I thought he loved me too.

We had been together for three years, since I was a small pup, and I had been incredibly happy. I thought he was too. What had happened to make him fall out of love with me? I let out a howl of despair. I would do anything to turn the clock back and undo whatever it was I had done to make Javier leave me in this place. I loved him, he was my owner, my entire world and, quite simply, I would die for him.

I felt a fresh wave of horror as I realised that now Javier had left me here I would never see him again. The thought of a life without my precious owner and best friend, as I came to think of him, was terrible. As the image of his handsome, Brazilian face appeared in my mind, I howled. I loved him, I missed him, and a life without him was unthinkable.

I thought back to my behaviour over the past few days and weeks and was unable to pinpoint anything I had done that was particularly naughty. In fact, I thought I had been good, ensuring I refrained from sitting on Javier's girlfriend, Gabriella's clothes, not making a loud noise when I chewed my kibble or bothering either one of them for too many walks to the park.

I howled again and suddenly heard the door to the room open, and footsteps pad gently towards me. I could tell from the scent of whoever it was that a human had entered. But who they were or what they wanted held no interest for me. I wanted to remain here, with my paws flung over my eyes for ever and nothing anybody could say or do would change my mind. As the human reached my side, I became aware of them bending down, their jean-clad knees brushing against the side of my face. There was a pause, and then I felt soft fingers, which had to be a woman's, run over my head and along my back.

'How are you feeling today, Percy?' she asked gently.

'Horrible,' I yelped, paws still clamped over my eyes.

'I'm not surprised,' she said gently, 'you've had a terrible thing happen to you. It's bound to be a shock, but I'm here to help you cope with it all, I promise.'

'I don't believe you,' I woofed again. 'There's nothing you can say or do that will make any of this better. My owner doesn't love me any more and I miss him. I will never be loved ever again.'

'Oh Percy,' the woman sighed, 'I promise, you will be loved again. And we will make sure of it. My name is Kelly, you may not remember, but I checked you over when you were dropped off last night by your old owner.'

'I remember,' I whined quietly.

'Now, I'm going to make it my own personal mission to ensure I find you the very best family to take care of you. People, who will love you for ever and ever,' Kelly said gently.

It was unusual to find a human who understood what we dogs were trying to communicate with our barks, but Kelly, unlike Javier or Gabriella, had understood straight away. There was something about this woman's voice I found soothing, and I prised my paws from my eyes to get a better look at her. She had a warm, open face, and was small, with a button nose and strands of grey hair intertwined with her blonde mane. Kelly was smiling down at me and I sensed she had an air of someone who had seen and done it all. Just being around her made me feel relaxed.

She continued to stroke my soft fur, and bent her face close to mine. 'You won't have to wait long for a home, Percy. Everyone loves pugs, you'll see.'

I licked her cheek in response. I knew she was just trying to be kind. After all, if that were true then Javier would never have abandoned me.

'I've got a secret I want to tell you, Percy,' she continued. 'I've always had a real soft spot for pugs, and I've been crazy about you ever since you arrived yesterday. I'm going to make sure someone very special adopts you, because I want you to have the happiest of lives.'

She scooped me up with her soft, warm hands, then gently covered my little face with kisses. Her lips felt like tender butterflies fluttering gently across my fur and I wrinkled my face with pleasure before Kelly put me down.

'I know you've had a shock. Being abandoned by your owner isn't nice, but I want you to understand that while I'm out there searching for a very special family to look after you, I will be the one taking good care of you, do you hear me?' she said in her silky, smooth voice.

I barked a little more enthusiastically than I had since I arrived — I wanted to let her know I had heard her loud and clear. I liked the sound of Kelly looking out for me.

'Now, I like to make sure my special friends have a good time while they're here, so I encourage playtime as much as I can,' she said with a chuckle, as she walked towards the large window and beckoned me to follow. The window overlooked a large yard at the back of the shelter, which I had seen briefly when I arrived, but I had felt so bewildered then that I had been unable to take anything in properly. I peered out and saw several other dogs playing with humans in green uniforms like Kelly, while others were sitting around chatting to each other. They did not look even a little bit sad. In fact, as I watched one particularly overexcited cockapoo run wildly from one end of the square to the other, sending the fallen crisp leaves flying in his wake, I noticed he seemed positively joyful.

'You see how some of them are running riot?' Kelly asked, once more reading my mind. 'Well, that'll be you too a bit later on. You'll have cuddles, walks, runs in the yard and friends to make. It won't be so bad, and I'll look after you.'

I rubbed my head against her legs in gratitude. Just being around Kelly was making me feel stronger and although I still desperately wanted to go home, I had a feeling that with Kelly on my side, she really would look after me as if I were her own.

'Now I'm going to leave you to it as it looks as though your neighbours, Barney and Boris, are back.' Kelly grinned as she ruffled my ears once more. 'I'll see you a bit later.'

As Kelly waved me goodbye, I saw a young West Highland terrier walk into the room on my left and a fairly fed-up looking elderly beagle enter the room on my right. I padded over to the big sheets of clear plastic that divided my room from each dog's and introduced myself with a welcoming bark.

'I'm Boris,' the Westie replied.

'And I'm Barney,' the beagle explained mournfully.

I noticed Barney was still wet from the bath he'd obviously been given, with a sore-looking scratch on his belly. He flopped on the floor in front of me, looking decidedly sorry for himself.

'How did you get that scratch?' I barked curiously.

'Trying to get through a cat flap,' he replied mournfully, his long ears making his sad brown eyes look even more doleful. 'I wanted to see if I could move into the house next door when my owner died. But when I got stuck in the flap, the neighbours brought me here.'

I shook my head in amazement. Beagles were supposed to be intelligent, and this was not one of the smartest moves I had heard a beagle make. Still, I realised this was not the best time to tick Barney off. Instead, I barked sympathetically and gave him the once-over. When his tummy had healed, no doubt he would be a handsome fellow and snapped up. I wasted no time telling him so.

'Do you think so?' Barney asked, brightening a little, his sad brown eyes looking slightly less miserable.

'Oh, yes,' I said knowledgeably, realising immediately that Barney could be a lovely-looking dog with a bit of TLC. 'They'll be beating the door down to take you in.'

'Percy's right,' Boris barked loudly through the plastic. 'You won't have to wait long for a home.'

Barney's tail thumped against the floor excitedly. 'Awww, really?' he asked. He paused for a moment, then looked at me. 'Well, I don't think it will be long before someone takes you in either. Everyone loves pugs, don't they?' Barney said, echoing Kelly's earlier sentiments.

Boris slumped to the floor. 'That's true as well. You two will be snapped up and I will be all alone for ever.'

'Of course you won't,' Barney reasoned.

'I will,' Boris barked. 'I'm a bad dog, my old owner Sam and his wife Emma could never be bothered with me. I was always getting under their feet or in their way.'

'I'm sure you weren't,' I replied. 'So many dog owners think that all we need is a bowl of food, and a couple of walks. They don't realise we need company, affection and — '

'Love,' Boris interrupted. 'My owners never

loved me. They thought they did, but when it came down to it, I was just too much trouble for them.'

I felt a pang of sympathy for the young dog. Barely out of his teens, he was just a little younger than me, and despite my own fears about the future, I wanted to make Boris feel better.

'You've seen how lovely Kelly and the rest of the carers are here. She will love you, play with you and listen to you, all while helping find you a good home.'

'She'll be lucky,' Boris barked darkly. 'My owner Sam used to tell me I was such a pain, nobody else would want me.'

I growled under my breath. This Sam appeared to be unfit to lick Boris's paws, I thought darkly.

'You're not a pain,' I barked in anger. 'You're a lovely dog, Boris.'

'Don't pay any attention to your old owners,' Barney added. 'Any family would be lucky to have you.'

Boris rolled his eyes. 'Easy for you to say, you're both a lot cuter than I am. Nobody will want me.'

'But it wasn't always like that,' I protested. 'I felt as bad as you do now when my old owner Javier dropped me off here yesterday.'

'What was he like?' asked Barney.

I sighed and flopped to the floor, unsure where to start. When I thought of Javier, I felt wretched. Even though he had dumped me here, I still worshipped him and would do anything he asked if he walked through the doors right now.

'Javier was a doctor from Argentina, who liked the finer things in life and he treated me like a king with the best food, treats and toys money could buy,' I told Boris gruffly. 'We lived in a flat in Battersea overlooking the River Thames, after he adopted me from my mum three years ago when I was a few months old.'

'Sounds like a nice life,' Boris barked appreciatively.

'It was,' I woofed. 'I would nap when he was working, then when Javier returned, he would drink a cold beer straight from the fridge, before taking me out for a walk in the park, where we would chat and I would chew tennis balls. If Javier was working long hours, then his girlfriend, Gabriella, would take me instead, but it was never the same as she couldn't wait to get our walk over with.'

'So what happened?' Boris asked, interrupting my trip down memory lane.

'I was watching television one night,' I barked gloomily, 'when I saw they were both filling their suitcases with their belongings.

11

Once the cases were filled, Javier picked me up, gave me a cuddle, told me he loved me, but that he and Gabriella had to go home to Buenos Aires, as their visas had run out.'

'Why didn't they take you with them?' Barney quizzed reasonably.

I shrugged my little shoulders and felt my bottom lip tremble. I had wondered the same thing as I had barked my throat out at the time, begging him to take me, but Javier ignored my pleas. Instead, he gathered my things together and then called a taxi and dropped me off here.

'That's horrible,' Boris said quietly. 'You must have been terrified.'

Sadness coursed through my fur as I remembered watching Javier walk away and how my little body had pulsed with fear as I realised he really was going to desert me in a shelter, somewhere in the far reaches of South London. My wrinkled cheeks burned with shame as I recalled how I had barked at him not to leave me, that I was sorry for whatever I had done and that I would be a good boy, if only he would come back for me and take me with him to Argentina. But my undignified and desperate barks had fallen on deaf ears as my former master climbed into the back of the taxi, without so much as a backward glance.

'I was terrified,' I barked quietly. 'I still am.'

In fact, I was so terrified I had not yet confessed my greatest fear to anyone here, not even to Kelly. That even if she did find someone who would love and adore me, there was nothing to stop them leaving me too. Who was to say that they would keep me for ever and ever? Javier had taught me one thing, that sometimes love was not enough.

2

As the days turned into weeks and most of the friends I had made left the shelter for pastures new, I wondered if Barney, Boris and Kelly had in fact been wrong and that not everyone loved pugs. Over the last few days, I had watched Frank the spaniel walk away with a lovely young couple from Cheam; Maggie, a Weimaraner, disappear with an elderly gentleman from Hove; and even Daisy the Highland terrier, with flatulence evil enough to clear a room, adopted by a seemingly lovely family from Chelmsford.

Now it seemed Barney was all set to leave me too, as he had hit it off with a young single lady from Clapham, who was now here to take him home. As the woman bent down to fondle his ears, Barney whined and wagged his tail with such excitement he made the floor vibrate beneath me. Of course I was happy Barney had found someone to give him the love he deserved, but deep down I was sorry it was not me.

As Barney walked away with his new owner, he shot me a hopeful stare. 'A special family are coming for you, I promise.'

I watched him walk through the large glass doors that opened up to the exercise yard and the outside world beyond. Deflated, I trotted back to my squishy bed, and dived under my soft blanket. All I wanted was to shut everyone out. Even though it was Saturday and I knew the shelter would be full of prospective families, I was not in the mood to perform. Over the past few weeks, I had done all the cute pug-like things you could imagine to try and get a family to take me. I had uncurled my tail to give it a little waggle, exposed my belly to show I loved a stroke and even stared longingly with my big brown eyes at passing children. Of course I had received my fair share of cuddles and, as my time here grew longer and longer, I had even stopped moaning when the bigger children pulled my tail or stepped on my delicate paws. But while everyone had been kind enough to shower me with love, I had heard them talk in hushed tones about the health problems my short face would cause, along with worries about gassiness.

I was broken-hearted. I had lost my home, my owner, and hope was deserting me. Kelly had done her best to cheer me up, by telling me how lovable I was, but I knew that was untrue. I no longer felt like putting a brave face on my little snout. Instead, I shut my eyes and dreamed of a different life. Little walks in big green parks, tummy tickles with a loving child, snuggles in bed with a cuddly mum and man-to-man chats with the dad of the house in a shed at the bottom of the garden.

But those thoughts seemed little more than fantasy to me now, and I closed my eyes tightly, wanting nothing more than to forget the world. My time here at the tails of the forgotten had been fine, nice even, but it was no substitute for a real home. Seeing all my friends apart from Boris adopted left me with a lot of questions, namely, what was wrong with me?

Since revealing the story of how I had arrived at the shelter with Boris and Barney all those weeks ago, I had been unable to forget how Javier had ignored the way I begged him to take me with him and had gone over and over all the things I could have done to upset him. I knew Gabriella had never been particularly fond of me and perhaps that was the reason he had not fought to take me to Argentina, to start a new life.

Doubt nagged away at me as I realised that even if I found a family who would take me in, there could still be one person who disliked me enough to send me away again.

There were so many reasons a dog could end up at the tails of the forgotten, I wanted to howl in despair. It seemed to me we pooches were doomed no matter how adorable or well behaved we were. Feeling sad, I did what I always did in a crisis and gave in to the land of nod, hoping against hope that when I woke there would be a change in fortunes.

* * *

'Oh, isn't he gorgeous,' a woman's voice murmured, gently waking me with a start from my slumber.

Turning around, with sleepy eyes, I looked at the woman peering through the glass. Short and thin, her brown hair fell in soft waves around her shoulders and her blue eyes radiated a kind of warmth and love I had not seen in a long time. I felt a sudden sense of hope and, glancing up at Kelly, who was standing with a smile a mile wide next to this woman, I shook the sleep from my eyes, got out of bed and trotted over to the glass to let out a little bark of welcome. The woman grinned as she crouched down, her red-wool coat pooling on the floor behind her. She tapped excitedly on the glass.

'Hello, young man.' She grinned before turning to look back up to Kelly. 'I think I'm in love. Can I go and see him, please?'

Kelly laughed, fishing into her pocket for one of the treats she knew I loved. 'Of course. This is Percy,' Kelly explained to the woman as I snaffled the treat from her warm palm. 'He's very special to me — handsome, gorgeous and bursting with love, he's my idea of a perfect man.'

After picking me up, Kelly gave me a comforting squeeze and invited the woman to sit on the old easy chair in the corner. When she was settled, Kelly placed me gently on the woman's lap and tickled me under my chin.

'This is Gail,' Kelly explained to me. 'We've just been talking nineteen to the dozen about you, because like me, Perce, she's a woman with excellent taste who loves pugs.'

I barked appreciatively. This was the most promising news I had received since I had arrived. Shuffling around in Gail's lap, so I could get a proper look at her, I drank in her appearance. She appeared to be in her late thirties, her skin was creamy white, and the few freckles on her nose gave her a cute, vulnerable appearance. But the soft lines around her twinkling blue eyes and the grey circles that were forming underneath told me life had not always been kind and that perhaps, like me, she was tired of battling to find her place in the world. I liked her immediately and, as Gail looked back at me, her blue eyes teeming with warmth, I felt a whoosh in my tummy and a pang in my heart. I sensed Gail was a woman who was simply bursting with love and, as I let out another little bark of excitement, she tickled me gently behind the ears and laughed.

'How would you like to go for a little walk with me, Percy?' she asked, gently. 'I'd really like to get to know you better.'

I rubbed my head against her arm with gratitude, to show my enthusiasm.

'I think that means yes,' Kelly said, holding out my lead.

As Gail slipped it onto my collar, I walked obediently alongside her and out into the exercise yard. As I felt the chilly air on my face, I looked up at Gail and uncurled my tail so it could wag freely with unbridled joy. Nobody else had asked me to walk with them, and I was determined Gail would like me as much as I liked her.

'So, Percy, Kelly has been telling me all about you,' Gail said in a soft, soothing voice. She wrapped her scarf tightly around her neck as the wind gathered speed. 'It sounds as though you've had a bit of bad luck.'

'You're not wrong,' I barked in reply, all the while trotting eagerly alongside Gail.

'I know what it's like,' she replied. 'My

family has had its fair share of bad luck too. It's not fair, is it?' Stopping at a bench, Gail sat down, then placed her warm hands around my little body to sit me on her lap. I breathed in the scent of her floral perfume and relaxed against her legs, the day's cool temperatures making me shiver. In the three weeks since I had arrived, the weather had taken a decidedly wintery turn and I was enjoying the chance of some human warmth and comfort. 'I'd love to take you home, Percy,' she said as she gently stroked my head. 'I don't think I'm imagining things when I say I think we've developed a bond in the short while we've been together.'

I snuggled deeper into her lap, to show her just how right she was.

'The thing is, boy — ' Gail laughed gently ' — once you've heard a bit about my family, you might feel you wouldn't want to live with us so it's only fair I tell you what we're like.'

The calm, relaxed and happy feeling I'd been enjoying since Gail had arrived left me.

'My husband, Simon, and I have been together twenty years,' she said nervously. 'We met at a party, shortly after he moved to Devon, and we've never spent a day apart. When we married fifteen years ago, we were blessed with a beautiful little girl, Jenny, who's twelve now.'

At the mention of her daughter, I saw Gail's eyes brim with tears. My little heart went out to her, and I gingerly rested my warm paw on top of her hand, urging her to carry on. The gesture wasn't lost on Gail, who looked at me fondly, then buried her face in my fur.

'Jenny's beautiful, kind, loving, and we adore her,' Gail continued, her voice thick with emotion, 'but she has a heart condition, and on top of that, we've recently moved from Devon back to London. Well, I say back, Simon's a plumber and originally from here so has lots of old pals, but I'm lonely with no job or friends and things are a little bit strained between us, if I'm honest.'

As she finished, Gail gently raked her fingers through my fur and looked at me expectantly. Meeting her eyes, I saw they were filled with genuine warmth and I tried to make sense of everything she had just said. All I had ever wanted was to be a part of a loving family, and it was clear that Gail needed love and care as much as I did. Even though we had only spent an hour or so together, I already felt bonded to this woman who had showered me with affection since we met.

But Javier's actions had cast doubt in my mind. I wanted to go home with Gail, I wanted to start again and find love, but I was scared. What if it was all too good to be true? What if this new family forgot about me, what if they decided to move back to Devon and refused to take me with them because Gail hated her new life in London? I was unsure what to do and so I burrowed my way deeper into Gail's lap, hoping to find the answers there. Nuzzling my face against her hands, I felt the love flood through her fingertips. I realised that nobody knew what the future may hold, but that I was already very attached to Gail. In that moment I tried to convey how much she already meant to me and how much I would be there for her family.

Gail was as tuned into me as I'd hoped. 'Well, Percy, you're on.' She grinned, setting me down on the ground and crouching down to look into my eyes. 'I think you and I will make a very good team. And although we don't know how things will work out, I can promise you one thing: I'll love you more than any other pug has been loved, if you let me.'

'I'd like that,' I barked in reply.

Walking back inside, I felt so happy it was all I could do not to dance a little jig. Finally, I was going to be part of a family again, someone wanted me and I wasn't going to let them down. As Kelly led Gail into the office to fill out some paperwork, I bumped into Boris, who was being led back inside after playtime.

'You look like the cat who got the cream,' he barked happily.

'More like the dog who got the big juicy bone,' I replied. 'I've been adopted.'

Boris sat on his haunches, raised his right paw to signify a human high five. Tongue lolling joyfully, I raised my left paw, remembering how Javier had taught me the trick, and propelled it forwards to meet the Westie's.

'Well done, buddy, I couldn't be happier for you,' he barked.

'Thanks. She's the nicest lady in the world,' I replied. 'When we met we just clicked and I knew she was the one for me.'

'Didn't Barney and I tell you there was someone special on their way?'

I nodded. 'You did, Boris, and I should have believed you. Now we just have to find you a nice new family.'

Boris shrugged his shoulders. 'You're a very special dog, Percy. You deserve be taken in by someone lovely. If I'm half as lucky I'll be one lucky Westie.'

'Well, you're lucky, and lovable, Boris,' I barked sympathetically. 'And until you find a nice new owner who will shower you with love, I want to prove to you just how special you are. Come with me.'

Excited, I trotted down the corridor back to my room, Boris following eagerly behind me, continually asking what was going on. However, I refused to tell him until we reached my quarters. With the door wide open, I went straight inside and saw just what I was looking for. I hadn't arrived with that much apart from a few toys. All that was left was my prized blue cashmere blanket and my bed. Boris had been unfortunate to receive a hard start in life with owners like Sam and Emma, and I wanted him to realise love was out there waiting for him, if he would only give it a chance. In the short time we had been together, I had become quite fond of the Westie and, looking at the blue blanket that had once meant so much, I padded towards it. I bit into the soft material and then dropped it in front of Boris.

'Winter's just around the corner and this will keep you warm at night,' I barked.

Boris looked at the blanket in amazement. 'But that's yours. Javier gave you that, don't you want it to remember him by?'

'I want you to have it as something to remember me and our friendship by,' I woofed truthfully. 'It's time for a new start, for all of us.'

3

I pressed my body against the sheet of cold, clear glass that separated me from the outside world and watched the comings and goings of the shelter. For the past two hours, I had carefully observed every car that had pulled up outside in the pouring rain, my fur standing on end in excitement as I waited expectantly for Gail.

Kelly told me yesterday that she had visited Gail's family and thought their home would be perfect for me. Since then I had been unable to stop thinking about my new family and had spent most of the night curled up in bed feeling excited one minute and anxious the next about my new life.

Now, as I watched a woman that definitely was not Gail get out of a red sports car, my heart banged against my chest in fear. Where was she? What if Gail had changed her mind? What if she no longer wanted me after all? I let out a growl of anxiety, waking Boris from his slumber.

'They'll be here, stop getting so excited,' he barked sleepily.

'But what if they don't come?' I asked in panic.

'What would happen between yesterday and today to make them decide they don't want you any more?' Boris asked sensibly. 'Now settle down so you're all nice and relaxed when they come to get you.'

I knew Boris was right, so reluctantly I returned to my bed, shut my eyes and tried to focus on anything else apart from going to a new home. But every time I tried to distract myself by thinking about my favourite things like chewing tennis balls or eating cheese, I imagined what it would be like if it was Gail throwing me a ball, or Gail feeding me treats. It was no good, my mind was in overdrive, and lying still was unhelpful. I got up from my basket, scampered back to the window and pressed my face against the glass — at least this way I felt I was doing something.

Suddenly, a silver car pulled up outside the front of the shelter and a middle-aged man wearing a green parka and jeans got out of the passenger side. Aside from his salt and pepper hair, I could just make out what looked like a pair of kind chocolatey eyes as he quickly walked to the rear car door and opened it. As the door swung open, a small girl, with pale skin and long dark brown hair that hung to her waist, clambered out, holding on to the man for support. Peering down, I saw she was the spitting image of

Gail and held my breath. Was it them? Had my family come for me? I shuffled my paws in eagerness, my claws tapping on the cool ground as I waited for the driver to reveal themselves.

I did not have to wait long, as the door opened and a woman with soft, wavy brown hair emerged — Gail.

'They're here, they're here,' I yapped, shuffling my paws even faster against the ground as I drank in my new family. One thing was certain, they looked happy to be here. The little girl, Jenny, was smiling and chattering away excitedly as she looked around at the shelter, while Simon looked animated and engrossed in everything his daughter was saying. As for Gail, she looked lovelier than ever, dressed simply in jeans and boots, and her now-familiar red-wool coat, buttoned to the neck. She put her arm around her daughter, smiling broadly, and kissed her hair. Gail then raised her head from Jenny's and lifted her face to meet mine. Catching sight of me at the window, she waved and smiled, then nudged Jenny and Simon. They followed her gaze and, when they realised it was me, Jenny did the same as her mother, and I jumped up and down, wanting to give them my own version of a wave.

Watching them hurry through the rain towards the door to come and get me, my heart swelled with affection for this lovely new family that were going to be all mine.

'Told you they'd come,' Boris said sleepily. 'You worry too much, Percy.'

'I wasn't worried,' I barked, scampering my way back to the window that separated us.

'Course you weren't,' Boris teased as I scampered around my room checking I had all my belongings together.

Hearing the sound of footsteps coming down the corridor, I hurried towards the door waiting for it to open. Within seconds, I heard the familiar squeak of the hinges against the door jamb, and then Kelly's smiling face appeared.

'Look who I've brought to see you.' She walked towards me, grinning, and picked me up in her familiar way for a cuddle.

Holding me tightly in her arms, I caught the scent of her floral perfume as she turned me around to greet the family standing in the doorway. My eyes jumped from one face to the next and I didn't know which one to lick or bark at first. Thankfully Jenny made the decision for me as she rushed across the floor towards me.

'Mum, he's so handsome,' Jenny cooed, raising her hand to pat my head, before hesitating. 'Is it okay?' she asked Kelly, clearly not wanting to take anything for granted.

'Of course it is,' Kelly replied. 'Our Percy loves a good stroke, don't you, boy?'

'Absolutely,' I barked encouragingly, craning my head upwards to meet Jenny's palm.

As she affectionately placed her fingers on my head and ruffled my ears, I raised my big brown eyes to meet her smaller blue ones. Just like her mother, love and warmth radiated from every inch of her, and as she beamed at me, I hoped we would be the best of friends.

'Come on then, Jen, don't hog Percy all to yourself, I want to say 'hello' to my new mate,' Simon said, appearing at Jenny's side.

Just like his daughter, he had a welcoming, warm way about him, but his eyes had a spark of hesitation in them. I wondered if Simon was shy and, wanting to say hello, I pushed my face into his warm, calloused hand and let him tickle my neck.

'Welcome to the family, Percy,' Simon whispered. 'It's about time I had another man in the house — these women are always ganging up on me, so us fellas have to stick together.'

'You can rely on me,' I barked earnestly, as I pulled my snout away. Looking happily up at him, my heart lurched with joy, as a familiar face appeared at his side. With her beautiful chestnut mane and happy grin, I knew I was where I belonged.

'Hello, you,' she whispered. 'I've been so excited about bringing you home today I haven't stopped talking about you.'

I nuzzled against her, and remembered the simple pleasure of her warm fingers against my fur. I barked appreciatively. Gail was everything I remembered her to be.

'He's all yours now,' Kelly said gently, as she stroked the top of my head and kissed my fur. 'Let's get him downstairs for a last check-up, and then you can take him home.'

Kelly placed me in Gail's warm arms and I felt my brown eyes moisten as I glanced up at Kelly. She had been my lifeline here and I would never forget the care and kindness she had shown me.

'Thank you,' I yapped at her quietly.

'You're welcome, Percy.' Kelly smiled, her eyes meeting mine as she kissed my black fur one final time.

Safely stowed in Gail's arms, I gave my room one final glance. Catching sight of Boris, who was looking at me with joy in his eyes, I barked my goodbyes.

'Take care of yourself,' I told him. 'Stay strong, and remember your family are coming for you.'

'I will, Percy, and you,' Boris barked in reply. 'Keep in touch.'

Outside, it felt strange to be in this part of the shelter again. As my paws scurried across the cold concrete I realised I hadn't been in a car since Javier abandoned me several weeks ago. My fur stood on end at the memory of that dark day. But now, I realised this new journey in four wheels would be a very different and happier experience.

As Gail unlocked the back door, I saw she had arranged a special dog carrier that was secured with seat belts for me. Usually I hated travelling in anything so restrictive, preferring to roam free in the back, but looking up at Gail's face, so full of concern, I knew she was only doing what she thought was best. Reluctantly, I scrambled inside, and as Gail checked I was safe and secure, she bent down and kissed my head.

'You okay in there, boy?' Gail whispered, her lipstick smudged from where she'd given me a smooch.

I woofed at her encouragingly. Despite my reservations, the carrier was actually quite comfortable thanks to the sheepskin blanket Gail had thoughtfully placed inside. Best of all, the sides were open, so when Jenny slid into the car next to me, she was able to run her fingers over my fur reassuringly as Gail and Simon got into their seats at the front.

As Simon clunk-clicked his seat belt into place, Gail started the engine. Checking her mirrors as she manoeuvred out of the car park, she caught my eye and smiled. 'We're about forty minutes away, just out in west London, but it's definitely not the posh bit, I'm afraid.'

'She's right, Percy,' Simon called over his shoulder to me. 'It's definitely not the posh bit, and I hate to break it to you, but it'll be a lot longer than forty minutes, given the way Gail drives.'

'Dad!' Jenny fired, eyes furrowed in frustration. 'Stop being so mean all the time about Mum's driving.'

'Good point, Jen,' Gail replied. 'In fact, Simon, you're welcome to drive us home yourself, if you don't like the way I do it.'

'Come on, love. I spend all week driving around London; the last thing I want to do at the weekend is to get behind the wheel,' Simon protested.

Gail's gaze never left the road, but her tone was clear. 'Well then, stop having a go at me about it. You were bad enough on the way in.'

'It was only a joke,' Simon hissed. 'You need to get a sense of humour.'

'And you need to get a sensitivity chip,' Gail retorted. 'You're ruining this special moment with Percy.'

I looked over at Jenny. The little girl's eyes were downcast and fixed firmly on her lap as her parents exchanged words. She did not appear to be crying, but she was obviously upset at the fact the happy atmosphere we had all enjoyed just moments earlier had become frosty. I glanced at Gail and caught her reflection in the rear-view mirror. Her mouth was set in a determined line while Simon had turned his head and was looking firmly out of the passenger window.

I wondered if this was evidence of the strain Gail had mentioned. More than anything, I wanted to help, this was supposed to be a happy day not a sad one. Observing Jenny, an idea formed and I remembered one of the tricks Barney had taught me to try to get new families to like me. Rolling onto my back in the carrier, I exposed my tummy and yelped, a bit like a human baby.

Jenny looked across and her face creased into a delighted smile as she saw my trick. 'Mum! Percy thinks he's a baby.' Not waiting for an answer, she reached her hand into my carrier and tickled my belly, just as I hoped she would. 'Oh, his tummy's so soft,' she squealed.

Simon looked around to see what all the commotion was about, and laughed. 'Oh,

Percy, I can see you've already got a way with the women. You're going to have to teach me a thing or two.'

'What's he doing?' Gail begged as she navigated a particularly busy junction. 'I can't see.'

'He's rolling over, pretending to be a baby,' Jenny explained, her hand still tickling my belly, much to my delight.

Quickly glancing around, Gail burst out laughing as she saw me. 'Percy!' she exclaimed. 'Oh, my goodness, you're adorable.'

'He's more than adorable,' Simon said, chuckling. 'He's bloody brilliant. Look at you women going all mushy; Percy's going to be the ace up my sleeve against you two.'

'No, he isn't.' Jenny giggled. 'He's going to be my friend.'

'And mine,' Gail said, meeting my eyes as I rolled over and got back on my feet.

Looking around at the smiling faces, I was delighted to feel the atmosphere in the car had thawed.

Glancing into the rear-view mirror, I caught Gail's delighted eyes. 'Thank you,' she mouthed.

4

As the car crunched over a gravelled driveway and came to a halt, I craned my neck through the carrier, to assess my new home. It was not a big house, and it was far from glamorous unlike Javier's old flat, but with its red brick exterior, black front door and smart, curved bay windows, it looked warm, cosy and inviting.

While Simon helped Jenny out of the car, I peered out of the window and felt relieved it had stopped raining. The early November grey clouds were doing nothing for my mood. As Gail opened my door and reached inside to pull me out, the feel of her warm hands around my middle helped settle my nerves. I had spent weeks longing for a new life, now it was finally here I felt scared.

'Welcome home, Percy,' Gail whispered, holding me close and gently stroking my head. 'I know this will all feel a bit strange at first, but we already love you so much, we will do everything we can to make you happy.'

I turned my brown eyes to meet Gail's, and stretched out my paw to lie across her forearm. *Thank you,* I communicated silently as we walked across the gravel and into the house. What was it about Kelly and now Gail, I wondered, that they always seemed to know just what I was thinking?

Once inside, I sniffed the air and got my bearings. I could make out the scent of coffee and laundry as I looked around what I assumed was the hallway. I was pleased to find it already smelt like home. I saw a console table filled with keys and mail underneath a large gilt mirror. To my right, I saw a host of what looked like family photos above the stairs. There was a big picture of a young-looking Gail holding Jenny when she was born, while above it stood prints of older couples surrounding Gail and Simon, and I guessed they were Jenny's grandparents.

In the middle, in pride of place, was a picture of a beaming Simon and Gail alongside Jenny. Peering closer, it looked as though the photo had been taken recently outside this house and although the couple was beaming into the lens, the wrinkles around Gail's eyes were prominent, and Simon's smile did not meet his eyes.

'Tea, love?' Simon called from what I guessed was the kitchen.

'Yes, please, and a big bowl of water for Percy,' Gail replied, as she sat me down on the floor.

'Already done,' he called. 'His lordship will want for nothing.'

I chuckled inwardly at Simon's use of the word. Gabriella had often used the same phrase, but it never sounded friendly. The way Simon had said it felt completely different — not only was the word loaded with affection, but the gentle teasing already made me feel as though I belonged.

'Hey, what about me?' asked Jenny as she came down the stairs.

'As if I could forget.' Simon emerged from the room at the bottom of the corridor, grinning. 'I've made you your favourite hot chocolate.'

Jenny's smile widened. 'Thanks, Dad. Can I go and show Percy my room now?'

I barked willingly at Jenny. I couldn't wait to explore and spend some time with the little girl. Looking up at Gail, I saw her exchange glances with Simon but I couldn't understand what she was trying to say.

'Go on then,' she said eventually, with a smile. 'But not too long — you need a rest as you'll be tired after all the excitement this morning.'

'Muuuum,' Jenny whined, 'I'm fine. I was only in the car.'

Gail looked at her daughter with determination in her eyes. 'Exactly, just a few minutes with Percy and then bed, please.'

'Okay,' she sighed, obviously realising this was a battle she was unlikely to win.

As I trailed behind Jenny up the stairs, I glanced behind me and saw Gail's eyes were still filled with worry. I knew I had only just arrived in their home, but I did feel my new owner was overreacting a bit. Jenny was right, she had only been in a car for a couple of hours, she had hardly been chasing rabbits all morning.

As we reached her room, Jenny pushed open the door and I gazed in wonder at the posters of Justin Bieber and One Direction that lined every wall. Opposite the window stood a single bed with a patterned bedspread and a big stuffed cuddly teddy bear, which was propped up against the pillows. I glanced to my right and saw the bookshelf on the wall nearest the door was filled with books on horses and ponies. I could see at a glance it was a girl's room and one Jenny was obviously very proud of.

'Welcome to my room, Percy.' She grinned down at me.

'Thank you for inviting me,' I barked solemnly.

'What do you think?' she asked, whirling around the room.

'It's very nice,' I yapped as she scooped me

into her arms and sat us both on her bed.

'I knew you'd love it, Percy.' She smiled, settling me onto her lap.

Once we were both comfy, she lay down and I stretched out along her legs.

'We're going to have such a good time together, I've got it all planned out,' she said excitedly. 'We're going to play brilliant games, and I'm going to be the one that lets you out for a wee every morning. Dad says that even though I'm poorly, I've got to learn responsibility, whatever that means.'

I uncurled my tail with pleasure. This sounded wonderful already, and I rather liked the idea of me and this little girl spending some precious alone time together, even if it was just so I could spend a penny.

'I've also made you a special sort of bedroom in the kitchen downstairs, where I've put your bed, your food and water,' she continued eagerly. 'And Mum's knitted you a new blanket to keep you warm and Dad's got you a brilliant new collar with your name and our phone number engraved on it.'

This was getting better and better and I let out a little enthusiastic bark, wanting to show Jenny just how much I approved of everything she was telling me. Javier had never gone to such trouble, but then he and I preferred napping on the sofa to going out too much. Perhaps this spelled the start of more walks and I wondered if Gail might be persuaded to kit me out in one of those cute little coats when winter arrived that I'd seen other pugs wear in the park. My mind wandered as I imagined myself trotting next to Jenny, Simon and, of course Gail, dressed in a checked waterproof jacket that would not only keep me cosy and dry, but complement my glossy black fur. I was so busy imagining myself looking stylish at the park, I lost track of what Jenny was saying and only caught the last part of it.

' . . . so when I'm in the hospital next month, I'd really love it if you could keep a special eye on Mum, please, Perce,' she said quietly.

I barked at her again, trying not to sound alarmed. I knew Gail had mentioned something about Jenny being poorly, but hospital sounded serious. I yapped again, trying to get her to tell me more, but just as I opened my little mouth, the door opened and Gail's beaming face appeared around the door.

'How are you two getting on?' she asked.

Jenny smiled down happily at me. 'Brilliant, Mum. I've just been showing Percy my room and he loves it.'

'That's great, sweetheart.' She smiled. 'But

it's time for a nap now.'

'No way!' she protested. 'Me and Perce are having the best time. I want us to play a game now.'

My eyes met Gail's and I saw her eyes were still filled with worry. I turned to Jenny and realised she looked exhausted. Her eyes appeared grey instead of a sparkling blue and her skin was sallow. With a start, I wondered if the hospital visit Jenny had mentioned a few moments ago had something to do with the reason Gail was keen for her daughter to take a nap. I wanted to help. If Jenny had to sleep, the last thing she needed was me distracting her. Opening my mouth wide as if to yawn, I slumped my face onto my front paws and shut my eyes as if I were ready for bed. The action was not lost on Gail, who, I was relieved to find, quickly took advantage of my actions.

'Well, look at Percy,' she said gently. 'He needs a nap because he's had a big day. He's falling asleep on your legs, so how about I take him downstairs and let him have a little rest in his new bed. Then you can play games and we'll give him a full tour after you've both had a nap.'

'Okay,' Jenny replied sulkily.

As Gail picked me up, she planted a kiss on Jenny's forehead and then mine. Turning back to glance at her as Gail shut her bedroom door, I was delighted to see the little girl was already fast asleep.

Gail drew her head back and regarded me curiously. 'I've no idea if you can understand what I'm saying, but that's a couple of times now you've helped me out of a sticky situation.'

'I can understand you loud and clear,' I replied with a soft whine.

As we padded down the stairs together, Gail beckoned me to follow her. 'Come on then,' she said encouragingly, 'time to see where you'll be sleeping.'

I trotted eagerly behind her and into the big square kitchen/diner. There was no denying it, Simon was right again, Gail and Jenny had indeed created a luxurious corner for me so I could relax. My large new bed was right next to the radiator so I'd be warm, while the bed itself was dressed in blanket after cosy-looking blanket, with a softer than soft hand-knitted patchwork blanket on top. I realised they smelled of Gail and felt instantly comforted, I was so excited to dive right in. I turned around and looked over at Gail and Simon who were standing at the kitchen doorway, arms wrapped around each other, smiling indulgently at me.

'Go on,' Gail coaxed, 'this is your home

now, Percy, just shut your eyes for a bit and have a rest.'

Excited, I turned back to my new bed and placed first one paw then another into the blankets. Soft, squishy and oh so warm, it felt like heaven as I walked around in little circles to try to get comfortable. Once I had found the perfect spot, I sank my head into the nice warm space I had carved out for myself. I needed very little encouragement, as I glanced once more at a delighted-looking Gail and Simon, I shut my eyes and immediately fell asleep.

⋆　⋆　⋆

'If I've told you once, I've told you a thousand times, Gail, we can afford it,' Simon said, his rasping tones waking me from my slumber.

'I know you keep saying we can afford it, but I just don't see how,' Gail protested, as I opened my eyes and saw her emptying the dishwasher. 'Holidays are expensive, and I know it's just a week away in the Lakes but, if we go back down to Barnstaple instead, we can stay with my parents for free.'

'But then it's not a holiday, love. We'll get bogged down seeing friends, looking after your parents and doing the things we used to do when we lived down there. If old Mrs Shand finds out I'm back, she'll have me servicing her boiler for free and you know I won't be able to resist.'

'That Mrs Shand won't just want her boiler serviced if she finds out you're back! You're too kind for your own good.' Gail grinned, swatting him with a tea towel. 'And I know we need a proper holiday, love, but now I've given up my job in the café to home-school Jenny, every penny counts.'

'So why did you decide now was a good time to get a dog, if money is such a worry?' Simon spat.

I felt a stab of alarm as I opened one eye and saw Simon rest his back against the sink, his arms folded in what looked like fury.

'That's not fair, Simon,' Gail whispered angrily. 'You know how long I've wanted to get a dog, and how lonely I've been since we moved to London. We both agreed to take Percy on.'

Simon shook his head despairingly. 'We agreed to give him a chance until Christmas and see how it goes, before deciding whether to keep him for ever. We've a lot on our plates with Jenny as it is, without taking on any more responsibility.'

Fear coursed through my fur as I realised my instincts were right. This had all been too good to be true; Javier had proved to me how fickle humans were. How stupid I had been to think things would be different with Gail and Simon. I wanted to howl as I realised that within a few short weeks I could be back at the tails of the forgotten. Would I never be good enough for someone to want me and love me for ever?

I closed my eyes tightly, just as I heard Gail walk across the kitchen floor to join Simon at the sink.

'You have to give Percy a real chance,' she said warningly. 'He's a wonderful dog and could be just what this family needs. He doesn't cost that much, and he'll certainly give us a lot more joy than a few days away in a caravan.'

Opening my eyes again, I felt a rush of love once more for Gail as I saw her face was filled with an earnestness I had never seen on a human before.

Simon cocked his head to one side and regarded his wife. 'Love, I will give Percy a real chance, I'm just asking you to keep an open mind too. It may not work out with him and all of us have to be prepared for that. Let's see how things are after Christmas.'

'Fine,' Gail sighed. 'But I want you to know, if you won't keep Percy, then there's a real chance I'll go with him. He's a lifeline to me.'

'Even more reason we need a break, love,' Simon begged, reaching for his wife's hands and clasping them tightly. 'But Percy aside, Gail, I can provide for my family, and part of that means I can treat us all to a holiday, even if it's just a few days in a caravan in wet and windy Keswick.'

I glanced up at Gail, who was now biting her lip. She rounded the table and drew out the chair opposite Simon's to sit down.

'I know that, love, but the other good thing about going back down to Devon is that if Jenny has a problem, Mum and Dad are there to help us out. Plus, all the staff at the hospital have dealt with Jenny over the years so will be able to treat her quickly. She's going into hospital in a couple of weeks for another procedure and we don't know how successful that's going to be. I think we should wait and see how that goes before we even think about holidays.'

Simon looked across at his wife and clasped his hands over hers. 'Nobody knows more than me how sick Jenny is. I grew up worrying about heart conditions remember? My old man was always in and out of hospital with a dodgy ticker and after his fifth heart attack I realised I couldn't control his health by worrying. I knew I had to make the most of my time with him, which is why one of the best things I ever did was take him golfing in Spain just before he died. I'll never regret doing that. It made me realise that if we wrap Jenny and ourselves in cotton wool we won't enjoy life and the time we all have together.'

Thoughts flooded my mind as I realised Jenny was perhaps more poorly than Gail had initially let on. This heart condition, whatever it was, sounded serious. I watched Gail's back stiffen in her chair as Simon finished his passionate speech. His words had clearly struck a chord and she was torn between wanting to make Simon happy and doing what she instinctively thought was right for her only precious child.

'You make it sound as though Jenny doesn't have long left,' she hissed. 'It's as though you've already given up and expect her to die just like your father did.'

Gail screwed her face up into an ugly scowl, and I was astounded to see her look so upset. Her body was shaking with anger, and all I wanted to do was sit on her lap and try to calm her down.

'Don't be daft,' Simon said swiftly, 'of course I don't think Jenny's going to die. It was my idea to move back up to London, wasn't it? I wanted to make sure she had the chance to get to Great Ormond Street quickly, so she would be on hand for top quality care. I wouldn't have suggested that if I thought she wasn't going to make it, would I?'

Gail said nothing as Simon took a deep breath. 'Gail, I know it's hard for you up here. That you miss our friends and your family, but we've got to make a go of it for Jenny's sake and we can't keep tripping up and down to Devon. Our lives are here now.'

'Easy for you to say,' Gail spat, 'your mum's just around the corner and your old school friends are streets away.'

Simon leaned back in his chair and took a deep breath before he spoke. 'That's true, but we're not here for me. Things have changed. We're here for Jen, and I know it's rough on you, but you will make friends soon. Why don't you go line dancing with Mum on Wednesdays? She's always inviting you.'

'Because I've got two left feet,' Gail sighed. 'Not only that, I haven't the time. Now we're home-schooling Jenny, I have to make sure we follow the curriculum. I'm determined that her education won't suffer any more than it has to because of her health.'

'Which is why we need to make the most of our time and appreciate each other again,' Simon reasoned.

Gail looked into Simon's eyes and then back at her lap, shaking her head sadly. 'I understand, Si, but surely our friends and our family down in Devon are all a part of making the most of that time we have together,' she said, the frustration creeping into her voice. 'I know how hard you work, and I know how tired you are working round the clock all the hours. I know you've been sleeping in the spare room lately when you've crept in late, so you don't disturb me, but it's not necessary.'

'I don't want to wake you,' Simon said, shrugging. 'Taking care of Jenny, schooling her, running this house, it's a full-time job in itself Gail. You need your sleep.'

'And I need you beside me.' Gail smiled, as she lifted her hand and tenderly stroked Simon's cheek. 'You, Jenny and now Percy are my family and my life. I'd do anything for any one of you.'

At the mention of my name, I decided this was as good a time as any to try to ease the tension. I opened my brown eyes wider and barked a little yelp of hello.

'Oh, look, Percy is awake.' Gail beamed, pushing back her chair across the parquet floor and heading straight for my basket. 'Hello, gorgeous, how did you sleep?' she asked softly, crouching on the floor her face pressed close to mine.

'Fine,' I barked gently, licking her cheek by way of greeting. I wasn't sure how long I had napped, but what I did know was that I felt an awful lot better for forty winks. I stretched my front and back legs out to wake them properly and felt my back click into place. Getting to my paws, I felt my tummy gurgle with hunger and realised it must have been hours since I had eaten. I looked at Gail, worried it was too early in our relationship for me to start complaining about my appetite. But, thankfully, she had filled a bowl with my favourite food.

'This is your home now, Percy,' she said, as I scampered across the floor towards my grub. 'You must do exactly what you like.'

I looked up at her again as she nodded reassuringly at me. Was this really my home? The conversation I had heard between Simon and Gail made me wonder. But my growling tummy stopped me from pondering any more as I chewed hungrily at my late lunch. Smacking my lips together, I realised now would be the perfect time to have the tour of the house I had been promised. So far I had only seen a fraction of the place and was eager to see more. Licking my mouth to ensure I had caught every last crumb, I walked towards the table where Simon was still sitting and nuzzled my head against his leg. We had not spent much time together yet and given he was the one who was considering sending me back, I wanted us to get to know one another.

'Why don't you give Percy that tour?' Gail suggested as she caught my affectionate gesture. 'You can show him your man cave, otherwise known as the spare room.'

Simon looked down at me and grinned. 'Good idea. Percy, it's time for you to see my hideaway where I get a bit of peace and quiet away from these nagging women.'

'You should count yourself lucky you've got two women who love you enough to nag at you,' Gail teased.

As Simon got to his feet and walked out of the kitchen, I followed closely behind. 'Here's the living room,' he explained cheerfully, throwing open the door to the room we had passed earlier.

I took in the large flat-screen television, real fire and squishy leather sofas that stood opposite one another. With more family photographs and a hand-knitted red throw strewn across the back of one of the settees, the place looked warm and inviting. With the chilly weather outside, I was all set to step inside and head towards the rug in front of the fire, but Simon had other ideas.

'This way, mate. Tour's not over yet,' he said, beckoning me up the stairs.

After a quick peek at Gail and Simon's bedroom, and the bathroom, which seemed nice enough, Simon proudly led me past Jenny's room to what looked like a spare room at the other end of the corridor. As we stood outside, Simon reminded me of a little boy on Christmas morning as he stood grinning and hopping from foot to foot.

'You're going to love it in here, Perce,' he chuckled. 'There are no girls allowed in this room, and I want you to think of this place as being yours as much as mine from now on. Any time those women get too much, you're welcome to pop in.'

I barked in approval, delighted Simon wanted to share what was obviously a very special place with me. He opened the door and stepped inside with obvious enthusiasm. I sniffed the air and realised this room smelt very different to the rest of the house. I couldn't put my paw on what it was, but the room was musky. I glanced up at Simon, who was standing by the window, hands in his jeans pockets looking proudly around him. I could see why. The room was a boy's paradise, with posters of Bob Dylan and Oasis lining the walls, while row after row of DVDs such as *Reservoir Dogs* and *The*

Godfather stood on a black metal shelving unit above a glass mini-fridge, filled with beer. Another large flat-screen television was mounted on the wall next to a rail filled with jeans and shirts, while an outstretched futon with a rumpled duvet stood next to it.

I glanced up at Simon. He seemed more relaxed now than he had all day. Worry coursed through me. I didn't know much about families, but what I did know from chatting with other dogs like Barney was that most couples spent their nights together. I knew from the conversation I had just overheard between Simon and Gail that she believed he was sleeping up here because he sometimes worked late, but looking at how much happier Simon seemed in this space, I wondered briefly if that was true. I furrowed my wrinkled brow, trying to make sense of it all before glancing back up at Simon. He was watching me intently, and seemed to be waiting for a response. The last thing I wanted to do was upset him.

I thought quickly. As far as bachelor pads went, this was a pretty good one, and barked appreciatively as I sat on the floor by the bed.

Simon sat cross-legged on the floor beside me. 'I'm glad you approve, mate. I'm hoping you and me will become pals because, you know what, I could really use one in this house.'

I licked his chin, urging him to carry on, his bristles rough against my tongue as he bent his face down towards me.

'The thing is, Perce, since we moved back up to London, well, our whole lives revolve around Jenny and her illness. It's heartbreaking. All I want is for Jenny to be well again and for us all to go back to how things were.'

Glancing up at him, I saw his green eyes moisten as he mentioned his daughter's condition. I was unsure just how sick Jenny was but it was beginning to sound more serious by the second. My heart went out to him and Gail as they were obviously coping in very different ways. Gail by bringing me into the family and Simon, I realised glancing around me, by shutting himself away from his family in this man cave. I nuzzled my face into his lap and tried to let him know I understood.

'I'm here for you, Simon,' I barked noisily. 'I'm here for you all.'

5

In the days that followed I began to settle into a routine with my new family. I was usually woken early by Jenny who would gently ruffle my ears, then open the back door for me so I could spend a penny. When I returned, I would find she had always made breakfast for me, and as I tucked in, she often liked to sit and watch me eat as the house gradually came to life.

After good morning strokes and kisses from Gail, Simon would throw on his old wax jacket and I would whimper in delight, knowing our early morning walk to the park was imminent. Patiently, I would sit by the front door and wait as Simon clipped on my lead, then we would trot down the road together chatting away about the day ahead. Although the ground was now covered in a thick frost, this morning was no different. As he yawned and stretched, jerking my lead so my collar caught my throat, I let out a yelp of agony.

'Oh, sorry, mate,' Simon said, loosening my lead. 'I'm a bit knackered this morning, didn't sleep all that well. Me and Gail had a row last night.'

I woofed in sympathy. I had been out like a light last night and had not heard a peep from either of them.

'To be honest with you, Percy, it feels like me and Gail are always having words,' Simon confided. 'This week we've rowed about the washing-up, the car and the fact I'm apparently always out with my mates in the pub after work. It's all doing my head in to be honest, I like a quiet life.'

As we walked up the lane dodging the icy patches on the pavement, I turned my face to meet his and barked again, encouraging him to get it all off his chest.

'Course I'm not stupid like a lot of blokes, Perce,' he continued. 'I know Gail, and I know what she's really upset about is the fact Jenny has to go back into hospital; but every time I say that to her, she bites my head off. I don't know what to do for the best.'

I said nothing and just listened as we walked along the road. I'd come to know Simon well enough to realise he said more when he was uninterrupted by my woofs of support.

'Since Jenny was diagnosed with dilated cardiomyopathy, Gail's been different, permanently on edge, you know. I thought moving back to London so we could be nearer to the hospital would make life easier. I mean, we were spending all our time on the motorway as it was with various appointments. But at least this way we've got my mum around to help.' He sighed, scratching the bristles of his day-old beard. 'The truth is, I think she blames me, Perce. My dad had heart trouble and this heart condition Jenny's got is genetic. Gail's never come out and said anything, but I think deep down, she feels it's my fault. When Dad passed away because of his ticker last year she was more upset than me. I think she thought it would be Jenny next.'

He stopped, then bent down, his eyes meeting mine. 'I'm sorry, Percy. You're such a terrific dog, you don't deserve all this rubbish. You deserve a home that's happy and carefree.'

My eyes widened. Did Simon want to send me back to the tails of the forgotten already? It wasn't Christmas yet, I still had at least six weeks to prove myself.

'Don't make me go back,' I yelped frantically.

'Oh, mate,' Simon said, kissing the top of my head with his cold lips, 'despite what you may think from all my moans and groans in the morning, you've changed our lives for the better, Perce.'

My cheeks puffed with pride as we reached

the safety of the park. 'You're my family too,' I barked, licking his face as he unclipped my collar. 'Which is why I'll be the best dog in the world if you'll just let me stay with you for ever.'

'Go on, mate,' Simon called loudly, ignoring my barks of plea, 'run free for a bit.'

I hardly needed any encouragement and ran across the green space that was rock-hard thanks to the wintery frost. Despite the cold, a visit to the park was one of the highlights of my day. There were lots of trees to have a tinkle behind, plenty of grass to run around on, not to mention loads of abandoned tennis balls that were begging to be chewed. Seeing one now, I pounced on it in delight just as a young, boisterous Border collie raced towards me.

'I'm Bugsy, but you can call me Bugs,' he said, panting excitedly. 'Me and my gang have seen you here every day for the last few days, and have wondered who you are. I said I'd find out, so I've come to introduce myself and bring you back to meet the others. Do you want to come now?'

His wild-eyed enthusiasm and endless stream of chat was both impressive and exhausting. Watching him run around me in circles reminded me of some of the dogs I had met at the tails of the forgotten and I

58

realised he was barely more than a pup.

'I'm Percy,' I replied slowly, trying to calm the youngster down. 'I've just moved in with Simon and Gail in Barksdale Way.'

'Cor! Barksdale Way's a bit fancy. Full of families that think they're no better than they should be — least that's what my owners Johnny and Bella say — but I don't know what that means. Do you want to come and meet my friends now?' Bugs barked relentlessly.

I thought my head would explode with laugher. You could always rely on a young pup to tell you just how it is, I thought wryly.

'I'd love to meet everyone,' I woofed agreeably, following behind as he raced to the other end of the park.

'This is Percy,' he puffed, rounding up all his pals. 'He's just moved in with a new family in Barksdale Way.'

'Very good, old boy. Welcome to the gang,' woofed an elderly-looking spaniel. With his greying whiskers, he reminded me a little bit of Kelly at the tails of the forgotten and was clearly a dog that had seen and done it all.

'I'm Jake,' he continued, 'out and about most mornings, hips allowing.' With that, he shifted his lower half from the wet, dank grass and wriggled his bottom to get more comfortable.

A sweet-looking German shepherd looked at Jake. 'Are you all right, lovey? Your hips look like they're playing up more than usual this morning.'

'Oh, I'm fine,' Jake barked in reply. 'It's this cold December weather. Christmas is no fun for old dogs like me.'

'Don't talk soft,' the German shepherd replied gently, before turning to me. 'And you're Percy, I just heard Bugsy say. Well, it's very nice to meet you, Percy. I'm Heather and you're welcome to come and hang around with us of a morning any time you want to. Who are your owners?'

'Gail and Simon,' I barked again, gesturing towards Simon, who was busy chatting to a small blonde woman at the corner of the park.

The two looked as if they had known each other for years by the way they were gassing away. I was about to ask the others if they knew who she was when I became distracted by the lead the woman was holding. Straining impatiently at the leash, was the most beautiful pug I had ever seen. Blonde, with dark markings and trademark big brown eyes, her paws looked tantalisingly beautiful, and the set of her jaw left my own hanging open in longing.

'That's Peg, old boy,' Jake barked quietly,

as he sidled up to me. 'She's just a young thing, and spoiled, a bit like her owner, but she's a good girl at heart.'

'Jake, she's a sweetheart,' Heather protested, as she scratched her ear in frustration. 'Don't put Percy off before they've even met.'

'Oh, Heather,' Bugsy barked affectionately. 'You always see the best in a dog, even me, and I'm always getting it wrong and I know you tell me it's just my age, but it's not always and anyway, I don't think Percy's about to be put off any time soon. His jaw's on the floor and he's dribbling. Is he sick, Heather?'

'No, sweetie,' Heather woofed affectionately. 'He's just got a bit of a crush, the poor thing.'

Bugsy grimaced. 'Yuck! On Peg? But she's a girl.'

I'd heard enough of this nonsense and turned back to face the others, who were all looking at me agog.

'I don't have a crush. I just think it's nice to meet another pug, that's all,' I objected, hoping my traitorous, thumping heart wouldn't give me away.

I turned back to look at Peg, only to find she was scampering towards us. I gulped noisily and felt my nose moisten with nerves as I turned to Heather. 'How do I look?'

'Like a prince, pet,' she barked kindly.

'Come and meet our new boy, Percy,' Heather barked as Peg approached. 'He lives around the corner in Barksdale Way.'

'Ooh, that's a bit posh,' Peg panted, echoing Bugsy's words as she scampered to join me. 'It's lovely to meet you, Percy. Can I come around and see your place sometime?'

'Steady on, old girl,' Jake barked sagely. 'Perce here has just arrived. It's a bit soon to be inviting yourself over for a bowl of Pedigree Chum.'

'Sorry, Percy,' Peg woofed a little shame-faced. 'Where are my manners? It's just rare to meet another pug, especially not one that lives in such a nice part of town. I got carried away, that's all.'

'That's okay,' I replied, her beauty leaving me almost barkless. 'I'd love to have you visit. I'll see if I can encourage Simon to invite your owner over.'

'Oh, our Sally doesn't need much encouragement,' Peg barked knowingly. 'She's a sucker for a pretty face that girl. I suppose that's where I get it from.'

Heather turned to Peg. 'How is your Sally now?'

Peg rolled her big brown eyes in despair. 'She's all right, Heather. But it doesn't take much for Sally to start turning on the old waterworks. She'd only been on a couple of dates with this latest one but she's been sobbing on my fur all week about how she thought he was the one, whatever that means.'

'She's been looking for love in all the wrong places again,' Heather barked sympathetically.

'You can bark that again,' Peg replied. 'Honestly, she's getting on my nerves with all these tears. We always have such a nice time when it's just the two of us, I can't understand why she wants to ruin everything by chasing after every man in trousers.'

'It's not our job to understand, Peg,' Jake barked wisely. 'It is ours merely to be there for our owners whenever they need us.'

'And I am, Jake,' Peg insisted, her little tail curling and uncurling in frustration. 'But all these tears are making my fur soggy and cold.'

Jake patted her much younger paws with his old wizened ones. 'I do understand, my dear, but such is our lot. Into this life a little rain must fall.'

'Literally, when it comes to our Sal,' Peg barked mutinously. 'Anyway, what about everyone else? I can't be the only one with owner problems.'

Being new to the group, I didn't want to speak first, but the others wasted no time comparing war stories.

'Well, I'm sure it's no secret that mine are getting divorced,' Heather barked matter-of-factly. 'It's been a long time coming. Pete's been convinced for years she's been cheating on him so he finally got fed up and hired a private detective to do some digging last month.'

I rolled my eyes in amazement. Was that really something humans did? I looked around the rest of the group, but they did not appear remotely surprised.

'And he found some evidence that she'd been with someone else?' Peg woofed compassionately.

'No, she hadn't been cheating at all,' Heather barked with exasperation. 'But when she met the private detective, she fell head over heels and has now moved in with him, so Pete really has got something to worry about and is either moping about the house or throwing plates in the garden. I have to be careful when I pop out for my evening tinkle.' Heather shook her head in disgust. 'What about the rest of you? I can't be the only one suffering thanks to my daft owners.'

Bugsy cocked his head and let his tongue loll to one side, an unattractive pool of drool gathering at the corner of his mouth. 'My owners have just had a baby,' he barked.

'Jasper's really sweet and cute and I like to look at him when my parents have gone to bed, but he's not asleep very often when it gets dark. In fact, most of the time he's awake and he's crying, and screaming and waking everyone up because he shouts so loudly. I never get any sleep and neither do Mum and Dad and they're tired, and I'm tired and all I want to do is go to bed. Sometimes I think I could sleep standing up, but then I know I'd fall over and probably hurt myself. My owners say they haven't got time to play with me any more because they're so tired and I miss going for walks with my parents in the morning because instead I've got the neighbour's son, Maxwell, taking me and he's horrible and listens to his headphones all the time and I'm fed up!'

With that, Bugsy slumped to the floor, his head on his paws in despair. As he let out a howl of frustration, Jake and Heather rushed to his side and encouraged him to his paws.

'Come on, Bugsy, lovey, don't take on so,' Heather barked soothingly. 'Jasper won't be a baby for long and Johnny and Bella will be playing with you again before you know it.'

'Absolutely, old boy,' agreed Jake. 'My owner's son, Patrick, was a baby once, made a huge racket night and day for months. Thought it was never going to end, but it did, and now the boy's almost a man. Mighty fine chap too, I might add. Stick with it, Bugsy, this baby phase won't last for long and your owners will come to rely on you once more over the years.'

'But it's so horrible,' Bugsy groaned, 'I liked it better before he came along.'

I scratched my ear thoughtfully with my hind leg. Bugsy's people were probably just a bit distracted at the minute, but they still loved him. Bugsy just needed to figure out a way to try to get his family a little sleep, then they might have a bit more time for him.

'How about we try to help you, Bugs?' I barked. 'There must be something we can do to give your family a bit of a rest.'

'Oooh, what were you thinking, Percy?' asked Peg, turning her pretty face to meet mine. 'I love a man with brains and beauty.'

My heart fluttered nervously in my chest. Was Peg flirting with me?

'There's no point,' Bugsy barked once more, interrupting my thoughts. 'They don't care about anyone else apart from Jasper. I might as well move out and live at the tails of the forgotten. At least I would get some peace and there would be other people to care for me.'

'That's enough,' I barked reprovingly. 'Your family are just a bit distracted at the moment that's all. There's no need to go wishing yourself to a shelter, if anyone knows it's me, I've just come from there.'

The others looked at me in surprise before Heather broke the silence. 'You never said, lovey.'

'Well, I want to make the best of my new start,' I woofed in explanation. 'I'm looking to the future now, not at the past.'

'Quite right, old boy,' Jake barked in agreement.

'Yes, Percy, ignore me, I didn't mean to pry,' Heather barked apologetically before looking at Bugsy. 'Now, it sounds to me that if we can get you and your family some sleep things will improve for all of you. In my experience, the best thing to get a child to stay asleep is a lullaby. How about we all gather outside your house tonight Bugsy and sing Jasper to sleep.'

'Can you sing, Heather?' Peg barked incredulously.

Heather looked at the floor and toed the ground self-consciously with her paw. 'Well, I don't like to brag, but I always used to sing my owners' girls to sleep when they were very little and they drifted off to sleep immediately.'

'I was once a member of the Welsh Dog Voice Choir,' Jake yapped. 'We had the children of the Valleys asleep in seconds. Of course, that was a few years ago now and my lungs aren't what they were.'

'Nonsense, Jake, you've a lovely voice,' Heather barked warmly before turning to me. 'What about you, Percy? Can you bark a tune?'

'I've never really sung. Perhaps the odd note in the bath,' I barked. 'But I'm willing to try, if you think it will help, Bugsy.'

'Me too,' barked Peg, sidling closer to me. 'Percy's right, we've all got to stick together.'

'Then it's agreed,' yapped Heather delightedly. 'We'll meet at Bugsy's at six tonight, so we're ready for Jasper's bedtime and can have a practice. I'll rap out the usual three barks for you.'

'What shall we sing?' Peg asked.

'How about 'Baa Baa Black Sheep' or 'Hush Little Baby'?' suggested Jake. 'In my experience, those two songs always get the children off to sleep quickly.'

'Good idea. Now can everyone get away? Percy, Bugsy lives on the next road to yours so we could meet at the corner of your street if that suits?' asked Heather.

I looked around me and saw barks of assent all around. Quickly, I thought how I would make my escape. Gail, Simon and Jenny usually ate their dinner at six so it would be quite easy for me to wriggle through their old cat flap.

'Sounds good,' I barked excitedly.

'Excellent,' Heather yapped delightedly again. 'Now, just one thing, not a word to anyone. No matter how lovely your owners are if they find out we're performing our very own dog quartet they'll be furious.'

'Or at the very least, we'll end up on the front page of one of the tabloids,' added Jake. 'And the last thing we want is the press camped out whenever we go to the park.'

'Quite right, Jake,' agreed Heather. 'Remember when old John got caught rescuing his owner from a fire? He couldn't move for journalists for weeks! None of you breathe a word, especially you, Bugsy.'

At the sound of being singled out, Bugsy groaned. 'Honestly, Heather, I won't say a word. I know there was that time I told Saul the shih-tzu around the corner that we wanted to do something nice for Jake's birthday and then there was a massive party, which Jake didn't want — '

'And always made it clear to you, old boy, I never wanted,' Jake insisted, cutting across him.

'Which Jake never wanted,' Bugsy admitted, 'but it was an accident, I've learned my lesson. I swear to you, Heather, I won't let you down, I promise.'

As Bugsy looked at us beseechingly, it was all I could do not to bark with laughter. The poor youngster looked so earnest.

'Don't worry, Bugs. We trust you, and all of us will keep our mouths shut, won't we?' I woofed.

'Course we will. Percy, looks like you and me are wanted,' Peg barked as she looked over at Simon and Sally who were waving like a pair of mad things, calling for us to join them.

'Until tonight then,' I barked.

'Until tonight,' Jake replied. 'And remember, all of you, not a word to anyone.'

6

Together with Peg, we hurried towards our grinning owners. As we got nearer, I saw Sally unlink her arm from Simon's and bend down to give Peg a stroke.

'Come on, you two, are you ready for home?' Sally asked, flicking her blonde mane behind her shoulder.

'I am. I'm freezing,' Peg barked, looking adoringly at her owner.

'Me too,' I woofed.

'I'm glad we're all agreed.' Simon grinned as he ruffled my ears, snapped on my lead and turned towards home. 'I need a hot toddy to thaw me out, I think.'

Sally snapped on Peg's collar. 'Do you mind if we walk home with you?'

'Course not,' Simon replied. 'Are you still around the corner in Denby House?'

'Oh, yes. And I'm still working as an accountant from home as well. It must be about ten years now since I bought the place. Me and Peg aren't going anywhere soon are we, girl?'

'No, we're very happy,' she barked.

I turned and looked at Peg. She hadn't

mentioned she lived so close by.

'We're in the garden flat on the hill,' she barked. 'Pop over any time.'

'I'd like that,' I replied enthusiastically. 'Shall I call for you on the way to Bugsy's later?'

'Yes! Give me two barks when you're outside and I'll come right out. Sally's always watching her soaps at six while she's cooking, so she won't miss me slipping out the back door, which she always opens to let the steam out.'

'But how will you get back in?' I asked. The last thing I wanted was for Peg to get stuck outside.

'Oh, if she's shut the door by then I'll just bark outside and she'll think I just nipped out into the garden somewhere. Our Sal doesn't think too deeply about anything,' Peg woofed.

Just then Sally let out a high-pitched tinkling laugh. The sound gave me a real fright. The last time I had heard anything like that was when the fire alarm went off by accident at the tails of the forgotten. I looked around and saw Sally was giggling at something Simon had said. Simon too was boasting a smile that reached the corners of his eyes and he had an air of jollity about him he never had at home.

'I'm telling you, Sally, that Filofax is still up

there on the roof of the science block,' Simon insisted. 'Last I heard, Mr Herring was still trying to find out whodunit, despite it being over twenty years ago.'

'Well, the rotten sod deserved it.' Sally grinned. 'Herring was a horrible teacher. He was surgically attached to that Filofax, d'you remember?' Sally shook her head at the memory. 'He looked destroyed when someone nicked the thing and it ended up on the rooftop. D'you know who did it?'

Simon shook his head. 'I heard the rumours. Someone told me it was Steven Michaelson, and someone else said it was Tasha Franks, but I never found out for sure. I just remember it being the only thing people ever talked about in the fourth year for months.'

'I hid my tracks better than I thought then.' Sally chuckled.

I turned to observe them both. Simon had a look of incredulousness on his face as he stopped and gripped Sally's shoulder.

'You're not saying it was you, Sally Hopkins?'

Sally nodded, her lipsticked smile, giving her face a happy glow. 'It's true. I did it after he put me on detention for a week after I didn't wear a school tie. I missed a date with Jamie Busby because of him! I was so tired of him having a go at us all, I snuck into his office one day, nicked the Filofax, and then flung it high in the air. I will confess even I was surprised when it ended up on the roof.'

Simon stood there open-mouthed, gazing at Sally in wonder. 'I can't believe it was you. You're a dark horse, that's for sure.'

'That's me all right,' Sally replied, smirking, as she started walking with Peg by her side.

'Finally, the mystery of Perivale Comp solved,' Simon chuckled as we rounded the corner and reached Sally's road. 'I wasn't expecting that today.'

'And I wasn't expecting to see you either. I had no idea you were back in London.' Sally grinned as she stood outside her flat.

'Yes, been back a few months now. Me and Gail have moved to the city so Jenny's closer to the hospital,' he explained.

Sally cocked her head in sympathy. 'I heard your daughter had a heart problem. I hope it's not as serious as it sounds.'

Simon raked his hands through his hair and grimaced. 'It's quite serious if I'm honest, Sal. Jenny has something known as dilated cardiomyopathy, it's genetic and basically means that her heart is enlarged and can't pump blood round her body properly. My dad died from heart problems and we think that's how she may have got it.'

'Goodness, Si, I'm sorry,' Sally said. 'Did you find out when she was born?'

I looked up at Simon and watched him shake his head. 'No, she was fine for years. Then when she was about nine she started fainting, was always struggling to catch her breath and was always tired. We took her to the doctors', but it took ages for them to work out what was wrong. Eventually, X-rays told us the news and since then we've been in and out of hospital.'

Sally shook her head in horror. 'Poor Jenny, and poor you and Gail. Can't the doctors operate or something like that to fix it?'

'If only it were that simple.' Simon smiled sheepishly. 'Sadly, Jenny's tried almost all the tablets under the sun as well as a pacemaker, but she's still having trouble, which is why we've moved up here so she can get to the hospital quickly. She's back in soon for an overnight procedure, which means more tests. The hope is we can crack this problem with drugs once and for all. The last thing we want is for her to have a heart transplant, she's only a little kid, I want her to live a normal life . . . '

As Simon trailed off, I saw Sally lightly pat his arm in sympathy. 'I'm sorry, Simon. Let me know if there's anything I can do.'

'Thanks, Sal. Though, to be fair, you've done something incredible already by cheering me up. I haven't laughed like that in ages,' he laughed.

'Any time. Me and Peg will look forward to seeing more of you and Percy in the park,' she said, grinning.

'We're there every day, aren't we, mate?' he asked, looking down at me.

'Every day,' I confirmed with a swift bark.

'And Gail usually takes Percy out in the evening. I'm sure she'd love to see you as well,' Simon continued hurriedly.

Sally smiled as she glanced down at Peg. 'I'd love to see her too. It's all been far too long, but in the meantime, we had better be getting inside. Nice to see you again.'

'And you, Sal.' Simon smiled as he waved her goodbye. 'See you soon.'

Simon turned and walked quickly away with me by his side. 'Well, I never expected to bump into Sally Hopkins this morning, boy. She was the class looker when I was at school, but was never interested in me, even though I asked her out nearly every day.'

As we turned into Barksdale Way, I glanced into Simon's eyes and was delighted to see he appeared a lot happier than he did when we left. Perhaps coming to the park was as good for him as it was for me.

The rest of the day passed quickly. After Gail had guided Jenny through maths, which she hated, and English, which she loved, the little girl passed out on the sofa with exhaustion and it was all I could do not to join her. But, as I watched Gail clear away Jenny's textbooks, pens and pencils, I could see the worry etched across her face. As she went into the kitchen to make a cup of tea, I followed her and sat by the side of the table waiting for her to join me.

'You must be a mind-reader, Perce.' Gail grinned, as she pulled out a chair and sat down with a cup of tea. 'I honestly don't know where I'd be without you and a decent cuppa.'

After resting her mug on the table, Gail bent down, scooped me up in her arms and set me down on her lap. Nuzzling into her, I rubbed my head against hers and looked into her eyes. Gail seemed more tired than usual, if that were possible, but knowing she and Simon had rowed last night I wasn't surprised. I reached my paw out and laid it on the back of her hand in comfort. Wordlessly, she stroked it and grinned.

'Fancy a quick game of tennis balls in the garden?' she asked.

Barking with enthusiasm, I jumped down from her lap onto the cool kitchen floor and scampered across to the big French doors. As we both went outside, Gail grabbed her coat and one of the balls from the grass, throwing it across the garden before she put her coat on.

'Thing is, Percy,' Gail said, as she picked up the ball I dropped on the ground in front of her, 'I know I'm a bit like a bear with a sore head at the minute. But Jenny hasn't had to stay overnight in hospital for such a long time, and I'm worried about it.'

'That's understandable,' I barked.

From the conversations I'd heard between Gail and Simon, and sometimes Jenny, too, I knew the procedure was not as serious as I had feared. The doctors just wanted to monitor her with a special heart machine for twenty-four hours to check how things were going. Yet Gail seemed to be taking this hard, and aside from the obvious, I was unsure why.

Gail threw the ball across the grass for me again. 'I don't know what it is that's upsetting me about all this to be honest, Perce.'

As she watched the ball fly through the air, she sank her full weight onto the wooden bench behind her and shielded her eyes from the early afternoon sunshine. With great restraint, I ignored the ball, hopped up onto the bench with a bit of help from Gail and settled quietly beside her. It was obvious to me why she was so upset. Jenny was her daughter, it was only natural she would be worried.

'I suppose I just feel like Jenny's getting worse, not better,' Gail continued. 'She's so pale and tired all the time and sometimes passes out with sheer exhaustion. Worst of all, the doctors can't seem to find the right medicines for her. I've lost count of all the ones we've tried. I suppose I'm worried what this means and what's next for us.'

Looking up at her, I saw the fear written across her face. I resolved to make an extra special effort to find some way of cheering her up.

As the sunshine disappeared behind the clouds, we went back inside. Gail made a start on the dinner and, when Jenny woke, the two carried on with more maths at the kitchen table, much to Jenny's disgust. I tried to spur her on, by giving her a woof of appreciation each time she got an algebra sum right. But although she appreciated my efforts, I could tell she'd had more than enough.

'Seriously, Mum, can't we call it a day? It's almost six, we never work this late at school,' Jenny reasoned.

Gail sighed. 'I do know that, love. But I

don't want you getting behind. Once we get this heart condition of yours sorted, you'll have a bright future ahead of you and I want you to have a proper education.'

'But we both know maths isn't my strong suit, Mum,' Jenny protested. 'Look, even Percy knows I'm never going to be a maths professor or an astronaut or anything like that. He always gives me way more encouragement when we're doing sums than when we're doing anything else.'

I looked out of the window, not saying a word. This was not a row I wanted to be drawn into, but Gail surprised me and her daughter.

'Fair enough, love,' she said, pushing the textbooks to one side. 'Let's leave it there for today. Why don't you go and watch telly, your dad will be home any minute.'

Jenny's face instantly brightened as she got down from the kitchen chair. 'Nice one, Mum! Thanks. You coming, Percy?'

Panic rose. A cuddle on the sofa with Jenny while watching *The Simpsons* sounded like heaven. But, on the other hand, I knew Heather would be barking for me any minute and I didn't want to be late.

Right on cue, I heard the sound of Heather's dulcet tones just as Simon walked through the door.

'Evening all,' he said, as he shucked off his coat.

'Hi, love,' Gail replied, as she walked towards him and kissed his cheek. 'Let's try and forget last night, shall we?'

'Sounds good to me.'

As the two leaned in to one another and hugged, I seized my chance, walked back into the kitchen and slipped through the cat flap. By no means was I a fat dog, but the flap was a tight squeeze and I was terrified at one point I was going to end up like poor Barney at the shelter. Thankfully, my paws bounced onto the concrete floor. After wriggling my hind legs out to meet my front, I wasted no time racing up the path and out into the cold night air.

I had never been out alone before and the pitch black left me terrified. Reaching the top of the road where Peg lived, I felt a surge of relief to see she was already waiting for me. Together we scampered up the road towards Heather's woofs, reaching her side within minutes.

'Hello, you two,' she barked in welcome. 'Jake's gone on ahead to see Bugsy and check he's ready for us. Are you two okay to go now, or do you need a couple of minutes to get your breath back?'

I looked at Peg. Like me, she was

wheezing, but determined.

'We're fine,' I barked in reply. 'Let's do this.'

'Okay then, Percy,' Heather woofed.

The German shepherd had a dogged steady pace as she set off before us, and Peg and I struggled to keep up as we ran through the streets, our shorter legs doing us a disservice. I tried hard to catch my breath as I glanced at a slightly younger Peg who seemed to have a lot more puff. How was she doing it? Thankfully, I didn't have to wonder for too long as Heather abruptly came to a halt outside a modest two-up, two-down terrace.

'Here we are then, loves. Jake said he'd be around the back waiting for us if he wasn't out the front so go quietly okay. We don't want to wake the baby,' Heather barked quietly.

'There's no chance of that,' I woofed. Jasper's screams were already ringing through the house and out to the street below.

As we followed Heather down the dark passageway behind the house, we soon saw the Border collie sitting excitedly next to Jake.

'Can you hear him? It's like that every night! Please say you can fix this, Heather,' Bugsy woofed, looking at each of us in turn for reassurance.

'We'll do our best, Bugsy,' Heather barked. 'Now, everyone knows 'Baa Baa Black Sheep', don't they?'

We all nodded as Jake led us further down the alleyway towards a large bush opposite an open window.

'That's the baby's room,' Jake barked once we were hidden behind the shrubbery. 'Now then, dogs, let's keep our tones gentle and keep in time. On my count: one, two, three.'

With that, the five of us started to bark out the tune of the well-known lullaby. Only, despite our best efforts, we sounded more like birds being choked to death than the Welsh Dog Voice Choir to which Jake had once famously belonged. Not only were we out of tune, we were out of time, and it wasn't long before Jasper's cries became full-blown shrieks.

Quickly, Jake interrupted with a furious bark. 'What on earth do you call that? We're dogs, not cats scrapping down an alleyway, screeching to all and sundry that this is our territory. Now let's try again.'

Suitably reprimanded, we shot awkward glances at one another before Jake opened his jaws wide and began barking the sweetest rendition of the lullaby once more. His barks were beautiful and, feeling encouraged, the rest of us opened our mouths, sure we could do better this time. However, within just a few woofs, we realised we were even worse than before with our barks resembling a pack of rabid foxes going in for the kill.

'That's enough,' Jake barked sharply, silencing us immediately. 'If I wanted to spend my evening damaging my hearing, I would have stayed in with Giles for the night and watched a cast of hopefuls on *The X Factor.*'

'Don't you want to give it one more try?' Heather barked nervously, as Jasper's cries became ever louder.

I looked across at Bugsy, who had sunk to the floor in despair, paws over his ears. 'I just can't take it any more,' he whimpered. 'I didn't think it was possible for him to wail any louder, but listen.'

'It's God-awful, old thing, but you can see how we're fixed,' Jake barked sympathetically, jerking his head towards us. 'None of you can carry a tune and I'm afraid if we continue, old chap, we'll make your situation worse.'

'That's okay,' Bugsy barked quietly. 'I understand. Thank you for trying.'

'Well, chaps, it wasn't what we planned or expected, but it seems as though our work here is done,' Jake barked helplessly.

I wished he was wrong, but unfortunately the spaniel was right. We were awful and I worried any further attempts would have Jasper roaring for the entire night. Glancing at Bugsy's downcast expression once more, my heart went out to him. I felt so sorry we had let him down and gave him an affectionate lick on his cheek, as I said goodbye, leaving the others to do the same.

'We'll see you tomorrow in the dog park,' Heather barked sympathetically as we turned to leave. 'Chin up.'

As we all nodded and said our final goodnights to Bugsy, we trotted down the alleyway towards home, each of us lost in our own thoughts. Tagging along at the back in silence, I reflected on the day. Even though our plan to help Bugsy had failed, I still felt remarkably positive. I had started out knowing nobody, but tonight had a group of friends and a loving family. I felt like the change in fortunes I had wished for at the tails of the forgotten was finally beginning to happen.

7

After saying goodnight to all my new friends, I ran as quickly as I could back to my home. Pausing outside, I surveyed the scene as if I were a plucky cat burglar, working out the best way inside undetected. From my position on the pavement behind a large bush, I saw all the lights in the front room were on while the rest of the house lay in darkness. Experience told me this meant Gail, Simon and Jenny had settled down together to watch television and, if luck was still on my side, meant I could scamper quietly down the alleyway and through the cat flap without any of them realising I had slipped out.

Quiet as a mouse, I put my plan into action. Holding my breath, I padded down the dark passageway taking care not to trigger next door's security light and quickly reached the cat flap. I pushed my nose against the plastic entrance, gave it a gentle shove, squeezed my head through and listened. Just as I hoped, the kitchen was silent. I slipped my front paws through the plastic and wriggled my body through, before my rear paws met my front ones on the cool kitchen lino.

Once again, I looked left, then right, before sniffing the air and once I was satisfied the coast was clear, I crept over to my bed and dived under the blankets. As I closed my eyes and breathed in and out, I tried to relax. Tonight might have been a failure, but I had to admit that I had enjoyed myself with my new friends, and it felt wonderful to have tried to help at the very least.

Settling back into the warmth of the blankets, I began to feel sleepy until I suddenly became aware of the hot breath of someone just inches from my face. I could tell without even opening my eyes that it was Gail, her warm, sweet scent instantly giving her away. She placed her hand gently on my head and stroked my forehead before giving me a kiss.

'I was about to ask if you wanted a walk,' she whispered in the darkness, 'but I see you've already taken yourself out for some exercise.'

My eyes flew open and my heart fluttered with panic. I looked at Gail in horror. How could she tell? I'd taken great care to slip in and out unnoticed.

Meeting my gaze, Gail shook her head and smiled. 'I'm a mum, Perce, nothing gets past me. Along with the fact I haven't seen you for the past hour. I was terrified something had happened to you and was just about to send out a search party.'

I got to my paws and hung my head in shame. I felt foolish for thinking I only had to worry about sneaking in and out. I had not intended to make Gail worry.

'I'm sorry. It won't happen again,' I barked softly. 'I had to help some new friends and didn't think you'd miss me.'

'You're freezing, boy,' she said, reaching for one of my blankets and wrapping it around me. 'I'm sure you didn't mean to worry me, but worrying is part of my job. If you disappear for just one moment, I'll fret. I love you, Percy, we all do, I can't bear the thought of anything happening to you.'

'Sorry,' I woofed again, as I licked her face and rested one of my front paws on her hand. I didn't know what else to say.

After patting my head one more time, Gail got to her feet and turned on the light switch, flooding the kitchen with a bright yellow glow. She reached into my food cupboard and got out a bone for me to chew. I tapped my little paws on the floor in pleasure as she handed me the treat.

'Anyway,' she said, sitting on the floor next to me, 'while you were out doing whatever it was you were doing, I wanted to tell you about the strangest thing I saw while I was on the phone to Mum earlier.'

I barked happily, slurping and chewing the lovely and unexpected bone. My adventures had left me with quite an appetite and I had to admit this juicy morsel was taking the edge off my hunger rather nicely.

'It was really funny,' Gail continued, in her soothing tones. 'Mum was just telling me about her neighbour's hip replacement when I suddenly heard this loud barking. At first I thought it was some of your pals from the park, nattering to one another, but when I poked my head out of the window I saw a group of dogs standing outside one of the houses a few streets from here.'

I stopped chewing my bone and brought my head up sharply to meet Gail's, my fur standing on end with trepidation.

'Anyway, I saw this group of dogs all yapping madly at first, and then suddenly they stopped, had what looked like a little conflab and started again with the same dreadful howling,' she explained, chuckling. 'I held the phone up so Mum could hear. She asked me to describe the dogs, Perce, so when I had a little look I saw a lovely-looking Border collie, a spaniel and a German shepherd and a couple of pugs. Then I had another look, Percy, as I don't think I've ever seen two pugs together, and that was when I really had to pinch myself as I could have sworn one of them was you!'

I opened my eyes wide in horror as I realised Gail had seen everything, and troublingly she had seen me. I was relieved to see her eyes were dancing in merriment.

'Remember, Perce, I'm a mum and have eyes everywhere.' Gail grinned.

Over the next few days, I half expected Gail to press me for more details about what she had seen the night I had gone missing, but to my great surprise and relief she let the matter pass. Instead we enjoyed happy trips to the park where we played tennis balls for hours at a time, and I got to know all my new friends better, especially Peg. The more time I spent with her, the more time I wanted to spend with her. Not only was she beautiful, but she was kind, funny and patient. Best of all, she made me feel good about myself and I often tried to bring her little presents like a bone or chew toy, which I would carry to the park for her to enjoy.

Today was no different and, as I saw Peg, I rushed up to her and dropped the bone I had carried with me as if it were precious cargo at her feet.

'For me?' she woofed appreciatively. 'Percy,

you shouldn't. I'm watching my weight!'

'Don't be silly, Peg. You're gorgeous, just as you are,' I barked in reply, meaning every word.

Peg gave me a grateful lick and started chewing on the bone. Turning my head, I saw Jake, Bugsy and Heather chattering nearby and I barked a loud 'Hello', keen to let them know Peg and I were here too.

Hearing my call, the trio trotted over, Bugsy leading the way, full of even more energy if that were possible.

Since our night-time escapade, Bugsy had gone from feeling forlorn to overjoyed almost overnight. It seemed that although our intervention had failed, a few days later, Jasper had discovered the art of sleeping through the night all by himself without a bedtime story or lullaby from our little dog choir.

'Jasper's still sleeping through the night,' he barked joyfully, 'and Bella and Johnny have a lot more time for me now with cuddles and walks, and everyone's a lot less tired, including me as we're all getting a decent night's sleep, which means everyone is ever so much happier and I've got more and more energy.'

As if to prove the point, Bugsy bounded off to the nearest tree, chasing what looked suspiciously like a squirrel, which thankfully bolted up the trunk of a large oak and rested on the branch.

'So our mission was a success after all,' I woofed as Bugsy rejoined me.

'A huge success,' he yapped, his mouth full of drool. 'Everyone's more content, even baby Jasper, who smiled at me for the first time ever yesterday! It was brilliant! I know you didn't help me and made things worse, Percy, because it was your idea, but I'm still grateful to you for encouraging everyone to help me. It's the thought that counts.'

My cheeks flushed with embarrassment. I was unsure quite what to say. 'It was nothing, Bugsy, we all wanted to help.'

'Course we did,' Heather agreed. 'Nobody could be more delighted than me, Bugsy, to see it all work out for you.'

'It's lovely news, Bugsy,' Peg barked happily. 'I take it the horrible Maxwell isn't always bringing you to the park now?'

Bugsy shook his head, sending drool flying everywhere. 'Nope! Johnny's brought me today. Look!'

As he gestured towards his owner sitting peacefully on a park bench, watching us all bark away, my heart burst with pride. Bugsy was finally top dog having got what he always wanted: his loving and happy family back.

Although we had been particularly unhelpful, I wondered what else we could do as a team.

Heather seemed to read my mind as she looked at us all with intent. 'So what's next then?' she yapped. 'Jake's not having the best of times with his owner, Giles, at the moment. He's so old, bless him, that he struggles to take poor Jake to the park for a walk these days.' She scratched her ear with her hind leg and paused. 'That means poor Jake isn't always getting the exercise he so badly needs, and with his hips it's vital he stays active.'

I looked at Heather, her face a picture of concern. 'Do you think we should try to find someone else to help walk him?'

'Well, as long as you don't ask Maxwell,' Bugsy replied gloomily. 'He's useless at bringing you to the park. You can never get him off his phone 'cos he's always playing games, chatting to his friends or watching some stupid zombie show on it, so he never throws balls and it takes ages to actually get to the park because he never takes his eyes off his stupid screen. His mum says he's a little angel, but if that's what an angel looks like I hope I never go to heaven because he's rubbish!'

'Bugsy!' Heather admonished. 'You might have a point, but there's no need to say things like that! No, I think we can do better than Maxwell to take Jake to the park. The question is who?'

'I could ask Sally but she's so scatty it's a small wonder she remembers to bring me to the park let alone anyone else,' Peg barked sharply.

'Where is she now?' I asked, scanning the grass for signs of Sally's blonde mane.

'She's parked herself in the coffee shop over there,' Peg replied, gesturing towards the large stone building behind the trees. 'Our Sal's not a fan of hanging about in the park, unless there's a man about.'

'Oh, Gail was in there a few minutes ago, getting one to take away,' I woofed. 'Looks like she's getting to know Johnny now.'

I looked over at the bench where Gail and Johnny were now sitting and looking at us with undisguised curiosity. If only they could talk dog, I thought unhelpfully and not for the first time. It would be the easiest thing in the world to explain that one of our number was having problems and I knew Gail would jump in and help immediately, or at the very least know what to do.

'Gail and Simon would be perfect, but they're so busy with Jenny about to go into hospital at the minute I don't think they'll have a minute.'

Bugsy turned his attentions from the stick a passer-by had thrown in our general direction and looked up at me with concern. 'You never said anything about a hospital.'

I furrowed my face, making my features even more wrinkly. I had not meant to tell them all about my problems so soon. 'Yes, Jenny, the little girl, has a heart condition and is in and out of hospital for care. I think it's quite serious, but she's going in tomorrow for more tests and my owners Gail and Simon are beside themselves.'

'Oh, Percy, that's awful news,' Peg barked, her dark eyes meeting mine, rich with compassion. 'You must let us know if there's anything we can do for you. You're one of us now.'

'Peg's right, Perce, you should have told us,' Heather barked sympathetically. 'And you shouldn't have come out with us the other night, you should have been at home with your owners, they needed you.'

'I know,' I woofed quietly in reply. 'But Bugsy needed us more and look how happy he is now.'

Heather and I gulped back waves of laughter as we looked at Bugsy running happily after his owner Johnny, who was teasing him with a big stick he was about to throw.

'Is there anything Jenny needs?' Heather barked softly, turning her attention back to me.

I was about to bark a quick and polite no, but the truth was I didn't know. I wanted to help but had no idea how. All I could come up with was being there whenever Jenny needed me so I'd lie next to her on her bed as she watched television or snuggle up with her as she fell asleep. I'd been wracking my brains to try to think of ways I could do more for Jenny, not to mention Simon and Gail but so far had drawn a big blank.

'I'm not sure,' I yapped.

Heather nodded, her face full of compassion. 'It's hard on you too, though, Percy. You haven't been with them long, and this is a very big deal. You don't have to do everything on your own, so let us know if you need anything at all.'

My little heart could have burst with pleasure at their kindness. 'Thank you, both of you.'

'I think I've solved Jake's problem,' Bugsy woofed, rejoining us. 'Me and Johnny were just playing games and he looked over and saw us all, and realised Jake wasn't here. Well, Johnny asked Gail if she knew where Jake was and she said she didn't and that she had only occasionally seen an older spaniel here with an even older colonel, but she had only been coming to the park the last few weeks as a regular, as they hadn't had you, Percy, for very long so she said she wasn't sure of who everyone in the gang was.' Bugsy paused for breath, his tongue lolling out of the corner of his mouth, before continuing his speech. 'Anyway, then Johnny said that Jake was definitely part of our gang and that he was a lovely old boy, as was his owner, who he realised had been suffering from ill health lately. Then your Gail said that she didn't know that and asked if there was anything she could or should do.'

As Bugsy gathered his breath, I turned to look at Gail. Catching my eye, she gave me a smile and a little wave. My heart burst with pride that she belonged to me. How selfless was she to offer to help when she had so much of her own to cope with.

'Anyway,' Bugsy continued, 'I barked very loudly when Gail said that and Johnny looked at me, and that's when he said perhaps he and Bella could try to look in on Jake and his owner as they've known him for years.'

'That's true, they have,' Heather woofed. 'And you have to pass Jake's house on your way to the park.'

Bugsy's face lit up. 'That's what Johnny said, and I agreed very loudly. So we're going to call in on Jake on the way home, and offer to bring him with us when we go to the park. Johnny said that since Jasper was sleeping through the night now, they had more time and energy for things and their lives were much happier and easier, so it would be no trouble for him and Bella to look in on Jake and also check the colonel's okay. I told him that was a brilliant idea by barking in all the right places and so it's all sorted now. We've solved another problem.'

'That's brilliant news, Bugsy,' Peg barked delightedly. 'Well done, you.'

'Yes, well done, Bugsy,' Heather agreed. 'It's a logical solution, and sounds like you helped Johnny reach the right conclusion.'

'I really did,' he agreed. 'Even Gail said it looked as though I thought it a marvellous idea, and that dogs were capable of more than humans gave them credit for.'

'Well, she would know,' I barked darkly, 'she saw us the other night outside your house.'

Peg looked at me in shock. 'No! I thought we were all so careful.'

'We were,' I barked in reply, 'but Gail saw us all when she was on the phone to her mum. She's not going to say anything. I think the most she's going to do is pull my leg over it, but we have to be careful if we do anything like that in the future.'

'Quite right, Percy,' Heather agreed. 'But are you sure Gail won't say anything to anyone?'

I shook my head. 'She definitely won't. Gail's not like that.'

'Thank goodness for that,' Heather barked with relief. 'She does seem to be a nice lady. She gave me a treat earlier in the week.'

'And me,' barked Peg.

'And me, a minute ago,' Bugsy woofed. 'Are you sure there's nothing we can do to help you or Gail?'

I regarded them all with gratitude. 'Not now, but in the future, possibly. There's so much going on between Simon and Gail, and the toll Jenny's health is taking on them all as a family. Today, I'm just hoping that Jenny's hospital visit goes well.'

'I'm sure it will, lovey,' Heather woofed supportively. 'The hospitals do marvellous things these days. All you hear humans go on about when hospitals are mentioned is all that new technology.'

'Exactly,' Peg barked, giving me a gentle nudge and resting her blonde paw on mine.

Feeling her fur on mine, I felt a pang of longing. How much better everything would be if I could cuddle up with Peg for a little bit.

'Well, keep us posted,' Heather barked, interrupting my daydreams. 'We're here for you aren't we?'

'Definitely,' Bugsy agreed. 'We're a team.'

'Too right we are,' Peg yapped. 'And we're all in this together. We're rooting for Jenny tomorrow.'

I looked at my new friends with delight. Things might be tough for my new family, but I had a funny feeling it really did look as though between us we could solve anything.

8

As Gail and I wandered home, I couldn't help admiring all the lovely Christmas decorations we passed. Houses were literally lit up like Christmas trees with fairy lights strung from windows, inflatable Santas hung from guttering and fluorescent reindeer loitering outside in people's gardens. Turning a corner, we stopped in our tracks as we saw one house with neon lights flashing from every window and door, while 'Santa Claus is Coming to Town' was playing at high volume from a speaker hooked up to the roof. The front garden was filled with giant illuminated Christmas trees, while a large Father Christmas shouted, 'Ho, ho, ho,' from a floodlit sleigh.

'My goodness,' Gail marvelled as she turned to me, unable to contain her laughter. 'What do you reckon, Perce? Is Christmas a few weeks away or something?'

I looked at Gail's shaking shoulders and immediately picked up on her sarcasm. 'I've never seen anything like it,' I woofed. 'Looks like they've used the entire street's Christmas decorations.'

Gail chuckled again as we carried on walking. 'Honestly, Perce, I must tell Simon not to bring Jenny down this way. She'll be on at us to light our house like that; she loves the holidays.'

At the mention of Jenny, Gail went quiet and started dawdling, the effort of putting one foot in front of the other seemingly too much for her. Despite the cold against my skin, I slowed down next to her. She was clearly deep in thought, and I had a fairly good idea what she was thinking about.

'Sorry, Percy,' Gail said, as she saw me loitering by her side. 'I'm all over the place with Jenny going into hospital. I'll just be glad when she's in there really and we're getting on with it. All this waiting about, well, it's doing my head in to be perfectly honest. Do you know what I mean?'

I knew exactly what Gail meant. She and Simon had been so worried about this that for days they had talked of little else, frantically changing the subject whenever Jenny appeared.

'It'll be fine,' I barked reassuringly. 'You're bound to be worried, it's natural. But it's just a couple of tests, nothing more.'

'I've just got to stop worrying. Nothing bad's going to happen tomorrow, and who knows, it might even be good news as the doctors might be able to tell us why all these different medications aren't working and help us find one that will.'

'That's the spirit,' I barked approvingly as home came into view.

Once there, Gail hurried down the path towards the front door, and I waited patiently as she fished in her bag for her key to unlock it.

'Hello,' she called, closing the door behind us and flipping on the hall light. 'Anyone home?'

'Hi, Mum. Hi, Percy.' Jenny emerged from the kitchen in a huge furry rabbit onesie, beaming. 'How was the park?'

'Lovely, thanks, sweetheart.' Gail smiled then kissed her daughter's cheek before bending down and unclipping my lead. 'Percy met all his pals, didn't you?'

'Certainly did,' I barked in agreement.

'And I had a nice coffee. Where's your dad?'

'In the kitchen, making spag bol,' Jenny replied, as she bent down to kiss my forehead.

She scooped me into her arms, carried me into the kitchen and set me down in my basket. I sniffed the air appreciatively. Simon always let me have a big piece of the Parmesan he grated whenever he made the meaty dish and I sat in my bed looking up at him, as he stood by the hob, stirring the sauce, curling and uncurling my tail in anticipation.

'All right, mate.' He smiled down at me. 'It's nice to see you too. Where on earth have you been?' he asked, as Gail arrived in the kitchen and planted a kiss on her husband's cheek.

'Just to the park to take Percy for his evening walk,' Gail replied, peering into the saucepan and nodding approvingly.

'Well, you're a bit late,' he replied, glancing up at the clock. 'You know I always make dinner for seven, it's ten past that now.'

Gail rolled her eyes. 'It's only ten minutes, love. It's not exactly a lifetime, is it?'

'No, but the pasta's going to be overdone and cold now,' Simon pointed out, gesturing to the saucepan full of cooked pasta that stood on the hob.

'Well, give it a blast in the microwave,' Gail said, as she turned to the sink and washed her hands in readiness. 'It'll be fine.'

'It won't be fine. It'll be ruined, but I don't expect you to care about the fact I've been slaving over a hot stove after a day on the tools,' Simon snapped, pulling plates out of the cupboards.

Gail dried her hands on the towel under the sink. 'Oh, for heaven's sake, you're always telling me how much you like cooking and how much it helps you unwind after a day sticking your hand down someone else's loo.'

'Er, yuck, Mum!' Jenny groaned, as she sat at the chair and beckoned to me to join her side.

'Sorry, love — ' Gail smiled, looking down at her daughter ' — but that is how your father makes a living.'

'And a bloody good job I do,' Simon grumbled, 'without my wages we'd be stuffed.'

'And that's my fault, is it?' Gail fired.

'Here we go,' Jenny muttered quietly as she scooped me onto her lap.

Simon paused, clearly regretting his outburst. 'I'm not saying that, I'm just saying it would be nice if my efforts around the house weren't wasted that's all.'

Gail took a deep breath and pinched the bridge of her nose. 'Your efforts are appreciated, Simon. Just because me and Percy are ten minutes late back from the park doesn't mean I don't appreciate you. For heaven's sake, why are you being so difficult?'

'I'm not being difficult. I'm just saying, Gail. Why were you so long anyway?' he asked, pulling cutlery from a drawer and laying the table.

'I just got chatting with Johnny, one of

Percy's doggy owners. He was telling me how worried he is about this elderly colonel, who he used to see every day walking a spaniel called Jake,' Gail replied as she stood at the sink and filled a jug with water. 'Anyway, he was telling me how he was going to offer to take Jake to the park for walks if the colonel was struggling to get out, so I said we'd help too.'

'Why did you say that?' Simon fumed as he laid the final fork on the table. 'Don't you think we've got enough at the moment to keep us occupied, without you sorting out everyone else's problems as well?'

Gail whipped around from the sink and slammed the water down on the draining board. 'Don't be so childish. What's wrong with wanting to help someone besides ourselves?'

'I didn't say there was anything wrong with it, I said we've got more than enough on our plates at the minute.' Simon sighed. 'What with Jenny, Percy — who I'm still not sure we should keep, by the way, there's too much going on here. Why don't you listen to anything I say?'

At the mention of the possibility of me returning to the tails of the forgotten, I felt a shiver of fear. I had started to fall in love with this family — was it possible they would never love me enough?

'You can forget any idea about Percy going back to the shelter!' Gail blasted, her shrill tone interrupting my thoughts. 'He's here to stay, he's a complete treasure. You want to think about someone besides yourself for a change.'

'I didn't say Percy wasn't a treasure! Christ, Gail, I need this like a hole in the head. I'm just saying we need to prioritise, that's all, and Jenny has to be our priority.'

I looked up at Jenny, who was unnaturally quiet. The last thing she needed was to hear her parents rowing, tonight of all nights.

'Settle down,' I barked crossly, lifting my head from her lap, 'you two aren't helping Jenny.'

Gail glanced at me and her expression softened. 'It's not fair to do this in front of Jenny. Let's discuss this later.'

'Fine by me,' Simon said, furiously ladling three plates with spaghetti and sauce, and banging them on the table.

Jenny's head snapped up. 'Well, it's not fine by me. All you two ever do is argue. You're never nice to each other and always row about stupid stuff. I don't want to listen to it any more! I'll eat in my room.'

With that, Jenny reached for a plate of food before storming out of the door. I looked at

Gail, whose face was now flushed with anger.

'Now look what you've done, Simon,' she spat. 'Thanks for cooking, but I've suddenly lost my appetite.'

With that Gail fled from the kitchen and followed Jenny upstairs.

Simon looked at me and shrugged. 'Women, Perce!' he said, shaking his head and sinking onto a chair.

I didn't know what to say. The argument had clearly been so petty, but had caused so much damage. The trouble was, Gail and Simon were behaving like children, I thought crossly. My family might be having problems, but they had no business upsetting Jenny like that. I cocked my head and heard the sounds of Jenny sobbing on Gail's shoulder, as she did her best to soothe her daughter.

Looking back up at Simon, I saw his face was red with anger. More than anything, I wanted to help this family I adored, but why on earth could they not do more to help themselves?

★   ★   ★

I woke the next morning early to find Jenny sat beside me in her pyjamas waiting for me to stir.

'Do you need a wee?' she whispered in my

ear. 'Just let me know when you want to go out and I'll open the door.'

I felt drained after last night's dramas and ashamed to admit that a part of me wanted to pretend I had simply not heard Jenny. But I could not ignore the little girl's gentle tones, and I got the feeling she wanted the chance to spend a few precious moments alone with me this morning so I shook myself awake. Once I had blinked the sleep from my eyes, I greeted Jenny eagerly by licking her soft cheek before she got up to open the door.

As my paws padded across the frosty lawn, I shivered in the freezing December air, and was as quick as possible before hurrying back into the warmth of the house. Padding over towards Jenny near the sink, I saw she was filling my bowl up with food and refreshing my water.

'I've made you breakfast.' She smiled, setting the refreshments in front of me.

As I tucked in, Jenny perched next to me, her long legs tucked underneath as she watched me eat. Sneaking a peek up at her between mouthfuls I saw her eyes were downcast and her skin looked grey. Over the past few weeks, Jenny and I had developed a routine where, once I had eaten, I would scamper up to her room and together we would lie on her bed, and snuggle up to each other. Sometimes Jenny would read a book or listen to music, but most of the time she just liked to talk to me, and nothing gave me greater pleasure than to listen. I loved to feel as though I was helping the little girl cope with her heart condition.

But this morning, even though breakfast was as ever, delicious, I felt we needed one of our talks immediately, so I stopped eating and turned towards her. I rubbed my head into her tummy and Jenny squirmed with delight, then I edged my way onto her lap and met her gaze. Today was the day she was going into hospital and I saw her eyes were filled with worry. I felt so helpless and would have done anything to make her day more bearable. But all I knew I could do was be there for her, so I gently rested my paw on her arm and tried to coax her to talk to me.

'Oh, Percy, I'm so scared,' she said, her low voice trembling. 'What if they find something seriously wrong with me and I have to keep going back into hospital?'

My ears pricked with alarm. Over the past week I had watched Jenny tell her parents over and over that she felt fine about going into hospital, that it was a good excuse to get away from her mum and dad and hang out with kids her own age. Of course, Simon and Gail had not believed her and neither had I.

Yet it was still a shock to hear her reveal her true feelings. To me, however, a problem shared was a problem halved, so I looked up at her again and let out a soft whine, encouraging her to keep going.

Sadly, she planted a kiss on my face. 'It's not just me I'm worried about. Mum and Dad haven't been the same since we moved up here and I know it's all because of me. You saw what they were like last night.'

Last night had been unbearable. Gail and Simon had managed to be civil to one another after Jenny had stopped crying and said how sorry they were for upsetting her. But once Jenny had gone to bed, they had continued their row in the garden until the small hours, when Gail had gone to bed and Simon had slept in his man cave.

'They act like they hate each other,' she continued flatly. 'Sometimes I think they're only staying together because of me. Before I got sick everything was perfect. Dad didn't have his stupid man cave and Mum used to laugh all the time. Now, they hate each other and it's all my fault.'

I rested my head against her heart and listened to its irregular beat. How could Jenny think her mum and dad's problems were anything to do with her? Jenny was already facing a difficult enough day, and she needed to be in a more positive frame of mind if she was going to get through what lay ahead. I thought quickly — sometimes the tough love approach worked best. I lifted my head from her chest and shuffled around in her lap so I could look at her properly.

'Nonsense,' I barked quietly. 'Your parents love you, and whatever they're going through, you mustn't blame yourself. You have to concentrate on getting better and let your mum and dad look after themselves. They would be furious if they knew what you were thinking and to be perfectly honest so am I!'

Once I finished barking, I sank my head back against Jenny's chest. I had never said so much first thing in the morning and my little speech had quite worn me out.

Jenny raked her fingers through my fur. 'I know I'm just a kid, Perce. Mum and Dad have got to sort themselves out, but I don't like how we are as a family any more. I wish you could have seen us when we lived in Devon. We had a life: I had my friends, Mum and Dad had theirs. We used to have fun, go to the park, cinema, that sort of stuff, nothing special, but now everything revolves around my hospital visits, and it's not fair.'

As she paused for a breath, I listened to her heartbeat again. It wasn't very strong but it was going fast. The last thing Jenny needed was any stress, not when she was about to go into hospital. I looked up at her and saw her eyes were full of tears, running like rivers down her face. As they plopped onto my fur, I felt Jenny's anguish as keenly as if it were my own. More than anything I wanted to help. She was hardly asking for the world, merely a happy, loving childhood. Jenny was enduring far more than any child should and I vowed at that moment to try to make the little girl's dreams a reality.

I burrowed my way deeper into her lap and craned my head upwards so it lay against her neck, and gave her a lick. Her skin was damp with salty tears and I mopped them up with my fur, as I leaned into her with the full weight of my body and tried to reassure her.

'It's all going to be okay,' I whined quietly into her skin. 'I promise you, Jenny, everything will go back to how it was, I'll make sure of it.'

'I knew you would understand, Percy,' Jenny whispered in my ear. 'You're the best dog in the world.'

Jenny rested her cheek against mine and wrapped her long arms around me. 'Do you remember how I asked you to keep an eye on Mum? Well, do you think you could keep an eye on both of them?' she asked. 'At first I thought it was just Mum that wasn't coping, but I think it's both of them. Even though I hate hearing them row, at least if I'm here I know what's going on. I can't do that from my hospital bed.'

I barked a simple 'Yes', then snuggled back into her neck and felt Jenny's hot breath against my flesh. This had all gone on for too long now. A family should be coming together at a time of crisis not tearing each other apart. A little girl with a heart condition should not be concerning herself with the state of her parents' marriage. This was clearly a lot more serious than I had realised, and I considered my friends offers of help. I had not wanted to burden my new pals with my problems so soon, but perhaps that was exactly what I needed to do. I looked up again at Jenny and saw her eyes filled with a combination of fear and worry. I had to do more to help this family, but how?

9

I had never been left on my own before and, as I wandered from room to room, I had to admit the house was extraordinarily quiet without my family. They had left an hour earlier to take Jenny to the hospital and, as they had kissed and hugged me goodbye with promises to be back soon, I had licked each one with tenderness and soaked up the affection they offered.

Watching them all drive away left me feeling sad and fearful, not just for Jenny and the tests she would face over the next couple of days, but for the whole family. I was worried for all of them as things seemed to have gone from bad to worse between Gail and Simon and I could not help but worry about the effect their relationship was having on Jenny. I dived under the blankets Gail had lovingly made for me and rested my eyes.

I thought back to the day Gail had chosen me at the tails of the forgotten. I remembered the sorrow in her eyes as she had revealed how much she needed a friend and I had promised to do all I could to support her and her family. I let out a little sigh as I closed my eyes more tightly. Last night's row had been the worst yet and even though the couple were doing their best to be all smiles for Jenny this morning, it was obvious things were far from resolved.

I looked out of the window and saw that snow had started to fall lightly to the ground. I stood there, mesmerised by the soft flakes, and pondered about what to do for the rest of the day without Jenny and Gail to play with. Simon was due home later to take care of me, while Gail stayed overnight at the hospital, but until then I was a free man. If I was honest I was feeling a bit anxious about spending time alone with Simon, especially after what he had said the night before. Rather than use this as a time to bond with me, I was concerned he might use it against me. What if he ignored me or neglected me, and then told Gail I was difficult and it would be better for everyone if I went back to the tails of the forgotten? Turning away from the window, I felt a surge of despair, unsure what to do. But as I looked around the room, I felt my worries disappear as I saw that Jenny had overfilled my bowl with food and left me a stack of toys to play with. I scampered towards the pile and felt my spirits lift as I saw she had even included a rubber chicken with a very loud squeak that I adored but everyone else detested. Perhaps I would nap for a bit then play with my favourite toy before doing anything else.

As I snuggled deeper into my blankets, I heard the sounds of the radio drift from the living room. Gail had thought the little wireless might offer me some company while they were out, and I had to admit the soothing sounds were making me feel less alone. I let out a contented sigh and listened to the voices wash over me, when suddenly I noticed the background chatter getting louder and louder. Reluctantly, I opened my eyes and lifted my head as a woman's voice shrilled through the kitchen and a clatter of paws scampered across the lino.

'Percy! There you are, boy,' Sally gushed as she bent down to ruffle my fur, closely followed by Peg.

At the sight of the young pug, I felt my heart pound. Her glossy fur shone and her inky black eyes were alive with warmth.

'Hello. What are you doing here?' I woofed, trying to still my beating heart.

'We've come to take you to the park,' Peg explained. 'Simon told Sally that Jenny was in hospital and you weren't getting a proper walk this morning so Sally volunteered to help.'

As Sally clipped on my lead, I got to my

feet and felt a rush of excitement. Gail and Simon had not mentioned anything to me about going for a walk with Sally and Peg. With everything that was going on, I had resigned myself to squeezing through the cat flap if I needed a wee.

'I hope you don't mind me whisking you away,' Sally said, as she locked the front door, 'but I felt ever so sorry for you when Simon said he didn't think he'd be able to take you for a proper walk this morning, so me and Peg offered our services.'

Peg barked immediately. 'You should have told us yourself, Percy. I'd have made sure we came over and got you. In fact, why don't you come back to ours afterwards? It's no fun on your own all day, and we could get Simon to pick you up when he gets back. What do you think?'

The pug's kindness was leaving me hot under the collar. But the thought of a whole day with Peg was an offer too good to turn down.

'I'd love to. If you're sure you don't mind?' I woofed quickly, as we rounded the corner and turned into the park.

'Course I don't mind,' she yapped. 'It would be lovely to spend some real time with you, Perce. I'll suggest it to Sally in my usual roundabout way, which will leave her thinking it was all her idea!'

My eyes locked with Peg's in gratitude. There was no denying it, she was gorgeous and I could have stayed there all day drinking in her beauty.

'Go on then, you two.' Sally smiled as she unclipped our leads. 'Have fun with your mates. I'll be over in the café getting a coffee, it's far too cold to stay out here. I'll see you in a bit.'

Spotting Bugsy's owner, Johnny, heading towards the old stone coffee house, Sally rushed after him, leaving Peg and me to fend for ourselves.

'Shall we go and see the others then?' I asked, desperately trying to think of some way to break the silence.

Peg curled and uncurled her tail as she turned her gaze away from mine. 'Good idea. After all, we've got all day to spend together.'

My heart beat loudly in anticipation as we ran side by side towards the dog track where I caught sight of Bugsy and Jake already deep in conversation as the snow continued to fall.

'Hello, boys,' Peg panted as we reached a standstill, 'what are you gossiping about?'

'Oh, this and that,' replied Jake, dismissively. 'I was just asking Bugsy here to pass on my sincere thanks to Johnny and Bella for taking me out for a walk. I must say, regular exercise has made the world of difference to my hips, and it's less of a worry for Giles, knowing someone's able to walk me when he can't, not that he ever can these days.'

'How is Giles?' I asked.

'The same,' he woofed. 'Good days and bad days. That's the trouble with getting older — in your head you're still a teenager while your body feels about a hundred! Giles has a carer now that calls in every day with some of those meals on wheels.'

Heather scampered up to Jake's side. 'Good to see you, old boy.'

'And you, miss,' Jake replied, fondness bursting from his bark.

'Heather's right, admitting you need help takes courage,' I added, understanding more than most how true that was.

Jake lifted his hips from the floor and gave himself a little shake to get his circulation going. 'Yes, you're right, young Percy. Which is just what Bugsy and I were discussing. It was Johnny and Bella who organised the meal delivery, along of course with my walks. I couldn't be more grateful to them.'

'It was no trouble, Jake,' Bugsy woofed. 'After everything you all did to try to help me, it was nothing and I know Bella and Johnny are glad to help.'

'I take it Jasper's still sleeping well then?' Heather asked.

Bugsy nodded happily. 'He wakes up a couple of times in the night, but he gets off again really, really, really quickly! And Bella says that she and Johnny have to take equal turns at looking after him, which they do, so that means that when they get up, I get up and keep them company so I get lots of cuddles as we sing Jasper back to sleep. Last night they even let me get on their bed and they didn't say a word!'

'Well done, Bugsy,' Peg barked approvingly, 'that's lovely news. I'm delighted it's working out so well. So with you two all sorted, it seems it's time to turn our attentions to the newest member of our little group. What do you say, Percy?'

I shuffled from paw to paw. Although I was grateful for Peg's concern and had resolved to be more open with my new friends, I still felt it was a bit early to ask for help. Then I remembered how hurt and confused Jenny had been last night, and the fresh tears she and Gail had cried into my fur only that morning as they kissed me goodbye. For my family's sake, perhaps it was time to reveal the full extent of their troubles and see if anyone had any suggestions. Taking a deep breath, I glanced at each of my friends, wondering where to start.

'Come on, lovey, better out than in,' Heather coaxed, cocking her head to one side and regarding me sympathetically.

She was right. 'Well, I didn't tell you everything when I told you about Jenny's heart condition and her visit to the hospital.'

'What do you mean?' Peg demanded.

'Well, it's not just Jenny that's having problems. Simon and Gail are always rowing too,' I barked.

Pausing for breath, I looked at each of my friends' faces, their expressions a mix of curiosity and concern. Quickly, I told them everything Gail had told me when we had first met, along with how much worse things seemed to have become. I left nothing out — the rows, the tears and the amount of time Simon spent alone in his man cave. By the time I had finished, I felt quite emotional and, as the snow turned to sleet and rain , I realised I felt like joining in with the sky, shedding its own tears of sadness as the water soaked into my fur.

'Percy, I'm so sorry to hear that,' Heather barked first. 'That's an awful lot for you to cope with, never mind Gail and Simon. The poor loves, dealing with marital problems while their little girl is so poorly, it can't be easy.'

Jake wiggled his hips again, the length of my story obviously taking its toll. 'Sadly, it's all too common. Giles' first wife left him after the death of their son. Instead of turning to each other, they turned on each other. It was dreadful to witness. Since then it's just been me and the old boy rubbing along together in that great big house. I wish there was more I could do for him, but he's too old now. Family battles can cause terrible devastation, which is why you should do your best to help your loved ones now, Percy, before it's too late.'

Jake's speech left me reeling. I knew he was right, but the thought of my family enduring such terrible sadness was heartbreaking. Sensing my upset, Heather sidled over to me and nuzzled her face against mine in a gesture of sympathy.

'Jake's right, lovey. You do have to do something before it's too late, but we'll help. Try not to worry,' she crooned.

Peg trotted over to my other side and gave me a lick. 'Heather's right. You're not on your own. I'm glad you were able to tell us everything. Now we know we can all come up with a plan.'

'Won't be easy though, old boy,' Jake woofed. 'I don't wish to be the purveyor of bad news, but if the two people in a relationship can't fix things, I'm not sure how much help a few dogs can be. The best help you can offer may simply be getting them to accept that things are beyond repair and they're better off apart for everyone's sakes, particularly your little girl.'

Bugsy leapt up and down with exasperation. 'Jake! I can't believe you're saying that. We can do anything we put our minds to and we can help Percy, I know we can. His family is not beyond repair and we can fix this. They're a family and they should be together not apart. I'm going to show you, you'll see.'

I looked at Bugsy gratefully. He may have been young, but his enthusiasm was infectious and I started to believe that if we put our heads together we could have a happy ending.

'You're right, Bugsy,' Jake agreed reluctantly. 'Ignore me. At my age you tend to feel you've seen and done everything and there's no such thing as good news.'

'Just how old are you, Jake?' Peg woofed her question evenly.

Heather let out a whine of laughter. 'Good luck getting the answer, lovey. I've known old Jake over ten years and he's refused to tell me in all that time.'

'A gentleman doesn't like to reveal his age,' Jake yapped good-naturedly. 'Let's just say it's very difficult to teach an old dog new tricks, but that doesn't mean I don't like to give the odd one a try. Now, on that note, these old bones of mine are cold, and I think I might like to go home. Do you think Johnny might be willing to go now, Bugsy?'

'He's been looking over here tapping his watch for the last ten minutes,' Bugsy replied. 'I think he'll be very happy we want to go.'

'As will Pete,' Heather barked in agreement. 'He's working from home today and I know he didn't want to stay long.'

'We'll say goodbye then,' Peg barked. 'Our Sal's got a couple of days off and I know she'll want to get back in time for *Loose Women*. Come on, Perce, let's howl at her outside the coffee shop, and let her know we're ready.'

'No need,' I said, gesturing towards Sally who appeared to be waiting outside the café for us.

'Whoops!' Peg barked, her tongue lolling cheerfully from her mouth. 'Sal hates waiting. Never mind.'

I barked my goodbyes and quickly followed Peg to where Sally was standing.

'Had fun you two?' she asked, clipping on our leads. 'Let's get you both home.'

Peg shot me a look as we trotted alongside Sally and she barked up at her owner quickly.

'Or he could stay the whole day until Simon returns.'

Sally paused, clearly experiencing a brain-wave. 'You know what, why don't you just stay with us until Simon gets back, Percy. I'll send him a text and tell him where you are.'

As Peg gave me a triumphant glance, she barked knowingly, 'Told you Sal does what I want. Stick with me, Perce, I'll show you a thing or two.'

We quickly reached Sally's flat and, after she ushered us inside, she set down two bowls full of food and then retired to the living room to watch television. Peg and I ate as though we had never seen food before and afterwards I felt really very tired, the events of the day having quite worn me out.

'Do you fancy a nap?' I asked Peg, quietly.

'Always,' she barked. 'Let's go and have a sleep on Sally's bed.'

'Won't she mind?' Gail and Simon allowed me to sleep in a basket by their bed if I wanted to but under no circumstances was I allowed to jump up.

'She won't care,' Peg replied, leading the way.

I was too tired to argue and followed without question to a room filled with a large four-poster bed. The bed was very grand, but it also looked comfortable and inviting.

'Come on then, Perce,' Peg beckoned as she jumped up and sprawled her paws out across the middle.

'Okay,' I barked, feeling nervous as I hopped up beside Peg. Nestling next to her, I breathed in her unmistakable woody fragrance. The warm, comforting smell of her always made me happy and I started to relax.

'Hope you're not getting too close, Percy!' Peg admonished suddenly.

Fear exploded through my chest. Had I done something wrong? That was the last thing I wanted to do, and I inched away from my favourite pug quickly, keen not to cause any more offence.

'Oh, Percy, don't be silly,' Peg yapped affectionately. 'There's nothing I'd like more than to snuggle up next to you for the afternoon, I was only teasing.'

'Really?' I barked hopefully. 'I don't want you to think badly of me.'

Peg opened her large inky black eyes in amazement. 'As if I could think badly of you, Percy. I really like you.'

My tummy did a large somersault as I got to my feet and looked at her with undisguised hope. 'I like you too. You're one of the reasons I would hate to be sent back to tails of the forgotten.'

The blonde pug looked at me in surprise.

'Why would you be sent back to the shelter? You've only just got here.'

I let out a sigh of anxiety. I had not meant to bark quite so much, but something about Peg made me feel as though I could woof anything to her. Quickly, I explained the situation and saw Peg's features change from concern to disgust.

'That's low,' she yapped. 'I bet the shelter don't know that's what he's been thinking. What does Gail say?'

'She says I'm not going anywhere,' I barked. 'And we've already developed such a bond, I'm sure she means it.'

'Well then, in that case you won't be going anywhere,' Peg barked authoritatively. 'Trust me, Simon won't have a leg to stand on.'

'I know, but just having this weird deadline hanging over my snout makes me feel like I can't relax. I might be back at tails of the forgotten come the new year.'

Peg snorted. 'And pugs might fly! Gail will never let it happen.'

As her barks drew to a close, she padded across the bed to me, and leaned in towards my ear. 'And neither will I. I like you. You're the kindest, sweetest pug I've ever met. I'm going to make sure you stay here for ever and ever.'

My heart roared with pleasure. Something

told me she was serious.

'Thanks, Peg,' I woofed gently, licking her ear and then rubbing her nose with my wet snout. 'You don't know how happy you've made me.'

'Just trust me, Percy,' Peg barked again. 'You're far too special to slip away. So now that we've sorted that out, can we get back to our nap?'

As Peg shifted back to the middle of the bed and curled up in a ball, I nestled against her back, and softly threw one of my front paws around her neck. Breathing in that heady, woody scent once more, I sighed with contentment. Peg thought I was special. I never expected to hear that. Could this be a sign of happier times to come?

10

The closing theme tune to *EastEnders* blared from the television, causing Sally to stretch herself catlike from the sofa and reach for her glass of wine. As she took a long, steady sip of the red liquid she turned to me and Peg, who were curled up next to her long, jean-clad legs.

'What do you two fancy watching?' she asked, picking up the television remote and scrolling through the channels. 'Peg loves a nature programme, don't you, but I find them a bit boring. Prefer a good story myself.'

'Your whole life's one big story,' Peg barked good-naturedly before she turned to me. 'Don't waste your time even suggesting something, Percy, she won't listen. She'll be sticking *Corrie* on in a minute.'

I said nothing, contented enough sitting beside Peg on the sofa. We had spent most of our afternoon fast asleep, then gone for a quick scamper around the park just before the snow turned to rain. Returning to Sally's flat once more, we had eaten our dinner side by side before retiring to the front room to thaw out by the radiator and watch television.

I had to admit, I had never been happier. The afternoon with Peg had been sheer heaven and I would almost be sorry when it was time to go home. I regarded Peg quietly as she lay with her front and back paws outstretched. She had never looked lovelier and I was just about to tell her so when the doorbell sounded loudly.

'Ooh, that'll be Simon, Percy!' Sally exclaimed, moving her legs and rising from the sofa, much to Peg's disgust.

'I was enjoying that,' she yapped to Sally's retreating back. 'And now you're going to go as well. I've really loved you being here this afternoon, Perce.'

I licked her soft cheek as I heard Sally's and Simon's voices in the hallway. 'Me too. I hope we can do it again soon.'

'See, I made sure your boy's still in one piece,' Sally said, as Simon followed her into the living room.

'Percy! My man! How are you doing?' Simon rushed towards me and softly stroked my head before scooping me up in his arms. 'I've missed you today.'

At the sight of my owner, and his obvious enthusiasm to see me, I felt a burst of happiness. Had I been worrying about tonight for nothing?

'Hello,' I whined, covering his tired face

with a series of wet licks.

'Jenny's fine, mate,' he told me softly, perching on the chair opposite the sofa and settling me on his lap.

'Wine, Simon? Or are you in a rush?' Sally called from the kitchen.

Simon checked his watch, then shrugged. 'I'm in no hurry to return to an empty house, Sal. And a glass of wine would be a great way of taking the edge off the day, thanks.'

'My pleasure,' she replied, returning with a large glass of red.

Simon took a large gulp and shucked off his padded black jacket. 'Thanks, Sal. And thanks for looking after Percy today, we all really appreciate it. What a day.'

'It was no problem,' Sally replied kindly. 'I rather think our pugs have become quite fond of each other.' She grinned as I settled myself back onto Simon's lap. 'How has it all gone at the hospital?'

Simon paused as if unsure where to begin. 'Well, fine, I s'pose. The doctors are just assessing Jenny with a round of tests, monitoring her chest, that sort of thing, to see how well her heart is now. None of the drugs so far have worked for very long, as within a few weeks she's back to fainting and struggles to even get out of bed.'

'Poor love,' Sally sympathised. 'What do

the doctors think they can do?'

'They're not sure yet. All sorts of treatments have been discussed, including the possibility of a transplant, but Gail and I have kept most of them from Jenny. We don't want to worry her any more than we possibly have to.' Simon shrugged as he rhythmically started stroking my fur.

'Oh God! That's awful!' Sally exclaimed. 'I'm so sorry, Simon. How on earth is Gail? I can't imagine how she must be feeling.'

Simon sipped his wine and closed his eyes briefly before opening them again. 'Gail's okay. At least I think she's okay. She's doing her best to be strong for Jenny. She's staying with her tonight, pretending that their stay in hospital is one big sleepover. She even went to the supermarket across the road and got them some popcorn so they could do a movie night.'

I lifted my head and looked at Simon. He looked as if he had aged a hundred years in the past few hours. His salt-and-pepper hair seemed more salty than it had a few weeks ago, and his eyes were filled with despair. I thought about the transplant he had mentioned and began to realise Jenny's condition was becoming increasingly more serious. I was unsure exactly what a transplant was but the word sounded dangerous. Suddenly it hit me that Simon and Gail were dealing with a life-or-death situation, and, more than anything, I wanted to be with Gail and offer her support when she needed it most. I pictured her brave face, laughing with Jenny while masking her own emotions. I knew she would save the tears for later when Jenny was asleep. She would need me more than ever and I was desperate to see her tomorrow when I would lick her cheek and simply sit on her lap giving her all my love and comfort.

'And what about Jenny? How's she coping with it all?' Sally asked, draining her glass and reaching for the bottle for a refill.

At the mention of his daughter, I saw Simon's face break into a smile. 'Incredibly, she's fine. Actually, she's better than fine, she's blooming in the hospital.'

'Really?' Sally asked as she refilled their glasses.

'To Jenny, it's a chance to hang out with her mates. She loves all the nurses, and she knows most of the kids on the ward because she's been there so often. As she's home-schooled she doesn't get much chance to see other kids so for her it's a treat! It's almost as though she can't wait to get away from me and Gail. In fact, she even told us to make the most of our time without her and go on a date! She said we should take advantage of

134

the hospital babysitting service.' Simon chuckled softly.

I glanced at Simon once more. The thing was I had seen with my own eyes just how worried Jenny had been about her parents, it was no wonder she was encouraging them to go out on their own while they had the chance. I turned my head to Peg and saw that although she was now cuddled up to Sally, her face was filled with concern.

'Don't worry, Percy,' she barked tenderly, 'we'll get this sorted, I promise.'

I looked at her gratefully, but said nothing. I still wasn't sure of the best way to handle this and, while I wanted to help, I was also eager to glean as much information as I could before I came up with a plan.

'Honestly, she's a marvel that child, she really is,' Simon continued, grinning ruefully. 'Any selflessness she gets from her mother, not from me.'

Sally rolled her eyes. 'Oh, come on, Simon, enough of the pity party. I seem to remember you doing me a good turn every now and then when we were at school.'

'Oh, yeah?' he asked, raising an eyebrow. 'Such as?'

'Well . . . ' Sally paused, appearing to struggle to come up with something now she was put on the spot. 'Well, like letting me copy all your maths homework, for instance. I didn't have a clue about algebra, but you always let me come round to yours after school and help me out.'

'That wasn't entirely altruistic, Sal.' Simon laughed.

Sally frowned. 'How do you mean?'

'Well, let's just say I always hoped you were interested in more than my maths home-work,' said Simon. 'And, of course, it didn't hurt that most of the lads in our school were jealous you were always round at mine.'

'Oh, Si!' Sally squealed, swatting Simon's arm playfully. 'Was that the only reason you asked me over? Were you just trying to make yourself more popular at school?'

Simon looked affronted. 'Hey! I was popular at school, thank you very much. But let's just say that having you over at mine a couple of times a week didn't harm my reputation. I was just sorry my brain was the only thing you were interested in.'

'So the only reason you asked me over was because you fancied me?' I looked at Sally and saw her face was a picture of surprise.

'Don't tell me you didn't know that?' Simon gasped, leaning forwards in his seat causing me to hop down to the floor. 'My crush on you was the worst kept secret in our class!'

Sally's face flushed a deep crimson at the revelation. 'I had no idea at all, Simon! You were always so nice to me, I thought you just wanted to help me out.'

Simon sank back into his chair and regarded Sally fondly. 'Well, of course I wanted to help. But when you started seeing Martin Bradwell, I lost interest. You broke my heart the day you told me you were going up the Ritzy with him.'

'As if!' Sally protested as if she were back at school again. 'As I recall you were going out with Leanne Young and had been for quite some time.'

Simon laughed and took a slug of wine. 'Only because you weren't interested, Sal.'

'And I only went out with Martin because you weren't interested in me!' Sally finished, sinking back into her chair in triumph. 'The only reason I came over to yours for all those maths lessons was because I was hoping you would ask me out.'

The atmosphere felt charged as I looked up, first at Simon and then across at Sally. They both had a glow about them, as their eyes locked. Glancing at Peg, I saw she looked concerned.

'What is it?' I barked.

'Just Sal,' she replied, 'flirting as usual. Take no notice, she's always the same when she's had a couple of glasses of wine.'

Now I was more concerned than ever as I noticed both Sally and Simon's glasses were almost empty.

'Well, I never knew that,' Simon said eventually, breaking the silence. 'You were the prettiest girl in class, I never thought you'd be interested in a lad like me.'

'A lad that was thoughtful, selfless and kind,' Sally replied in a quiet voice. 'And from what I can gather still is.'

I watched Simon's face light up as he looked up at Sally and whispered, 'Thanks. It's a long time since I've heard anyone say anything like that.'

Sally nodded. 'You're welcome. So are things between you and Gail a bit iffy at the moment?'

'You could say that.' Simon grimaced holding his glass aloft as Sally poured them both another glass. 'It's not her fault, and it's not mine. We're both under so much pressure at the moment there's no time for us any more. Sometimes it feels like we're complete strangers, with only one thing in common — Jenny's illness. It's as though with everything that's happened, we've forgotten how to be a couple again.'

'Maybe you should have taken Jenny up on that offer after all,' Sally said.

Simon smiled as he shook his head. 'Maybe. She's perceptive all right is our Jen. I worry sometimes that she hears us rowing. We do our best to keep it down or take it outside, but sometimes an argument can flare up so quickly between us there's not always time.

Sally pursed her lips. 'You shouldn't argue in front of Jenny. The poor girl's got enough to cope with without worrying about you two as well.'

'I know, I know,' Simon groaned. 'Believe me, it's not deliberate. It's just, well, these days, it's the only way me and Gail seem to communicate. Hopefully after tomorrow we'll get some good news about Jenny and we can all move forwards.'

'And what if the doctors don't give you good news?' Sally reasoned. 'What if they say Jenny definitely needs a transplant for example?'

My heart lurched with fear. Sally was asking all the things I wanted to know.

'I honestly don't know,' Simon said, his voice thick with emotion. 'I sometimes feel like I'm asking for the world, but all I really want is for me, Gail, Jenny and Percy to be happy, Sal. Is it too much to ask for a healthy, happy child and for me and Gail to be like we were. It's eating me up all this.'

Glancing up at Simon, I was shocked to see

his eyes brim with tears as he sank his head into his hands.

'It's okay, buddy,' I whined, jumping up to rest my front paws on his legs and licking his face.

Simon looked up, his eyes meeting mine. 'Oh, mate, I'm sorry. I'm okay, honestly.'

Sally offered him a comforting smile. 'Things are going to get better, I promise. I know it doesn't seem like it now, but trust me.'

'Well, it feels pretty bloody bad at the minute,' Simon said sharply.

'That's because things are bad!' Sally smiled. 'But they won't always be. And you know what, Simon, they could be a lot worse because at least you've got Percy.'

I barked at the mention of my name and nodded my head in agreement to show Simon that Sally was right, he did have me and I hoped he always would.

'And you've got me,' she said quietly. 'Any time you need a chat, Simon, someone to look after Percy, a moan, anything at all . . . well, you know where to find me. I'm always here for you, I hope you know that.'

I watched as Simon clasped his hand over Sally's and leaned in towards her. 'I appreciate that, Sal. I can't tell you how good it is to find you again after all these years.'

'Likewise,' she replied, as she continued to hold him tight.

I felt uncomfortable watching the two of them together. There was something about the way they were locked together, which made me feel something wasn't right. I removed my paws from Simon's leg and padded over to Peg. I was being silly, and needed a distraction.

'Thanks for today,' I yapped, as I hopped up onto the sofa and nestled against her. 'I know I shouldn't have enjoyed it with everything that's been going on but I did.'

'I did too,' Peg agreed as she softly nibbled my ear. 'And you know what, Perce, it's okay to find a bit of happiness when you're having a bad time. It's what makes the bad times bearable.'

She really was a marvel. 'You're so wise,' I barked, causing Simon and Sal to break apart.

'Well, we'd better get back,' Simon said, getting to his feet. 'Thanks for everything again, Sal, Perce and I appreciate it, don't we, boy?'

'Course,' I agreed, barking my thanks at both Sally and Peg for making me feel so welcome.

'I've already said it was nothing,' Sally grinned as she walked us out, Peg close behind.

'See you tomorrow,' Peg barked at me.

Out into the darkness I shivered as Simon clipped on my lead. It was well past ten and I wasn't used to being out so late.

'Come on, Perce, it's nippy out here,' Simon said as if reading my mind. 'Sooner we get back, sooner we're in the warm. And I tell you what, as it's so cold tonight, how about you come and sleep in mine and Gail's bed with me? You can keep me company.'

'Really?' I barked in wonder. 'But I'm never allowed in your bed.'

'I know you're not allowed usually, but I reckon it's time you and me got a bit closer,' Simon said. 'So don't say anything to Gail.'

As we walked the short journey home, I felt a surge of hope. Was Simon thawing? Was this a sign that I wouldn't be going back to the shelter in the New Year? It felt like there were a million thoughts and ideas going around my little brain. So much had happened today but perhaps Peg was right, maybe the good bits of life helped you get through the bad.

I looked up at Simon in the moonlight and tried to gauge his expression. He seemed happy and content following his chat with Sally. It was an expression he never wore around Gail. I still found it impossible to put my paw on what had made me so uncomfortable about the sight of them together and, as I scampered after Simon, I tried to make sense of it all.

Perhaps I was reading too much into things. Perhaps the two had just bonded over a trip down memory lane, after all they had known each other a long time. But then what was all that about them both fancying each other when they were at school? Despite the thoughts and ideas swirling around my mind, I had clearly understood nothing about the evening, but hoped I had a couple of doggy pals who might.

11

As I heard the car pull up outside the house, I let out a bark of delight. I had been listening all morning for the sound of my family returning and rushed to the front door to welcome them. I struggled to contain myself as I heard Gail's gentle voice talking to Jenny while Simon opened the car boot and fetched the bags.

Hearing the doors slam shut, there was the unmistakable echo of three sets of footsteps getting louder and louder as they got closer to the front door. And then, finally, they stopped and I heard Gail fish inside her handbag for her keys.

'Come on, come on,' I barked excitedly, 'I've missed you, hurry up.'

'Percy! We're home!' Gail called as I heard her slide her key into the lock.

Within seconds, the door swung open and I saw all of my lovely family together. Gail ushered Jenny inside first and I drank in the sight of her. She looked the same as she had the day before; tired, and a bit paler, perhaps, but her face transformed into a vision of delight as she saw me.

'Percy! Percy!' she squealed, squatting down on her haunches, long hair swinging past her shoulders as she plopped a huge kiss on my forehead.

'Easy now, Jen,' Gail cautioned as she helped her daughter to her feet and cast her own delighted smile at me. 'No sudden movements.'

But I couldn't be contained. 'Hello! Hello!' I yapped, as I ran around them all in little circles, getting in their way as I scampered between ankles. 'I'm so pleased your home.'

'And I'm pleased we're home too.' Gail beamed, as she bent down to pick me up. She gave me a big kiss and then brought me closer to Jenny.

'Hi, Perce.' She smiled, running her soft hands over my face. 'I love you so much.'

'And I love you,' I woofed in reply. 'Don't go anywhere again; it's not the same without you.'

Although Jenny had only been away twenty-four hours, it had felt like so much longer and I had really missed her quiet, gentle presence around the house. Home had not been home without her or Gail, and even though Simon had let me sleep in the big, family bed, both of us had lain awake knowing something was amiss.

As I lay in Gail's arms, my head resting on

her red wool coat, I turned to look at her and saw her eyes bursting with love. 'Oh, Percy! I can't tell you how good it is to see you.'

'And me, you,' I yapped, craning my head upwards to rub her cold nose with my own warm wet one.

'All me and Jen talked about all night was you, wasn't it, love?' She laughed, turning to her daughter who nodded vigorously. 'We talked about how much our lives have changed for the better since you arrived in our house and all the fun things we're going to do now Jen's home.'

Gail's eyes rested on mine as Jenny leaned on her mother and stroked my head. Overwhelmed by so much affection, I reached out a paw and rested it on Jenny's arm, keen to return the loving gesture.

'First of all, Percy, we have decided it's time you met the rest of the family. Mum and Dad are desperate to see Jenny and they are also very excited to see you, so they're coming up from Devon later today. They can't wait.' Gail grinned.

'What about my mum?' asked Simon, as he came into the house armed with bags. 'She'll go spare if she's not included in party plans.'

Gail shook her head in exasperation as she put me back down on the floor. 'She's not here, love. She's cruising around the Caribbean for Christmas in case you'd forgotten.'

'Is she? Christmas is more than three weeks away, and besides, she just got back from South America last month,' Simon said, as he brought the rest of the luggage from the car.

'Well, she is on her own,' Gail pointed out. 'I can't say I blame her, to be honest. Still, no doubt she'll meet Percy soon, but in the meantime we'll have to make do with my parents.'

'When are they getting here?' Simon asked.

Gail glanced at her watch. 'Couple of hours I think. Mum texted me when they were leaving.'

Simon set the bags on the floor and turned to Jenny and Gail. 'Cuppa before they arrive?'

'Yes, please, love.' Gail smiled as Jenny shook her head.

'No, thanks, Dad, but think I might have a nap for a bit before Nan and Granddad get here if that's okay?'

Gail nodded as she slipped off her sheepskin boots. 'Course it is, sweetheart. Why don't you take Percy with you?'

I barked excitedly and bounded up the stairs as Jenny followed me. I was so happy to see her I did not wait for an invitation and instead leapt onto her bed. Jenny giggled and joined me.

'Percy! You are so cheeky,' she laughed, stroking my head. 'I wish you had been allowed in to see me in the hospital, we would have had a brilliant time.'

'I know,' I barked in reply. 'It wasn't the same without you here.'

'And I didn't sleep very well, knowing I wasn't at home to take care of you,' she said sadly.

'Good enough reason for us to have forty winks now,' I woofed.

Cuddling into the crook of her arm, I threw one of my paws around Jenny's waist and shut my eyes. Within minutes the two of us were fast asleep dreaming of better times ahead.

★ ★ ★

Suddenly the sound of the doorbell woke me from my slumber. Shaken, I got to all four of my paws and blinked the sleep from my eyes only to see Jenny doing the same.

'That'll be Nan and Granddad,' she said, stretching her arms overhead. 'Come on, it's you they've come to see really, not me.'

'I'm sure that's not true,' I replied, following Jenny down the stairs and out into the hallway.

Hearing the sounds of strangers bustling

about in the hallway, I felt shy. What if they did not like me? They might cause Gail and Simon to go off me, and then I might have to go back in the New Year once Simon's horrible deadline had passed.

Feeling nervous, I hid behind Jenny's legs as I took in the sight of her grandparents. Gail's mum was tiny, with grey hair that hung in a neat bob and a warm, open face. She wrapped her granddaughter and then daughter in a huge hug, and, with her face hidden, I observed Gail's dad. He was the spitting image of his daughter, with his chestnut hair, and like his wife had an air of openness about him that I immediately liked. Taking off his jacket and hanging it on the bannister, I saw him smile at his daughter and granddaughter, before opening his arms to give them both a cuddle.

'Hello, sweethearts,' he said in a broad Devon brogue. 'How are you feeling, Jen?'

'I'm fine, Granddad,' she replied, her face buried in his chest. 'It was just a few tests. It's nice to be home.'

'All right, Dad?' Gail asked, breaking away. 'Good drive up?'

'Not bad,' he replied. 'Bit of traffic coming off junction twelve, and there was a lorry causing a — '

'Oh, never mind all that now, Eric,' Gail's

149

mum interrupted as she elbowed her husband indelicately in the ribs and smiled at Gail. 'Where's Percy? I'm dying to meet him.'

'Oh, yes, never mind me, Doreen, having driven all the way up here,' Eric replied, rubbing his right side. 'Aren't I entitled to a moan?'

Doreen turned to her husband and smiled. 'A moan yes, but not six thousand of them, dear, which is roughly how many you've managed today. Is it any wonder I'd rather spend time with this blessed dog than listen to any more out of you?'

'Doreen, I — ' Eric began, before Gail interrupted.

'Percy's just here,' she said, picking me up and handing me to her mother.

'Oh, he's gorgeous,' Doreen cooed, looking into my brown eyes.

'Poor sod.' Eric smiled, leaning over Doreen's shoulder. 'Having to put up with you women gushing over him all the time.'

'That's what I said,' laughed Simon, as he emerged from the kitchen. 'Perce has got these women wrapped around his paws. I've asked him to show me how it's done, but he won't tell me.'

'P'raps he'll tell us over a bit of man-to-man time later,' Eric suggested as he ruffled my ears affectionately.

'You get off,' Doreen protested, as she kissed my forehead. 'Me and this boy have got a lot of catching up to do, your man to man chats will have to wait. And I'll tell you summit else 'n'all, Simon,' the older woman said, her gaze meeting Simon's as she nudged him sharply in the ribs, 'if you think this boy's going anywhere in the New Year you can think again. If you want rid, I'll take him in, but I've a feeling you'll be served your marching orders before this lad.'

Turning back to me, she planted a huge sloppy kiss on my forehead and gave me a big squeeze. There was something about Doreen that made me feel relaxed, and I got the impression the feeling was mutual, as she tickled my ears before glancing back at Simon, her green eyes twinkling. 'Any chance of a drink, love? I'm parched after that drive.'

'Oh, yes, of course, sorry, Doreen.' Simon asked quickly, 'What do you fancy? Tea? Coffee?'

'Wine, love.' She chuckled. 'After hours in a car with Eric, I think I've earned at least a bottle.'

Laughing, Doreen set me back on the floor and I followed the family into the kitchen and settled into my bed to watch them all together. I had to admit that I liked both Doreen and Eric. They seemed good for Gail, who looked instantly lighter and happier now they were here, while Simon looked at his wife lovingly. He seemed happy that she was happy and the worry I had seen etched on his face last night appeared to have vanished. As for Jenny, I noticed she was relaxed and happy to bask in the love and affection of her grandparents for a few hours. I felt the atmosphere around the kitchen table lighten and, with Eric and Doreen around, I felt I could take my eye off the ball for just a couple of hours and enjoy a nap.

When I woke up, I realised I must have been asleep for ages as Doreen, Eric and Jenny had all disappeared and only Gail and Simon were left. I sniffed the air and realised I could smell Chinese takeaway, the empty cartons in the bin a giveaway I had missed dinner. I looked back at my owners and was delighted to see they were sitting opposite one another, sharing a bottle of red wine, their faces still happy and relaxed.

'I wish Mum and Dad would just stay with us,' Gail whispered.

'You know they prefer a hotel; I'd let them get on with it.' Simon shrugged.

'But if they stayed with us then maybe they would stay longer. They're going in the morning as it is,' Gail protested.

'And maybe if they did, we'd all start

getting on each other's nerves. Enjoy the moment love,' Simon said sympathetically.

Gail sipped her wine. 'You're right. It just seems so wasteful when we've a perfectly good spare room upstairs.'

'I hope you're not talking about my man cave?' Simon gasped. 'That's no spare room that's a sacred space, like a man's shed.'

'Oh, yeah?' Gail chuckled. 'And where's my sacred space? And if you say the kitchen, I'll swing for you!'

'Okay, okay!' Simon laughed, holding his hands up in defence. 'Just a joke.'

I watched the two of them smiling at one another and felt a surge of joy. Despite all their problems it was good to see them enjoying one another's company. In fact, I realised, as I scratched my ear, this was possibly the happiest I had ever seen them together. As if to prove my point, Gail leaned over and kissed Simon on the lips.

'I've missed you.'

'Is that right?' Simon whispered, as he pulled his face from Gail's and beamed at her. 'And there was me thinking it was just young Percy you'd missed.'

At the sound of my name, I curled and uncurled my tail with pleasure and scampered over to Gail. I wanted some love too if there was some going around.

'Well, obviously, I missed Percy the most,' Gail said slowly, bending down and scratching my ears with her free hand. 'But I missed you just a little bit too.'

I wasted no time jumping up onto her lap. I'd longed to see Gail for what felt like weeks, and wanted to make the most of her now she was back. Cocooning myself into a little ball, I enjoyed the warmth of her legs and touch of her hand as she idly stroked my head.

'So, what did you get up to while I was away last night?' she asked, sipping her wine.

Simon shrugged. 'Not much. Came home, ate dinner, that was it really. I was exhausted.'

'I know that feeling,' Gail replied. 'Was Percy okay when you got back? I hated the idea of leaving him on his own all day.'

'Perce was fine. Actually, Sally — you know, from the dog park and my old schoolmate? — offered to take him for a walk so he wasn't on his own all day.'

'Really?' Gail brightened at the news as she looked from me to Simon. 'That was good of her; I ought to call her to say thanks.'

'No need,' Simon replied, 'I've already done it. He was good as gold apparently.'

'No surprise there,' Gail crooned warmly, rubbing my forehead with her nose. 'So what did you two do after dinner?'

'Nothing. I took Perce for a quick trip to

the park, so he could run about, then we came home and put our feet up in front of the telly and did our best to ignore the persistent carol singers at our door.'

'So much for a boys' night out,' Gail chuckled.

'It was so boring, it was barely a boys' night in,' he laughed.

I raised my head from Gail's lap and peeped over the wooden dining table to get a better look at Simon. Why had he not told Gail the truth that Sally had looked after me? And more, surprisingly, why had he not told Gail we had spent most of the evening over at Sally's flat, while he and Sally had drunk wine and talked about old times? As for carol singers, they had only existed in his imagination. I tried to read Simon's expression, but with his head bent he appeared to be studiously examining his coffee. Once again, that same uncomfortable feeling coursed through my fur as I tried to work out why Simon's version of last night's events didn't sit well.

'Anyway, shouldn't we discuss the elephant in the room?' Simon asked.

I felt Gail's body stiffen at the change of subject, and snuggled deeper into her lap. 'I suppose we should. But what can we say? Jenny might need a transplant. I haven't stopped worrying about it since the doctors told us.'

'But worrying won't solve anything, love.' He sighed, leaning across the table and grasping Gail's hands. 'The doctors know what they're doing and it might not come to a transplant.'

'I know that,' she replied coolly. 'But if they do, how long is it going to take for them to find a donor heart? How is she supposed to manage? And then supposing she has a transplant, what if her body rejects it? Then what?'

Gail's voice was getting higher and higher and I could feel the panic coursing through her body. I let out a low whine to reassure her just as Simon spoke.

'Love, we've been through this countless times already. Jenny will continue to manage as she has been doing. She will be monitored closely by doctors until the time comes. You're getting worked up over something that hasn't happened yet, and probably won't,' Simon replied, squeezing Gail's hands more tightly. 'Let's just take this one step at a time, okay?'

Gail removed her hands from Simon's grasp. 'This isn't a money worry or some sort of work problem, Si. We've just found out our only child may need a heart transplant.

Taking it one step at a time isn't something I'm sure I can do.'

'Because you think she's going to die?' Simon snarled, shock and fury in his eyes.

Tears coursed down Gail's cheeks. 'I'm afraid, Simon, why can't you see that?'

As she looked over at Simon, I was relieved to see his expression soften. He got out of his chair, walked around to Gail and pulled her into a hug. As her body weight shifted into her husband, I allowed myself to be pulled along with her.

'Course I can see that, love. And I know how you feel, but we'll get through this,' he whispered soothingly. 'But rather than snap at me, perhaps you could just try talking to me about your feelings? It might be easier?'

Gail sniffed and nodded. 'You're right. I'll try harder from now on.'

'Good,' Simon replied, kissing her tenderly on the lips, 'because we shouldn't keep anything from each other. That's how trouble starts.'

I could scarcely believe my ears and jumped down from Gail's lap and onto the cool floor. Simon's speech about honesty and secrets had made my fur stand on end in disgust. I knew first-paw how secrets could destroy lives. After all, if Javier had been more honest with me about why he was leaving, then I may not have felt so bad about myself when I was at the tails of the forgotten. As I wandered from the kitchen and into the living room, I simply failed to understand why he was keeping a secret himself. The worst thing, I thought as I flopped on the rug in front of the unlit fire, was why he would refuse to tell Gail we had spent most of the night at Sally's. I growled in frustration as I rested my head on my paws. I needed to talk to Peg and the others about all of this, and soon.

12

It was an unusually sunny December afternoon and, as the weather was so nice, Gail had suggested Jenny and I join her for a quick walk to the park to make the most of the fresh air after lunch. It had been a week since Jenny left the hospital and it was a treat to have her company. She rarely had enough energy to join us on a trip outside and so I walked rigidly by her side in case she felt faint or had a fall, much to Gail and Jenny's amusement.

Yet despite the laughter, Gail and I made sure Jenny took things slowly, and the little girl rested on Gail's arm for much of the journey. With Simon's agreement, they had both decided to let Jenny live a little. This not only meant short, slow walks to the park, but Simon had even taken Jenny to the movies and out for a pizza with one of her mates from the hospital.

Although there had been a shift in attitude, that did not stop me and Gail watching her every step like trained hunting dogs. By the time we reached the park, I was shattered from concentrating so hard, but the sight of

Peg at the track on the other side soon gave me a surge of energy. Quickly barking goodbye to Jenny and Gail, who were by now settled on a park bench, I raced off to join the pug. With the sun beaming down on her blonde fur, she had never looked lovelier and I wasted no time telling her so as I reached her side.

'You're so pretty, Peg,' I yapped quietly. 'I've missed you.' I walked towards her, rested my nose against hers and looked deeply into her chocolate brown eyes.

'Awww, Percy, you only saw me two days ago,' Peg woofed as she nuzzled her cheek against mine in greeting.

I knew she was right, but two days had felt like a lifetime. I was just about to tell her so, when Bugsy came bounding towards us.

'Hello! What are you doing? Are you kissing? That's disgusting! Look, Heather, Heather, Heather,' he barked as the German shepherd closely followed by Jake joined us.

'For heaven's sake, Bugsy, leave them alone,' Heather chided as she sat on the grass, her jaw loose and tongue lolling in happiness. 'It's lovely to see you both, how are you?'

'All good thanks, Heather,' Peg replied. 'And have you seen who's joined Percy at the park today?'

Heather gazed at the bench where Jenny

and Gail sat, and scampered up and down excitedly on the spot. 'Is that your Jenny? My, it's good to see her looking so well.'

'Thanks, Heather,' I barked. 'We're just taking it one step at a time, she needs a transplant and I'm just so worried about them all.'

'I understand,' Heather woofed.

'So do I,' Peg barked quietly. 'It's heartbreaking when your owners are hurting and you don't know how to help. Sally was devastated when she lost a baby last year.'

My eyes widened. 'You never told me Sally had been through something so traumatic. I'm really sorry to hear that Peg.'

'It was pretty awful,' Peg replied. 'I've been with Sally since I was taken from my doggy mum two years ago and we've always been inseparable. When she met this bloke six months after I moved in, she fell for him like a dog in a bone factory. Anyway, when she found out she was pregnant, she also found out he was married and I think the shock of that led to her losing the baby.'

'Poor Sally,' I barked, not knowing what else to say.

'That's why I worry about her so much,' Peg replied. 'Since losing the man and the baby overnight she seems desperate to find the happiness she lost and I fret she's throwing herself at any man to find that happiness.'

I rested a paw on Peg's and found she was freezing, despite the warmth of the winter sunshine. 'I suppose that's natural. She's still grieving and it's all a lot for anyone to cope with.'

'It is, but I do wish she'd wise up. Thankfully, Heather, Jake and, later Bugsy helped me through it all. That's what friends do.'

'I know,' I replied. 'You've all been wonderful.'

'Nonsense,' Peg woofed. 'All I'm saying is our owners have to take responsibility for their problems too, no matter how much we try to help. What's happened to Sally has made me realise that when I have puppies I need to be very careful about finding the right daddy.'

I nodded, instantly recognising what she was trying to tell me. Peg's heart was not to be taken lightly and I would never let her down, she already meant far too much to me as a friend for that. I rubbed her head gently with my own to show I understood before turning my gaze towards Jenny and Gail.

Watching them nestled into one another on the park bench, their faces turned towards the sun, I felt a pang of love for them both as

I remembered Simon's lies from last night. More than anything I wanted to protect them from any more hurt or pain than they already had to endure. Remembering Peg's advice about humans shouldering the responsibility of their own problems, I wondered if there could be a simple and reasonable explanation for Simon's actions.

I churned it over quickly in my mind, but still felt none the wiser, so decided to ask for a second opinion. Taking a deep breath, I told my friends everything that had happened since Jenny had returned from hospital. By the time I had finished, Peg gazed at me, a puzzled look on her face, while Heather and Jake exchanged a variety of expressions from shoulder shrugs to looks of sheer bewilderment. As for Bugs, he just looked plain perplexed before turning back to me.

'I hate to say it, Percy, but it doesn't sound good,' Peg barked matter-of-factly.

'It might not be as bad as it seems,' Heather yapped hopefully. 'Perhaps Simon just didn't think to tell her. You know what men can be like.'

Bugsy ran around us forming a little circle in excitement. 'What are men like, Heather? How are they different to women? Are men stupid or silly or something? Is that what you mean?'

Jake rolled his eyes in despair. 'No, Bugsy, old chap, that is not what Heather means. And Heather,' he barked in earnest, fixing his eyes on her, 'men may be forgetful, but they are not stupid. No, I'm sorry, Percy is quite right to be worried, there is a good reason Simon didn't tell Gail that he was with Sally and that's because he didn't want her to know.'

'But why?' I barked, frustrated by the lack of answers. 'I don't understand why he wouldn't be honest with Gail.'

'Who knows, but it can't be too bad, after all everyone seems to get on, don't they? Look, Sally's getting on famously with Gail and Jenny now,' Bugsy pointed out, trotting towards the edge of the dog park.

As I followed Bugsy's gaze, I saw Gail, Jenny and Sally together. In fact, Gail appeared as relaxed around her as she did her own mum and dad, laughing and joking along with Sally.

'Well, what's all that about?' I asked, turning to the others for more answers.

But each one looked as confused as me as they all woofed and yapped their concern. Only Peg remained silent, her eyes fixed determinedly on the grass.

'Peg, you're very quiet. What's up?' I asked. 'You know you can tell me.'

'I can't,' she yapped softly, 'you'll be upset.'

My fur stood on end in anticipation. 'Come on, Peg, you can tell me anything and I won't be upset. Unlike Simon, I truly don't believe in secrets.'

At that Peg looked up from the floor and met my gaze. 'Well, I wasn't sure if you knew, but Simon was round at ours again last night. He and Sally shared an Indian takeaway and bottle of wine.'

I rummaged around my brain for memories of last night. After Simon and Gail had their big talk, we'd all watched a film on the telly and eaten cheese. Well, they had eaten popcorn, but Gail had not wanted me to miss out and had fed me lumps of cheddar then we had all cuddled up on the sofa together. It had been sheer bliss, and the uncomfortable feelings I had felt about Simon had almost vanished as we lay contentedly together. The scene had felt so perfect, and I started to relax, feeling safe for the first time since arriving at Barksdale Way that I would not be leaving in the New Year. It had been a huge shame when his mobile had rung with an emergency job just as the film drew to a close. He had promised not to be long, but did not get back until after ten when Gail and Jenny had gone to bed.

'But there must be a mistake,' I barked,

feeling confused. 'Simon was out fixing a burst pipe last night. He said it wouldn't be long, but it took him ages.'

Peg looked down at the floor again. 'I'm sorry, Percy. Maybe Simon did have a job, but he was at ours last night for a good couple of hours.'

I could hardly breathe as I struggled to take in what Peg was telling me. I wanted to shout that she was wrong, but I knew Peg was telling the truth. Like me, I knew honesty meant the world to Peg. I looked across to Sally, Gail and Jenny still laughing and smiling on the bench.

That same feeling of discomfort I thought I had successfully shaken off coursed through my body. Aside from Jenny's illness, something serious was happening to my lovely family. Suddenly I felt a wave of tiredness creep over me, and as I saw Gail and Jenny get to their feet, I barked a series of quick goodbyes to my friends and promised to see them later.

As I raced towards my family, I heard the scamper of paws and turned around to see Peg just behind me.

'Percy, wait,' she woofed, her little heart clearly beating nineteen to the dozen. 'I just want to say I'm sorry.'

I stopped in my tracks. 'What have you got

to be sorry about?'

'For telling you Simon was at ours last night,' she barked, licking my ear affectionately. 'I didn't mean to upset you and I'm sorry.'

My heart burst with affection for this blonde pug standing before me. Peg had nothing to apologise for, all she had done was tell the truth.

'You were right to tell me, Peg, at least now I know Simon's telling lies to Gail. I just have to worry about why.'

'I'm sure it's perfectly innocent,' Peg barked, her brown eyes full of concern. 'All they did was talk.'

'If it was so innocent then why didn't Simon say anything?' I barked.

But Peg had no answer and, as she hung her head in sorrow, I felt a stab of guilt for snapping at her. 'Now it's my turn to be sorry, I didn't mean to sound harsh.'

Peg's brown eyes met mine. 'Life's too short for pals to fall out,' she barked. With that, she nuzzled her nose against mine and licked my cheek. At the feel of her fur on mine, my pulse raced. Boy oh boy, I felt as if I was on an emotional roller coaster, sad one minute and elated the next. One thing was for sure though, that with so much going on at home, the last thing I wanted was to fall out with Peg.

'Agreed,' I woofed, remembering only too well how awful Gail and Simon's rows were. 'You're too pretty to argue with.'

'Awww, Percy,' Peg whined as she batted her eyelashes at me, 'you're so sweet.'

I curled and uncurled my tail with pleasure. I was never more contented than when I made Peg happy. Giving her one final nuzzle, I turned to face Gail and Jenny and ran towards them with Peg by my side.

'Hello, you two,' Gail cooed, as she squatted down to greet me. 'Have you been having fun?'

Pushing my face into her hands, I squirmed with pleasure as I felt her palms on my flesh.

'These two always have fun together,' Sally chuckled, as she scooped Peg up in her arms. 'They're thick as thieves.'

'Well, they're very cute thieves.' Jenny smiled, as she leaned her face towards mine and showered me with kisses.

'Come on, love,' Gail said, turning to Jenny and setting me on the floor. 'Time to get you home.'

Jenny rolled her eyes. 'Mum, can't we stay for a bit and go for a coffee with Sally and Peg?'

'Sweetheart, no. You've just come out of

hospital. You need your rest,' Gail pointed out, as she exchanged a look of despair with Sally.

'Your mum's right, love,' Sally agreed as she gave Peg a kiss. 'We'll catch up soon.'

'Okay,' Jenny groaned, linking arms with her mother and waving Peg and Sally goodbye as they walked towards the park café.

As the three of us strolled home, with the sun dipping behind the clouds, I remained quiet, preferring to listen to the sounds of Gail and Jenny's chatter. The two of them sounded so happy, it was almost possible to pretend they were just a normal mother and daughter out for a walk. In truth though, they were far from normal, and the small faltering steps Jenny was forced to take was testament to that.

Despite Jenny's slow pace, she kept up a steady stream of chatter about the kids she had met in hospital and the games they had played once the adults had been out of earshot. Listening to her tell her mother about a young girl called Cassie, who had met Harry from One Direction, I felt a jolt of pleasure. In a funny way, I thought the hospital stay had done Jenny the power of good as she had enjoyed the opportunity to catch up with her pals and behave like a normal kid for a night. I shook my head as I slowed my paws to keep pace with Gail, who for once had forgotten to clip on my lead. Gail, Jenny, Simon, they all deserved a normal and happy life, the question was would they ever get it?

We soon reached home and, as Gail unlocked the front door, I scampered into the house and through to the living room. I pulled a soft red blanket from the back of the sofa with my teeth and dragged it towards Jenny, who appeared frozen.

'Oh, thank you, Perce. You are good,' said Gail gratefully, as she took the blanket from my mouth and wrapped it around Jenny. 'Why don't you two go and relax in the lounge and watch a film or something?'

'Brilliant idea,' I barked enthusiastically. I loved nothing more than the chance to curl up with the family and watch a film, but an afternoon movie was a rare treat indeed.

'Really, Mum?' Jenny sounded surprised, as she gathered the blanket more tightly around her 'What about schoolwork?'

Gail shrugged as she brushed a strand of hair from her daughter's face. 'Let's have a day off for a change. You've already worked so hard these last few weeks, I don't think a bit of time away from school work will hurt.'

Jenny's face broke into a delighted smile.

'Awesome!' she cheered. 'Come on, Perce, let's go and watch *Pitch Perfect 2*.'

I needed no further encouragement and, as I trotted behind Jenny and flopped onto the sofa, Gail came in behind us and selected the movie from the streaming service. As the opening credits rolled, Gail sank back into the sofa while Jenny lay lengthways and rested her legs on her mother's lap. Gathering me in her arms, she perched me gently between her and Gail, causing my tail to curl and uncurl with pleasure.

'Oh, Percy,' Gail said, chuckling as she ran her fingers through my fur. 'You're so easy to please.'

'And that's just one of the reasons you love me so much,' I barked softly in reply, turning my face towards her.

'Which is precisely why we love you so much,' she whispered, planting a kiss on my head.

As I went to look away, I suddenly saw a photo in a white frame resting on the coffee table I had never seen before. Peering over Gail's shoulder, I saw it was a picture of a very young looking Gail and Simon beaming happily into the camera. They were sitting on a tartan blanket surrounded by picnic goodies. Running my eyes over the image, I saw there was something unusual about it, because despite the fact the couple were enjoying a summery looking spread, they were wearing winter coats and there appeared to be snow on the ground. Catching me examining the photo, Gail picked up the frame and smiled at me and Jenny.

'Mum brought this with her last week after she'd cleared out the loft,' she told us. 'I'm not sure you've ever seen it, have you, Jen?'

Jenny gently took the photo from her mother and examined it. 'When was it taken, Mum? Must have been a long time ago, you and Dad look like kids!'

'Cheek!' Gail laughed and I barked at the same time.

'It was taken just after your father asked me to marry him,' Gail said, taking the photo from Jenny's hands and gazing at it wistfully, reliving every moment.

'It was such a wonderful surprise,' she said finally, looking at each of us and smiling. 'Your dad came to take me out the Saturday before Christmas, which just happened to be Christmas Eve. He usually picked me up and we'd go to the cinema or out for lunch or something, but this time he took me to the park, said he had something special lined up as it was Christmas.'

'Wasn't it a bit cold?' Jenny asked. 'In the photo it looks as though it was snowing.'

Gail nodded. 'Exactly, Jen, I thought your

dad had lost his marbles. But the more I asked what he was up to, the more secretive he became, refusing to tell me anything. Anyway, he led me to this lovely spot right under a tree, where a picnic blanket full of goodies was waiting for us.'

'In the snow?' Jenny asked, incredulous again.

'In the snow,' Gail confirmed, as she smiled fondly at her daughter. 'Well, your father had thought of everything. He'd got little cushions for us to sit on, blankets to keep us warm, and he'd bought all my favourite things, like Scotch eggs and those little rollmops that you and your dad hate — '

'Because they're disgusting,' Jenny protested, with a shudder.

Gail laughed. 'Anyway,' she said, nudging her daughter in the ribs, 'he'd also bought a bottle of champagne, and just as I was about to ask whatever he'd splashed out on that for, he got down on one knee, pulled a beautiful black ring box from his pocket and asked me to marry him.'

I felt a lump form in my throat as I saw Gail's eyes shine with joy as she relived happier times. I whined in awe, along with Jenny, who rubbed my head affectionately.

'That's so sweet, Mum,' Jenny cooed. 'Did you say yes straightaway?'

173

'Of course!' Gail laughed again, swatting her daughter's hand playfully as she gazed back at the photo. 'I knew I was on to a good thing the moment I laid eyes on your father at a party. I wasn't letting him slip through my fingers.' She beamed at me and Jenny. 'That was the happiest afternoon of my life. Even though it was freezing, we sat in the park for hours, drinking champagne and talking about our future. We had it all planned out. We couldn't wait to get married. It was the best Christmas present I could have had.'

Returning the photo to its place on the table, Gail glanced down at her left hand and twiddled her engagement ring thoughtfully. 'With Christmas just around the corner, I thought it would be nice for us to remember our first Christmas as an engaged couple,' she said brightly, before picking up the remote. 'Now, let's watch this film, shall we?'

As Gail pressed Play, I watched her face carefully. She looked so optimistic, I had a funny feeling the photo had been placed there, not just as a reminder of the Christmas Simon had proposed, but because Gail wanted her husband to remember the happier times they had once shared.

I rested my head on her lap, and wondered if there was a way I could make Gail's Christmas wishes come true.

13

I woke the next morning to find Simon standing over me in the pitch darkness, hands on his hips and an excitable grin on his face. Scrabbling onto my paws, I looked at him in surprise. Simon was usually the last one up, and he certainly never loomed over me like that. Panic rose through my body as I realised something had to be wrong.

'What is it?' I whined.

'I want you to help me. I thought we'd all go out for the day,' he whispered, bending down so we were eye level. 'Somewhere new, a bit of a change for the whole family.'

'Really?' I barked, a little more loudly. 'Is Jenny well enough?'

'I know what you're thinking,' he said. 'You're worrying about Jenny. Well, I've thought about that, which is why we won't go too far, so we can get back quickly if we need to. I just want us to spend some time together, Perce, as a family. What do you think?'

What I thought was that the plan sounded brilliant and I wasted no time telling him so with a loud, enthusiastic bark. After Simon prepared my breakfast and then finally let me out for a wee, I returned inside to find Gail and Jenny had also got up and were sat at the table drinking tea and eating toast.

'We're going to Marble Hill House,' Jenny said cheerily as she saw me come in. 'We can play together all day, isn't that brilliant, Percy?'

'It is,' I barked earnestly, licking up her toast crumbs from the floor.

'Well, maybe not quite all day,' Gail cautioned. 'It is the middle of winter.'

'Muuum, don't ruin this by being all serious,' Jenny grumbled.

'I'm not ruining anything,' Gail protested. 'I think we'll all have a great time. I just want you to keep in mind, we might need to come home earlier if you're not feeling well that's all.'

'Your mum's right, Jenny,' Simon called from the kitchen counter where I saw he was busy making sandwiches. 'The point of this day out is for us all to have a good time, not put your health in jeopardy.'

'Yeah, yeah,' Jenny replied, pushing back her chair. 'I'm going for a shower.'

An hour later and we were in the car driving to our destination. Once again, I was secured into the carrier, with Jenny beside me, while Gail sat in the passenger seat and chatted happily with Simon. As Jenny idly stroked my fur with her fingers, I relaxed in the warm, happy atmosphere of the car and enjoyed the sounds of my family getting on with one another.

I realised I had now been with my family for over a month, and an awful lot had happened in such a short space of time. I felt as though Gail, Jenny and I had become incredibly close, and on a good day, when I was feeling less insecure, I even felt as though Simon and I had bonded enough for me to forget worrying about returning to the tails of the forgotten. Of course, there were days I fretted that caring for me may simply become too much for them now I understood just how poorly Jenny was, but I hoped that by proving how useful and supportive I could be, Gail, Simon and Jenny would realise they could not live without me. I certainly would not want to live without them, I thought sadly. Once upon a time, Javier had meant everything to me, but these days I had a happy life filled with love and, although I still occasionally missed my former owner, I felt far better off with my new family, especially when they were all as cheerful as they were today.

'We're here,' Simon announced, abruptly bringing the car to a stop.

As Gail set me free from my carrier, I looked around and saw acres of green grass and what looked like hundreds of dogs were roaming free around the parkland without leads. To my right stood a huge lake and, even though I knew it was a freezing December day, I shivered in pleasure at the thought of diving right in, preferably to chase one of my favourite tennis balls.

'This looks brilliant,' I barked excitedly, curling and uncurling my tail in delight.

Simon bent down to ruffle my ears. 'Plenty of space for you to run about here, Perce, and plenty of space for me and Gail to walk, talk and just be together.'

'And what about me?' Jenny protested, hands on hips. 'When you're being all gooey with Mum, what am I meant to do?'

'Play with Percy!' Simon chuckled. 'I don't often get a chance to get gooey with your mum.'

As he bent down to kiss his wife lovingly on the lips, Jenny and I exchanged glances. They seemed so happy in one another's company, I had high hopes for the day.

'Come on,' Jenny said, eagerly turning to me, 'let's go and play on our own. The lovebirds can catch us up.'

Willingly, I scampered alongside Jenny, as together we walked along woodland paths. I looked around and saw that even though the trees were free of leaves, and the hedgerows were almost bare, the glow of the winter sunshine peeping out from just behind the clouds made our surroundings look beautiful. I felt a rush of happiness as I noticed that everywhere around us, families were out walking, their dogs padding alongside, all of them eager to make the most of the glorious day ahead. I turned back to look at Gail and Simon, and was delighted to find they were only a little way behind, their faces happy as they followed our trail, arms entwined.

'Mind if we sit down for a minute, Percy?' Jenny asked as she spotted a bench up ahead. 'I'm feeling a bit tired.'

'Not at all,' I barked. 'I'm feeling a bit weary myself.'

Together we walked to the bench a few steps away and, once Jenny was settled, she reached down to pick me up and I sat beside her, snuggling into her side to help keep us both warm.

'Percy, can I teach you a trick?' Jenny asked suddenly.

'Okay,' I barked, doubtfully. I had never been very good at tricks — the only one I had successfully been able to master was the high five Javier had taught me.

'It's really easy,' Jenny explained. 'It's called

peek-a-boo. We can impress Mum and Dad with it.'

Slowly, Jenny brought me around to face her, and then asked me for my paw. Next, she grasped it in her hand and raised it over my eyes before lowering it a few seconds later, only to repeat the whole thing again. There was no denying it, the thing was madness as far as I could make out.

'What are you doing?' I barked, unable to see a thing.

Jenny giggled at my confused face. 'It's a trick, Percy. I say, 'Peek-a-boo,' and then you raise your paw, and I say, 'Peek-a-boo,' then if you're really good, I give you a treat.'

I barked enthusiastically at the sound of a treat.

'Let's try again.' Jenny chuckled.

This time, as Jenny said the magic words, I raised my paw over my eyes and lowered it. Looking up at her I was delighted to see she was grinning broadly, and I realised this trick must be making her very happy. Perhaps it was not so mad after all.

'Brilliant, Percy,' she said, offering me a handful of treats. 'Let's show Mum and Dad how clever you are.'

As Gail and Simon neared our bench, their arms still wrapped around one another, Jenny waved enthusiastically. 'Look what I've taught Percy.'

'Go on then,' Gail said, expectantly.

'Better not be how to pickpocket five pound notes out of my jeans pockets.' Simon chuckled, as he bent down to kiss his daughter's head. 'Although if you could teach him how to snaffle them from your mother's jeans, I'm okay with that.'

Gail playfully nudged Simon in the stomach with her free elbow. 'That's enough out of you! Now, Jen, let's see this trick.'

I felt Gail's gaze rest firmly upon me and was keen to impress. Sitting squarely in front of Jenny, the moment she called the command I raised my right paw, then lowered it, before repeating the exercise just as we had practised.

Gail let out a squeal of delight. 'Percy, that's brilliant.'

'I told you he was bright didn't I, Mum?' Jenny grinned. 'He got that first go.'

'But I imagine a treat helped.' Simon smiled, spotting the open bag of dog snacks lying beside Jenny.

'Well, it would be the only motivation that worked for you.' Gail chuckled, as she walked towards me and scooped my face in her hands. 'You are so clever, Percy.'

I basked in her adoration and licked Gail's face appreciatively. Jenny joined in and kissed first the top of my head and then squeezed her mum tight.

'Hey, what have I done to deserve all this?' Gail asked.

'Nothing,' Jenny replied gently. 'I just love you, that's all.'

'Me too,' whispered Simon.

'And me,' I barked, wanting to join in.

I looked through Gail's hands and saw Simon had wrapped his arms around Jenny and Gail. Leaning forwards, he planted a kiss on the top of my head, and I felt a surge of delight at the unexpected show of affection.

'I just want to say,' Simon added gruffly, 'that I really do love you all. You're my family, you mean the world to me and I don't know what I'd do without you. Any of you,' he said, glancing at me this time.

Gail turned from me, and buried her face in her husband's chest. 'And I love you. This was such a good idea to get away for the day.'

'Yes! We should do it more often.' Jenny smiled.

'We should definitely do it more often,' I barked. 'Look, I would never have learned a new trick otherwise.'

Without waiting for Jenny's command this time, I raised my paw and lowered it, as my family stood back and watched in glee.

'I will never tire of watching that.' Gail

laughed. 'You were so clever to teach that to Percy, Jenny.'

Jenny shrugged. 'Percy was the clever one. Now can we carry on walking for a bit, I'm feeling less tired.'

Continuing our walk along the trails, my family enjoying the nature, bundled up in their heavy winter coats, I enjoyed sniffing out all the new smells that were all so different from the park. After a quick break for lunch, we continued to stroll along at a leisurely pace, with Jenny and I following Gail and Simon just a little way behind. It was nice to see they were still holding hands, and Jenny and I continued to exchange looks of joy as we watched Gail and Simon laugh and chatter away like any normal, happily married couple.

As the sun beat down and lunchtime turned into afternoon, I found myself drawn more and more towards the lake. It was only a couple of metres away and looked so inviting with the sun shining onto the water. Despite the cold, I could think of nothing I wanted more than to jump in. I looked at my family, who were all sat around one of the café's outdoor tables enjoying a cup of tea under one of the patio heaters. Where would the harm be in simply sauntering down for a little paddle while they finished their refreshments? Especially when I was so bored sat under the table.

Simon must have read my mind, as he caught me glancing at the water and bent down to stroke my head. 'Not today, Perce,' he said gently, 'we haven't got a towel to dry you off with.'

'That doesn't matter,' I whined, getting to my paws.

'Simon's right, buddy,' Gail soothed. 'It's winter, you'll catch your death if you leap in there.'

Disappointed, I slumped back onto the floor and looked longingly at the water once more. So what if it was cold? I was a dog with a nice warm furry coat, and I could quickly shake myself dry.

I glanced up at Gail and Simon, who were busy chatting with Jenny, and, sure they were distracted enough, I got to my paws raced towards the water and jumped straight in. I whined with pleasure as the cool water took me by surprise and then doggy-paddled around in little circles in delight.

Normally, I would never have been so naughty, but the water was calling my name like catnip to kitties and I was powerless to resist. Now I was in the water, I had no regrets even though it was so cold, and did my best to ignore the shouts from Gail and

Simon, who were now standing on the grass verge, hands on hips looking very cross indeed.

'Percy, get back here now,' Gail called firmly.

'Yeah, come on, Perce, not funny, mate,' Simon added angrily. 'We told you not to go in there.'

'It is quite funny,' Jenny chuckled, who had by now joined her parents. 'He's got mud all over his face and it looks as if he's having one of those face packs Mum uses.'

Gail and Simon craned their necks towards me and, as they saw what Jenny had witnessed, their expressions of anger changed into giggles of delight.

'You're right, Jen,' Simon chuckled. 'No doubt his skin's going to be super-smooth when he gets out. Let's just hope he hasn't got rid of his puggy wrinkles.'

'Have you got your mobile, Si?' Gail asked. 'That's definitely a photo for the family album.'

As Simon dug out his mobile and snapped me doggy-paddling in the water, apparently covered in mud, I looked up in delight at my family's faces and was overjoyed to see any feelings of anger had gone. Posing happily for the camera, I realised I had never expected to be a source of entertainment for my family;

but watching them laugh and hug each other as I swam to the shore, made me realise I would do whatever it took to see my family like that every single day.

14

As the sounds of One Direction pumped through Jenny's bedroom, I snuggled deeper into her lap. Giving her hand an affectionate lick, she stroked my head, making me feel relaxed and happy, causing my little tail to curl and uncurl with pleasure. Since Jenny had got out of hospital, I had wanted to spend as much time as possible with the little girl and this morning, once she had given me my breakfast and opened the garden door for my much-needed wee, we had returned to her bedroom for cuddles, lying in companionable silence reflecting on yesterday.

We had all enjoyed a wonderful day out with everyone seeming relaxed and happy. After I had soaked them all by shaking myself dry following my dip in the lake, we had returned home and Jenny had slept on the back seat.

From the moment Gail had shown me the photograph of her and Simon together, I had been wracking my brains to think of something nice to do for her, and Simon's bright idea of a day out had come at the perfect time. For the first time since moving in with the family, I had gained an understanding of what life had been like before Jenny became sick and they had to endure problems no family should have to go through. It was proof, if proof were needed, of just how much Gail and Simon loved one another and still had a marriage worth fighting for and saving.

Glancing up at Jenny, seeing her deep in thought, I had a feeling she felt the same. Gail's eyes had shone with happiness all day, as had Simon's and Jenny's. Best of all, Simon had not gone to bed in his man cave last night or stayed up watching television alone after Gail went to bed. Instead, he and his wife had gone up together and I fell asleep feeling sure this was the start of happier times to come, as long as Sally kept her distance.

Just the thought of what Simon might be doing with Sally sent waves of worry through my fur. I had tried to push the fact Simon had lied to the back of my mind, but it was impossible not to think about the fact Peg had told me Sally was looking for happiness anywhere she could find it. As an image of my beautiful pug pal flooded into my mind, I let out a little whine of delight. Peg was perfect in every way.

In fact, she had been very good at spying on Sally over the last few days and told me

Simon had popped over for a glass of wine after work every night for the past week, where they had chatted about old times. She said it had all seemed very innocent, but that did not change the fact that Simon had told Gail he had been working late every evening over the past week because everyone wanted their boilers working before the Christmas holidays. I wondered why, if it was all so innocent, Simon had not mentioned his trips to Sally's. Interestingly, I had noticed during some of my walks that Sally and Gail had been getting closer, enjoying a coffee and a natter on the park bench, while me, Peg and the others played nearby. I had no idea if Gail had confided in Sally about her relationship with Simon, or if Sally had told Gail that Simon often came round to hers for a chat too. If she had, surely they would no longer be friends and the arguments between Gail and Simon would be fiery.

Speaking of which, I could just about make out the sounds of a row between them starting from the kitchen. I turned to look up at Jenny, as I felt her stroking my head more furiously, and guessed she could hear her mum and dad arguing as well. Shuffling upwards towards her face, I nuzzled into her neck as I lay on my side.

Turning towards me, she gave a watery

smile and blinked back the tears. 'I thought that after yesterday everything was good again — just goes to show how dumb a kid I am!'

'You're not dumb,' I barked. 'I thought things were better as well, so if you're dumb so am I.'

Jenny smiled and ruffled my ears. 'Sorry, Percy, it's just I know they think I can't hear them when they're downstairs and up in my room, but I can.'

She blinked back the tears while I barked in agreement. I knew Gail and Simon did their best to conceal their problems, but Jenny was not blind or deaf. I had hoped that since discovering Jenny needed a transplant they had called a truce, but judging by the cross words being spoken downstairs it seemed the hostilities were back on. I lifted my head from Jenny's shoulder and heard them arguing about money yet again.

'Look, all I'm saying is that maybe it's not a case of affording a holiday but needing one,' Simon said.

'We've been through this,' Gail replied patiently. 'I really appreciate you working so hard, and I know you're doing this overtime for us so we've got more money, but Christmas is almost here. We need the extra for treats.'

'A holiday would be a treat, Gail,' Simon

growled. 'And, frankly, we need something to get us back on an even keel.'

There was a long pause and, for one blissful moment, I thought the row had stopped until I heard the sound of Gail's voice once more.

'What do you mean even keel?' she asked gruffly. 'I thought we were on an even keel as you put it, things were perfect yesterday. What do you know that I don't?'

'Nothing. It's just I think it's fairly obvious things between us haven't exactly been great, have they? This argument proves that,' Simon replied.

'And you think a holiday's going to solve all our problems?' Gail spat. 'It's not a holiday we need, Simon, it's a miracle!'

With that, there was the sound of the back door slamming, closely followed by Simon's footsteps on the path in the back garden as he headed towards the garden shed.

Jenny twisted her neck towards me and looked at me. My own heart lurched with despair at the sight of such sorrow in her eyes and I wrapped my paw tightly around her.

'Thanks, Percy,' she said quietly, 'you always know just what I need.'

I licked her cheek affectionately as Gail knocked on Jenny's door.

'Can I come in, love?' she asked, her voice

muffled through the wooden door.

'If you want,' Jenny replied quietly.

With that, Gail's beaming face appeared around the door. Glancing up at her red-rimmed features, it was obvious that she had been doing her best not to cry, and even now was putting on a brave face for the sake of her daughter.

'Just wondered if you two fancied coming out for a walk?' Gail asked gently.

'Yes, please,' I barked enthusiastically, getting onto all fours and giving myself a little shake.

'What about you, love?' Gail smiled as I jumped down from the bed and walked towards her. 'It's a nice sunny morning, shame to stay in bed.'

'No, thanks, Mum,' Jenny said, turning over onto her side so she faced the wall. 'I think I'd rather stay here.'

'Come on, love,' Gail wheedled as she entered the room.

She scooped me up into her arms and we padded over to Jenny's bed and perched softly by her side. 'Just a few minutes, with me and Perce, wouldn't you like that?'

But Jenny refused to turn around. 'Honestly, Mum, I don't feel all that well and I'd rather be alone, if you don't mind.'

Gail laid a hand on her daughter's

shoulder. 'Sweetheart, why didn't you say you felt poorly? I can take Percy out later if you want me to stay with you.'

Jenny shook her head and buried her face in her pillow. 'No, thanks, Mum. I think I just need some time to myself, and Dad's here if I need anything. You and Percy go. I'll see you later.'

'But love — ' Gail started as she tried to comfort her daughter.

'Mum, please,' Jenny interrupted, her voice now thick with exasperation, 'I'm fine, really, please just go.'

Removing her hand from her daughter, Gail turned to me and smiled falsely. 'Come on then you, just us this morning. Are you ready?'

'Always,' I barked, licking her hand to offer some comfort before she set me on the floor.

Together we walked towards the door, only for Gail to pause as she laid her hand on the door-knob to open it.

'You know how much I love you, don't you, Jenny? You're my world. I just want you to know that.'

Jenny said nothing as Gail opened the door reluctantly, leaving me to follow her down the stairs and out to the hallway. The weather was decidedly cooler this morning and much more wintery. As Gail slid on her parka, she

193

opened the cupboard door which I knew contained my lead and doggy treats and pulled out what looked like a small furry blanket I hadn't seen before.

'I got you this.' She smiled, squatting down so my eyes were level with her knees.

Looking up, I saw she had pulled out a fleecy blue dog jacket, which looked as if it were bursting with warmth. I could tell just by looking at it that the jacket would be a welcome treat today as yesterday's sunshine had long since gone, only to be replaced with clouds and cool winds.

'It's beautiful,' I barked gratefully, thinking back to the little jacket I had hoped Gail would buy for me when I was in the tails of the forgotten.

'But here's the best bit,' Gail explained, as she held the jacket up and showed me the back view. In red and white letters, PERCY was emblazoned on the back for all to see. I looked back up at Gail and was touched she had gone to such trouble for me when she had so much on her plate.

'I love it,' I woofed, resting on my hind legs so my front paws could lean on her knees. Leaning forward, I rubbed my nose against hers to say thank you.

'I'm so pleased you like it, Percy,' Gail said happily, as she helped me put it on. 'I saw it and just knew that you would look so smart in it, and you do.'

As Gail stood and looked at me approvingly, I walked towards the full-length mirror by the door and admired my reflection. The soft, furry fabric felt snug and warm against my fur and I looked up at Gail joyfully, curling and uncurling my tail in pleasure.

'Fit for a prince!' she pronounced, as she opened the door. 'Now let's go and show your friends, you're the king of style!'

Standing there in the hallway, proud as punch in my new jacket, I had to admit I felt cock-a-hoop and was looking forward to receiving many an admiring bark from pooches I passed in the street. Yet as I put one paw in front of the other ready to join Gail, I heard movement from upstairs and felt a tug at my heart. I turned my head back to look up at the stairs, and then turned back to Gail. She was looking at me quizzically, my lead in her hand, unable to understand why I was not my usual excitable self when I knew a walk was on the horizon.

But something told me it was impossible to leave Jenny when I knew she was so upset. Gail might be having a bad time with Simon yet she was an adult and more able to cope. The little girl needed me more.

'Sorry,' I barked in explanation to Gail.

'Can we go for a walk later? I should be with Jenny.'

Yet Gail did not seem to understand me. 'Percy, come on. It's going to rain in a bit and I don't want to get drenched. I need to pop into the supermarket on the way home and get some essentials, so please stop mucking about.'

'I'm not mucking about,' I woofed. 'You go to the shops and I'll wait for you here. I'm sorry, Gail, please try to understand.'

I looked at my owner, willing her to get the message my barks were conveying. But she just stood there looking puzzled, hands on hips, shaking her head.

'Percy, come on,' she persisted. 'I won't ask you again.'

'Sorry,' I yapped, rooted to the spot.

'Oh, for goodness sake.' Gail sighed impatiently. 'I'll see you later then.'

With a heavy heart, I watched her shut the door before I padded back up to the stairs towards Jenny's room. I felt so guilty for disobeying Gail, and a part of me fretted it would be a strike against me when the decision was made about whether I should stay or go at the tails of the forgotten. Yet something deep inside told me that my place was with Jenny this morning.

Reaching her bedroom, I pushed open the

door and saw Jenny was now standing up, peering at her bookshelf.

'What are you doing here?' Jenny chuckled, a huge grin lighting up her face as she caught sight of me.

'Thought you might like some company,' I barked, padding across the room to stand by her side.

'I'm glad you're here,' she said, bending down to fondle my ears. 'I was just trying to find a new book to read, but my head feels all mushy and I can't think straight.'

'Maybe you should have a rest,' I barked in suggestion, feeling worried about the little girl. Her face was very pale, and she looked tired all of a sudden.

'In fact, I think I might have a lie down for a minute,' she said. 'Will you join me for a nap?'

'I can think of nothing I would like better,' I replied eagerly.

As Jenny turned away from the bookcase and walked back across the room towards her bed, I followed just behind her, and watched as she wrapped her arms around herself. Then, without warning, I saw Jenny's legs buckle beneath her as she crashed to the floor on top of her One Direction rug.

'Jenny! Jenny! Can you hear me?' I barked frantically in her ear.

Slumped on her back, eyes shut and her lovely long hair spread all over her face, I expected her to stir briefly and get straight back up, but there was nothing. What was wrong? Could she be asleep? Was she so tired she had simply fallen to the ground in a kind of sleep fall rather than sleepwalk? Determined to get a reaction, I leaned in closer to her face, my hot breath bouncing off her cheek, then I licked her cheek with as much slobber as I could muster, and waited for a response. Still there was nothing, so I tried again. This time, taking great care not to hurt her chest, I sat on her arm, sure the weight of my body would at least cause her to push me off, but still she refused to stir.

Drawing my face back, I peered at her lifeless body and felt a flash of fear. Why would she not wake up? Had something happened to Jenny? I decided to try one last time and leaned over her face, licking every one of her features including her eyelids, which I knew she hated. Still there was no sign of life and I knew I had to act.

'I'm getting help, Jenny,' I barked. 'Hang on.'

I raced through her bedroom door and pelted down the stairs, barking my lungs out, desperately trying to find Simon. Bursting into the kitchen, I found him, sat at the coffee table, devouring the remainder of last night's pizza.

'Ah, Percy,' he said guiltily, as I caught him with half a Margarita slice in his mouth and tomato sauce all over his chin. 'Just having a little snack. You want some?'

'No! It's Jenny,' I woofed determinedly, as I ran to his side. 'She's collapsed. Something's wrong. You have to come now.'

'Mate, why are you wearing that coat?' Simon asked, taking another bite. 'I think Gail got you that to wear outside not inside.'

'I know that,' I woofed. 'Don't worry about the coat, you need to help Jenny.'

Simon smiled and put the pizza down. 'Ah, I get it.' He grinned, ruffling my ears with his hand. 'You want some as well. You should have said, there's more than enough for two. Hang on, let me get you some.'

Mistakenly thinking I was as excited as he was over the idea of leftover pizza, he pushed his chair back, walked to the fridge and pulled out a slice. Crouching down, he held it out to me, encouraging me to lick the corner.

'Go on, mate, it's delicious. Gail's gone out, she won't know.'

'For the love of Lassie! I don't want any stupid pizza,' I barked, pushing the slice away with my nose. 'Jenny needs help.'

Not for the first time I found myself feeling

frustrated Simon was unable to understand my barks and the sight of him eating pizza as though nothing was wrong made me feel angrier by the second. Perhaps I needed to show Simon rather than bark at him. Quickly, I turned around, yelping frantically as I raced out of the kitchen and into the corridor, all the while checking to see if Simon was following me. Turning my head, I was relieved to see he had finally put the pizza down, curiosity seemingly having got the better of him, and was following me into the hall.

'Mate, what is it?' he quizzed.

'This way,' I barked again, quickly bounding up the stairs, all the while checking behind me to follow.

Thankfully, he seemed to get the message and chased after me up the stairs.

'This better be important, buddy. I was enjoying that pizza,' he grumbled as I led him to Jenny's bedroom.

Bounding through the doorway, Simon hot on my heels, I heard him gasp as he saw his daughter lying on the floor. We rushed to her side. Simon crouched over Jenny and tried to shake her.

'Jenny, sweetheart, Jenny!' he shouted. 'Wake up, wake up!'

But still there was no sign of movement. I stood rooted to the spot, unsure of what to do or bark next to help. All I could do was watch Simon try desperately to rouse his daughter, tears streaming down his face as he realised his efforts were all in vain.

After a few attempts, Simon stopped, reached into the back pocket of his jeans and fished out his mobile. He seemed to press the device a few times and then held it to his ear.

'Yes, ambulance, please. My daughter's collapsed, she has cardiomyopathy and is being treated at Great Ormond Street. Quick as you can, thanks.'

He put the phone back into his pocket and swept the hair from Jenny's face, before planting a kiss on her forehead. The gesture touched me, and I found myself, licking the spot he had just kissed, desperate for Jenny to know how much she meant to me.

As I turned to look at Simon, I heard the sound of sirens. 'The ambulance is here,' I barked. 'Jenny's help is here.'

Quickly, Simon got to his feet and bolted down the stairs. Seconds later, he flung open the front door.

'She's upstairs. Please hurry,' I heard him say, before the sound of footsteps echoed up the stairs.

I just had time to give Jenny another lick on her forehead, before I saw Simon burst back into the room, with a man and a woman dressed in green.

They smiled at me, and got to their knees to work on Jenny. I looked at all the equipment in their hands and felt scared. There were so many frightening-looking devices I felt afraid for my favourite little girl.

'Don't hurt her,' I barked. 'She's only little.'

'Come on, Percy, out of the way,' Simon said, beckoning me to his side.

Padding towards him, it was impossible for me to tear my eyes away from the humans working on Jenny. The lady was placing a mask-like thing on her face, while the man was shining a bright torch into her eyes.

'That doesn't look very nice,' I barked to Simon.

'They know what they're doing, buddy,' Simon reassured me, as he stooped down to pick me up.

Holding me tightly into his chest, I heard his heart beating wildly. My own heart went out to him, he was as terrified as me. I looked up at him, and softly rubbed his nose with mine.

'What was that for?'

'Because you look like you needed it,' I barked gently in reply.

Simon smiled down at me through his

tears, then rubbed my nose with his.

The man and woman in green stood up and turned to Simon.

'Jenny's stable now but we're going to take her straight to the hospital. Do you want to ride in the back of the ambulance?' the man asked.

'Yes, of course,' Simon replied, setting me on the floor and wiping his eyes with the back of his hand.

As Jenny was placed on a weird portable bed type of contraction, the man and woman carried her out of the room and down the stairs, with Simon and I following closely behind.

Reaching the front door, I watched as Jenny was loaded into the back of what looked like a large van.

'Get well soon, Jenny,' I barked desperately, as Simon clambered into the van behind.

'Don't you want to shut the front door, sir?' asked the man in green, as he looked at me still barking madly at Jenny and the van.

'Oh God! Yes!' Simon gasped.

He jumped out of the van and ran towards the house. He was just about to shut the front door, when he suddenly smacked his hand against his forehead. 'Christ, I'd better leave a note for Gail.'

After running down the hallway and into

the kitchen, I watched him scribble a note on a scrap bit of paper and stick it to the fridge.

'Bye, Percy,' he said, hurriedly shutting the front door.

As the noise of the sirens grew fainter, I slumped to the floor and tried to gather my thoughts. I felt terrible, seeing Jenny like that had been so distressing. I would have traded places with her in a heartbeat if it meant she would feel better. Then it struck me, if I felt bad, how on earth was Gail going to feel when she returned and discovered her daughter had been rushed to hospital.

I shook my head, determined to make sure I was a shoulder to cry on when she got back. I had a feeling she would need it.

15

Alone again, I wandered from room to room, wondering what to do next. Gail would be back any moment, and my biggest challenge was being there for her as soon she returned. Without Simon, or her mum around to offer support, she would need a friend and I was determined to be the very best friend I could be.

I tramped into the kitchen and stared at the hastily scribbled note on the fridge that Simon had left. I had no idea what it said, but knew it would not be much judging by the few words that were etched onto the piece of paper. I was just wondering how to make sure Gail saw it straightaway when she returned, when the lady herself appeared at the front door.

Laden down with supermarket carrier bags, she looked as if she had enough food to feed the five thousand, rather than the few essentials she had apparently nipped out to get.

'Got a bit carried away with Christmas bargains,' she explained, dumping the bags on the floor and shrugging off her parka.

'Everyone likes a tin of choccies don't they, so I got six at half price! Bargain!'

'Never mind the chocolates,' I barked. 'You need to read this note.'

Gail picked up the bags and walked towards me, planting a kiss on my head as she passed me into the kitchen. 'And don't think I forgot you, my angel. I got you plenty of festive chews to get your jaws around.' She smiled, looking at me with bemusement. 'Now then, why hasn't Simon taken your coat off?' she asked, bending down to loosen the fastenings and slip my jacket off. 'That's better, isn't it? You must have been roasting in that.'

'Gail, the fridge, there's a note for you on the fridge,' I barked, as she stood up and put my jacket on the counter.

'You're welcome, Percy,' she said, as she began unpacking the groceries she had just bought. 'Now what have you been up to while I've been out? Did you get Jenny to come down and play?'

'No, she's gone to hospital, Gail,' I barked at her furiously again. I padded away from her side and over to the fridge and began jumping up and down. 'Look, here's the note.'

'Oh, sweetheart, I'm sorry, I'll get you some food now,' she said, spotting my empty food bowl and quickly refilling it with kibble. 'So where is everyone? The house seems very quiet.'

'That's what I'm trying to tell you,' I barked, ignoring my food bowl. 'They're not here, they're at the hospital.'

But Gail still did not appear to understand what I was saying, and walked out of the kitchen in search of her family, with me following closely behind, continuing to bark to get her attention.

'Hello? Hello? Anyone home?' she called. She wandered back out into the hallway and up the stairs, pushing open the doors to each room and discovering they were empty. 'That's weird,' she said, looking down at me. 'Maybe they're in the garden.'

'No, they're in the hospital,' I barked loudly.

'They'd have rung me if they'd gone out, and there have been no missed calls,' Gail said. She pulled her phone out of her jeans pocket and scrolled through the various screens checking for updates. 'No, no missed calls or messages.' She sighed, walking back down the stairs and into the kitchen.

Seeing no sign of them, she opened the back door and together we walked across the cold, hard ground towards the shed. 'Simon? Jenny?' Gail called again. She opened the shed door, only to find it bare.

By now, I was beside myself with frustration. What was it with these humans? What did I have to do to get them to understand me for once?

'Gail, please!' I woofed, as we returned to the house. 'Look on the fridge or give Simon a ring!'

Back inside, Gail seemed to have finally understood one of my barks as she pulled out her mobile, then hit speed dial to call Simon only to find it went straight to voicemail. 'Might as well have a cup of tea and a snack while we wait for them.'

Gail walked across to my side of the kitchen and pulled out a juicy new bone from my treat cupboard. As she pulled off the wrapper, my tummy rumbled appreciatively and I licked my lips in anticipation.

'Here you go, sweetheart,' she cooed, setting it down on the floor for me and stroking my head.

Bending down to lick the treat, I suddenly backed away from it with a start. What was I doing? This was not a time to be thinking about treats. How could I have allowed myself to become so distracted?

Quickly, I ran to the sink, where Gail was filling the kettle. This time I was determined to get her to understand once and for all.

'Gail, the fridge. Please look at the fridge,' I barked desperately.

My lovely owner paused. She smiled briefly before a flicker of concern crossed her features. 'Percy, what's wrong? It's not like you to leave a treat.'

'I've told you! The fridge, Gail! I can't eat at a time like this.'

Gail padded back across the kitchen, flicked on the kettle then went to the fridge. I held my breath as I saw her glance at the fridge door, then let out a squeal as her palm rested on the handle. Worry coursed through my fur as I saw she had gone very pale.

'No!' she groaned, pulling the note from the fridge. 'No, no, no, no, no. This can't be happening, not now. She's just come out of hospital,' Gail shrieked as her hands flew to her mouth. She scrambled frantically in her pocket for her phone. 'Simon! Simon! It's me. What's happened? What's happened to my daughter? I'm on my way to the hospital now but call me.'

Seeing Gail's shaking hands, I got to my feet and raced across the cool kitchen floor to her side. 'Jenny collapsed,' I woofed quickly, 'but a nice man and woman in green came and took her away in a van to make her better. Simon went with her.'

'Oh God, Percy!' Gail gasped, sinking to

the floor, and resting her head lightly on mine. 'Jenny's collapsed and been taken to hospital. Simon's just left me this note.'

My eyes went from Gail's to the note she was clutching fiercely in her hand. My breathing quickened as I struggled to find the right bark to offer comfort.

'I'm so sorry,' I whined quietly, not knowing what else to say. 'I love you, Gail. Just say the word if there's anything you need or I can do.'

Gail buried her face more deeply into my fur. 'Thank you for being here, Percy. Thank you for being you. But now I've got to be there for my darling daughter.'

She stood and walked up the stairs. I followed and watched as she started frantically throwing things into a bag, desperately trying to predict what Jenny would need in the hospital. As she rushed into her bedroom, she flung in spare clothes, her music player, laptop and, of course, her favourite stuffed bear: Big Ted.

Just the sight of him sent a fresh wave of tears spiralling down Gail's cheeks. I watched as she sank onto Jenny's bed and clung to the teddy. Burying her face in his neck, I noticed she inhaled her daughter's scent, which clung to Big Ted as richly as the handmade knitted jumper he was wearing. At a loss for barks, I did what I always did and hopped up onto the bed beside Gail and burrowed my way onto her lap beside the large bear.

'It's going to be okay,' I whined. 'Jenny's going to be fine, I know it.'

Gail pulled her face from the teddy and looked down at me. She smiled and wiped her eyes with the back of her hand. With a large sniff, she stuffed the teddy bear into her already bulging bag, then gave me a peck on the top of my head.

'Thank you, Perce.' She smiled again. 'Why is it you always know just what I need and when I need it, eh?'

'Because I'm your best friend,' I barked softly.

'I don't know what I'd do without you,' she replied gently. 'In fact, I don't know what any of us would do.'

Giving me a firm but final kiss on the top of my head, she set me down on the floor and got up from the bed. As she rose, I saw in her a gritty strength and determination that I had not seen before. It was as though this was the moment she had been rehearsing for since Jenny's diagnosis and now it was here and she had got over the initial shock, she was ready to cope with whatever else this cruel disease threw at her.

The tears that had streamed down her face

only moments earlier had now dried, leaving salty track marks down her cheeks. Although Gail's complexion was still a deathly white, there was a steely look in her eyes that said she was ready. She ran back downstairs, stuffed her phone and car keys into her bag before refilling my food and water bowls. After grabbing her coat, she sank down onto her haunches as I sat opposite and let her pat and stroke me goodbye.

'I don't know when I'll be back, Percy, but don't worry, I'll call Sally and ask her to look in on you again, and one of us will be home later.'

'Okay,' I barked, 'don't worry about me. I'll be fine, but drive safely and send my love to Jenny. Tell her to get well soon.'

Shooting me a smile, Gail got to her feet, gathered her belongings and walked towards the door. After she shut it firmly behind her, I heard the familiar sound of the car start, and jumped up to the window in the living room to watch her drive away.

'Bye,' I barked furiously as Gail gave me a wave. I wished more than anything that I could go with her and ran delicately along the windowsill continually woofing to let her know she, Jenny and Simon would never be far from my thoughts. I followed the red car all the way to the top of the street and watched Gail safely turn right into the busy road ahead. Once she was out of sight, I jumped down from the windowsill and onto the living-room carpet. I had been left alone before and was used to the sounds of the boiler, the house next door and the planes that sometimes flew overhead, but now, with everyone gone, the house seemed even quieter than usual, and weirdly had a somewhat eerie air to it.

Unsure what to do with myself, I ran from room to room, desperately looking for clues as to what had happened to Jenny, but found nothing. Everything looked just as it usually did, with Jenny's bed still unmade from the night before, the towels hanging on the bathroom radiator drying from the morning's showers along with the empty mugs on the side of the sink awaiting a space in the dishwasher.

A sorry, sick feeling gnawed away at me as I walked over to my bed and pushed my nose underneath the blankets. I hoped a nap might make me feel better as I was now feeling shaky from head to paw. I lay down on the soft covers trying to find a sense of calm. I took a deep breath then closed my eyes and waited for sleep to find me, hoping that when I awoke this awful nightmare would be over, or at the very least I would know what was wrong with my favourite little girl.

I tried to push all thoughts of Jenny and what she might be going through in hospital from my mind as I counted cats, then rabbits and finally all the different kinds of cheeses I would love to eat. But the more I tried to sleep, the more awake I felt and in the end I gave up. I wondered if I might have more joy sleeping in Jenny's bed, so I padded upstairs towards her room and hopped up onto her bed. Her bed was always so comfortable and reassuring, and, as I curled up under her duvet, I hoped being near Jenny's things might make me feel closer to her, but I still found it impossible to sleep. Frustrated, I opened my eyes, just to hear the front door open and the sound of Sally's voice echo from the hallway.

'Hello! Percy? Are you there? Where are you? Me and Peg are here.'

The thought of Peg waiting for me on the floor below was all the incentive I needed to get to my paws and rush downstairs. Just the sight of her sitting at the bottom was enough to send my heart and spirits soaring.

'Hello, you,' I barked, hopping quickly down the last couple of stairs to rush towards my love. 'Thank you for coming again.'

'Hey, Percy,' Peg yapped, licking my cheek by way of greeting. 'I'm so sorry to hear about Jenny. Do you know what's happened?'

'Not a clue,' I barked, hanging my head in sorrow. 'I don't suppose you or Sally have heard anything?'

Peg sank to the floor, the walk to Gail's clearly a bit much for her in the cold weather. 'Sally just had a call from Gail about half an hour ago telling us Jenny had been rushed to hospital by ambulance and Simon had gone with her.'

'So, Simon hasn't got in touch then?' I asked, sinking to the floor beside her.

'Not a word,' she replied quickly. 'Gail asked if we could look in on you and, of course, Sally agreed, so we came straight over. I'm so sorry, Percy. Let me know if there's anything we can do.'

'Thanks,' I whined quietly. More than anything, I wished Peg had the answers, but I had quickly learned that where Jenny's health was concerned, there was nothing any of us could do to make her better. We had to place our trust in the doctors and nurses looking after her and hope against hope that help could be found soon.

Peg rubbed her nose against mine. 'Well, you mustn't worry about being on your own. Sally told Gail that she was happy to bring you back to ours if she and Simon were stuck at the hospital.'

'That's kind,' I barked gratefully.

As Sally reappeared, I looked at her hands and saw she had gathered a bag full of my food and a couple of my favourite toys.

'How about we all go back to mine for a bit? You two can have a snooze in front of the radiator while I do some work, then we can go to the park if you fancy?'

I looked at the floor. I was unsure if it was a good idea for me to leave. What if Gail and Simon came back urgently or needed me for something? My mind raced as I pictured a worried Gail returning home only to think I had sneaked out of the cat flap again on a jolly with my pals.

Peg turned to me, her brown eyes boring into my soul. 'Percy, Gail and Simon know that you'll be with us so there's no need to worry. In fact, Gail is less likely to worry if she thinks you're with us rather than on your own.'

I knew she was right and, looking up at Sally, seeing her worried eyes flitting from me to Peg, my heart went out to her. Whatever was going on between her and Simon, she had always been there for me and I knew she was doing her best to put a brave face on everything and be enthusiastic. The least I could do was be grateful and so I barked my thanks.

'Let's go then,' she said.

Together, the three of us made our way to Peg's flat and, as Sally let us in, I had to admit the place was starting to feel a bit like home. Following Peg's lead, I curled up next to her on the striped chenille rug by the radiator and tried to relax, but it was just too difficult. Every time the phone rang, I lifted my head and listened out in case it was Simon or Gail with news. Sally must have noticed my despondent expression, because she crouched down next to me and stroked my back.

'I understand you want to know what's happening, but, honestly, Percy, no news is good news,' she said kindly. 'I'll make you a promise right now that if I hear something before you do then I'll tell you immediately.'

'Thanks, Sally,' I whined, licking her free hand in gratitude.

'Tell you what,' she said, looking out of the window, 'how about we all go for a walk? The sun's just come out and a bit of fresh air might do us all some good.'

'Now that is a good idea,' I barked, giving Peg a gentle nudge with my nose. 'Come on, Peg, we're going to the park.'

'*Phner*, leave me alone,' she whined, shutting her eyes even tighter, causing me and Sally to laugh. 'Peg, the sun's out,' I barked, more insistent this time, 'and it's really, really bright. You know what that means.'

Her eyes flew open. 'Shadows, lots of shadows.'

'Exactly!' I barked. 'Still want to stay here?'

Scrambling to her paws in excitement, I knew the answer and, as Sally shucked on her coat, we whined impatiently at the door, eager to get to the park.

'Do you think he'll be there?' Peg barked excitedly. 'If he's not going to be there, it will all be for nothing.'

'All we can do is hope,' I yapped encouragingly. 'You know Bugs, though. I bet he was whining at Bella to take him and the baby to the park the moment the sun reared its head.'

'Then let's go!' she barked more insistently, turning to Sally and tugging gently on her trousers.

'All right, all right.' Sally chuckled. 'I know you like the sun as much as me, girl, but a coffee in the park is not a cocktail on a Caribbean island so calm down.'

We got to the park in record time and, as soon as we crossed through the gates and onto the soft grass, Sally unclipped our leads and we raced across the park towards our usual spot.

'I can see him! I can see him!' Peg barked excitedly, her pace quickening as she got closer and closer to the Border collie.

'Is he doing it?' I panted, wondering once again why I wasn't as fit as my pug friend.

'Not yet,' she replied, as she slowed her pace to match mine. 'But, look, the sun's getting stronger, so it'll be any minute now.'

Sure enough, as we neared Bugsy's side, we saw his gaze fixed firmly on the ground and his body hunched over his shadow. Exchanging glances with Peg, we watched in anticipation as he drew his shoulders back, leapt onto his hind legs and then jumped onto his front paws, a determined look in his eyes.

'I'm going to get you! Stay there, you rotten thing,' he barked furiously at the ground. 'You always try to get me. Well, you won't get away this time. I'm going to stop you once and for all.'

With renewed grit, Bugsy hopped onto his hind legs, raised his front paws and quickly jumped once more onto his shadow before repeating his jump again, and again, and again, and barking at the ground, 'Stay still! Stay still! You won't beat me, you thug!'

'Hey, Bugsy,' I barked casually, 'how are you doing?'

'Fine, Percy,' Bugsy barked, his eyes never

leaving the floor. 'Be with you in a minute.'

'Okay, mate,' I replied, hardly daring to look at Peg.

The sight of my friend trying to do battle with his own shadow was just the medicine I needed to take my mind off what was happening at home. I turned to Peg and saw her tongue was lolling out of the corner of her mouth as she watched Bugsy try to win at least round one against himself.

'Do you think we should say something?' I woofed to Peg, who was by now transfixed watching Bugsy run around in circles, trying to catch his own shadow.

'Are you kidding?' Peg barked incredulously. 'This is the best entertainment I've had all day. I'm waiting until he catches himself. Who knows, maybe today's the day. The hundredth time's a charm?'

'I think it's more like the two-hundredth,' I yapped sarcastically. 'I'm just impressed at his stamina. Look at him now.'

Sure enough, Bugsy was no longer content to leap on his own shadow and instead had the bright idea of trying to outrun it before giving the thing chase, up the fence. Sadly for poor Bugsy, he had not quite worked out that it was impossible to do battle with his own shadow and gravity at the same time, and the Border collie quickly tumbled to the ground.

Seeing him sprawled on the grass, Peg raced over.

'You okay, Bugsy?' she asked.

'I think so,' he woofed, looking a little woozy as he gingerly got to his paws.

'That was quite a tumble you took there,' I barked, catching up with them both.

'I know, but I thought this was the time I'd catch that rotten black dog once and for all,' he yelped mournfully. 'I'm sick of him, taunting me when the sun's out, Percy. All he does is follow me around, copying my every move. He even follows me when I go to the loo and it's really getting me down.'

Poor old Bugsy. We had all tried explaining that there was no black dog and it was just his shadow, but he refused to listen. Since then, Heather had suggested that to make our lives easier, we just went along with whatever nonsense he came out with. Looking at him staring reproachfully at his shadow once more, it was hard to resist the temptation of explaining again, but I knew my words of wisdom would fall on deaf ears. Strangely, Peg didn't feel the same.

'Bugsy,' she yapped, 'how many times have we got to go through this? It's not a dog, it's your shadow. We've all got one. Look at mine and Percy's.'

But Bugsy remained unconvinced, as he

221

barked gravely, 'I don't know where you've got that from, Peg, because you're wrong. We've all got this big black double that follows us, teasing us and making our lives a misery. For some reason, it's bigger in the summer than it is in the winter, but he's real. You might not want to do anything about the bully that's got it in for you but I won't be made a fool of, not by anyone. Don't you agree, Percy?'

But I hardly heard him as my attention had been caught by the sight of a man walking towards me. As he got closer, I could see that it was Simon. Feeling a slight thrill, I bounded towards my owner, eager to greet him with a lick and a curl of the tail. But as he came to meet me, fear burst from my chest as I took in the sight of him. Simon's eyes were red raw from crying and his skin looked ashen. He bent down to scoop me up and I rested my head on his chest and heard his heart rate quicken.

'Oh, mate, it's so good to see you,' he whispered into my fur, squeezing me tightly. 'I've got something I have to tell you.'

Quickly, he set me back down and clipped on my lead, then together we set off for home, barely glancing at Sally. My little paws were shaking with dread as I imagined the worst.

'As you already know, Jenny collapsed this morning at home,' Simon explained, his voice shaking with emotion. 'But what you don't know is that the doctors are now running a thousand tests. We don't know what's wrong or why it's happened, but what we do know is that when we got to the hospital doctors found her heart rhythm was abnormal and her condition has deteriorated.'

I stopped walking and looked up at Simon, my mind a whirl with a thousand questions.

'Jenny's now going to stay in hospital for a bit while the doctors work out what's wrong,' Simon continued tearfully. 'Gail or I will always be with her, but all we can do now is wait and hope.'

A rush of sadness coursed through my fur. Poor Jenny, I would do anything to ensure she lived a normal life. Suddenly, we stopped walking and I felt Simon's hands around my middle as he scooped me from the ground and tucked me into his coat.

'Sorry, buddy,' he wept, burying his face into the top of my head. 'I just need a hug.'

Me too, I thought desperately. *Me too*.

16

Since Jenny's collapse a couple of days earlier, I had quickly got used to spending time alone and had even developed a little routine. After Gail or Simon left for the hospital, desperate for news, I would return to my bed for a doze then I would get up and try to do a bit around the house.

I knew there were specially trained dogs known as Canine Helpers who helped make their owners lives a bit easier by assisting with domestic chores. I remembered how Javier used to tease me that he should have got a pup that knew their way around a washing machine, rather than a pug who liked to create enough mess to fill one.

I had felt quite affronted at the time. After all, it wasn't as though he used the machine himself, instead preferring his cleaner Gloria to do all the housework. But Gail and Simon had no money for Glorias, so I did what I could and put my little paws to good use. Although I avoided the washing machine and dishwasher because they looked like huge scary machines that had the potential to eat me alive, I was able to clean and tidy.

I would straighten beds using my mouth to tug the duvets and pillows straight. Then when each one was just so, I would dust off the Christmas decorations, straighten the cushions on the sofa, sweep the pine needles away underneath the Christmas tree, stack the television remotes away tidily and clear away any other mess that I could. Of course being small, I was unable to reach most things, like the top of the dining table, so I had to challenge my balancing skills and hop up onto chairs so I could reach the things I needed.

Once everything was clean, I would go into the kitchen and open the door to the cupboard under the sink. It was there that all the cleaning goodies were kept, so I would pull out a duster and give the surfaces a good going over before Sally and Peg came to take me for a walk. I usually managed to finish before they arrived, but this morning they caught me red-pawed and were amazed to find me with a feather duster in my mouth.

'Blimey!' Sally whistled incredulously, as she stood in the doorway, hands on hips and eyebrows raised in wonder. 'Could you pop over to mine and help me out with the housework when you've finished here, Perce?'

'Don't give her ideas,' Peg barked unsym-pathetically, as Sally bent down to remove the feather duster from my mouth and tickle my ears. 'She's a lazy so-and-so as it is, more interested in sitting on the sofa than cleaning it.'

Peg had a point, and I tried not to laugh, but it was fair to say you could write your name in the amount of dust at Sally's place. I looked up at the woman to see if she had realised her pug was trying to tell her off, but, as ever, Sally did not appear remotely concerned.

'Oh, Peg,' Sally chuckled, as she turned from me to my pug friend, 'are you giving me lip again, girl? Honestly, I don't know why I keep you sometimes!'

'Because nobody else would put up with you the way I do!' Peg barked, giving me a gentle lick on my ear as she went into the kitchen to admire my handiwork. 'I must say, you're doing a smashing job. Look at the shine on that wood, you've surpassed yourself.'

I felt my cheeks flush red with pride beneath my fur. 'It's nothing. Gail and Simon have such a lot on at the moment, a bit of cleaning's the least I can do.'

'What's the latest on Jenny?' she asked. 'Any change since she was rushed in?'

I sighed. Since Simon met me at the park and told me how seriously ill Jenny had become I had thought of little else. 'No change,' I yapped forlornly, 'we're still waiting for test results to work out what's happening next. Gail and Simon are with her round the clock, and we're all hoping and praying for a miracle.'

'It'll come, Percy.' Peg nodded wisely.

'I hope so,' I barked, joining her on the floor.

It had been a difficult few days all in all. Simon and Gail were usually here fleetingly, with one or the other popping back to either collect clothes or sleep while the other stayed by Jenny's bedside. All rules about me not sleeping on Gail and Simon's big double bed had gone out of the window, as I usually snuggled up with one of them until morning, my presence offering them gentle reassurance through the night.

The only good thing about all of this was that they were both too tired to row as often as they had before Jenny collapsed. On the rare occasions they were at home together, they ate a late dinner then flopped in front of the sofa in contented silence before one or the other went back to the hospital. Of course they exchanged the odd cross word, which was only natural, but it was nothing like before. With a heavy heart, I realised Gail and Simon's improved relationship was the only good thing to come from this sorry situation, but Jenny's life hanging in the balance seemed a hefty price to pay.

I was about to say as much to Peg, when I heard footsteps coming down the path. I got to my feet and barked a welcome with Peg following eagerly behind me. I knew that sound anywhere and I wagged my tail excitedly as I stood next to Sally and let out another bark as my beloved owners unlocked the door and stepped into the hallway.

'Blimey, we weren't expecting a welcoming committee.' Gail laughed, her face a picture of surprise.

'Yeah, you didn't have to roll out the red carpet, you know.' Simon chuckled as he emerged behind Gail clutching a bag of what looked and smelt like dirty laundry. 'How did you know we'd be here?'

'We didn't.' Sally grinned as Simon kissed her on the cheek. 'It's called perfect timing. How are you both?'

Gail turned to Simon and shrugged before smiling warmly at Sally. 'There's no change. Jenny's in good spirits even though she's hooked up to goodness knows how many machines. She sent us home together for the night, said we were cramping her style and it was time for us to spend a bit of time with Percy.'

'That's teenagers for you,' Sally said. 'You can always rely on them to tell it how it is.'

'And make you feel good in the process,' Simon added, as he dropped the bag of laundry on the ground and turned to each of us expectantly. 'What's been happening around here then?'

'Not much,' Sally said, smiling. 'We were just on our way out to the park.'

'Oh, well, don't let us stop you.' Gail smiled. 'But before you go, we wanted to give you these.'

I watched with interest as Gail handed Sally a huge bouquet of flowers.

'For you.' Gail grinned. 'We just wanted to say a huge thank you to you for everything you've been doing. What with Percy, and all the cleaning, it's not necessary you know.'

Sally looked confused. 'Cleaning?'

'Yes, you don't have to be modest, Sally,' Gail said gently. 'The house is always spotless and I haven't had time to run a duster around the place for days now.'

'And I certainly haven't,' added Simon.

Sally took the flowers and sniffed them appreciatively. 'They're beautiful, guys, thank you. But honestly, it's a pleasure to look after Percy, and it's not me you should be thanking for cleaning — '

229

'No, Sally!' Gail interrupted firmly. 'We won't hear another word about it. This is the least we can do. And as for you . . . ' She smiled, turning to me. 'We didn't forget a treat for you either.'

Reaching into a carrier bag, she pulled out a delicious-looking bone fresh from the butcher's. 'I think you've more than earned this now.'

As Gail set the bone on the floor, my tummy rumbled appreciatively. I was just about to bend down and start nibbling when I caught Peg glaring at me from the corner of my eye.

'Would you like first chew?' I barked, in what I hoped was a gentledogly fashion.

'Why, Percy! I thought you'd never ask,' Peg replied sweetly.

She wasted no time nibbling it as I stood back waiting for my turn. Looking up, I saw Gail beaming at me fondly, while Sally and Simon roared with laughter.

'What a diamond!' Sally chuckled.

Simon shook his head at me, in mock disgust. 'Honestly, mate, you're giving us blokes a bad name by letting your girlfriend devour your treat like that!'

'You leave him alone,' Gail admonished playfully.

'All right, all right,' Simon said, laughing,

holding his hands up in a gesture of mercy.

I watched the two of them, enjoying the gentle banter and my heart soared. Peg may well have been demolishing my bone, but seeing Gail and Simon enjoy a laugh together was present enough. The only one who looked slightly miffed, I noticed, was Sally. Although her mouth was turned upwards, the smile failed to reach her eyes and, as she did up her coat, I got the impression she was keen to leave.

'Well, we'll get out of your hair and let you have a bit of time to yourselves,' Sally said quickly. 'Come on, Peg, let Percy have a bit of his treat for heaven's sakes.'

Reluctantly, Peg pulled herself away from my bone and surveyed the damage. In the few minutes she had been let loose with it, Peg had managed to tuck into more than half. My eyes bulged in shock. Peg might only have been a little thing, but she had an appetite to match some of the biggest canines.

'Sorry, Percy,' she barked apologetically, 'I think I might have got a bit carried away.'

'That's okay,' I whined adoringly. 'It doesn't matter.'

Sally let out an impatient sigh. 'Will you come on, Peg? I want to get home before the soaps start and Gail and Simon want a bit of time with Percy.'

With that, Peg growled at her mistress, 'All right, all right.'

After giving me a quick lick on the cheek, she pushed past Sally and sat beside the closed front door.

'Well, that's my cue to leave.' Sally grinned, doing up her coat to guard against the miserable winter air. 'Stay in touch, won't you? Let me know if anything changes.'

'We will.' Gail smiled, as she opened the front door, letting a cool blast of air into the house. 'And thanks so much for everything.'

Sally smiled, this time her eyes crinkling with her mouth. 'Any time.'

Simon joined Gail as she waved them both goodbye, and then she shut the door quickly and rubbed her hands together to get warm

'Tea, love?' Gail asked.

'Go on then. And I'll have one of those biscuits while you're about it,' Simon said, picking up the bag of laundry and making his way to the tiny utility room.

Gail walked into the kitchen and set her car keys on the hanger especially designed for the job, while I followed eagerly behind, my little tail curling and uncurling with pleasure. It was such an unexpected pleasure to see Gail during the day at the moment, I weaved in and out of her legs excitedly, desperate to make the most of every second.

'Easy, Perce,' she said, flicking on the kettle, 'you nearly had me over then.'

'Sorry,' I woofed earnestly.

Sitting on the floor, I watched Gail plop two tea bags into mugs then open a pack of custard creams before she bent down and kissed my head. 'I know I'm not around much, Percy, but I miss you. I just want you to know that.'

My tongue lolled out of my mouth in pleasure at the kiss. 'I miss you too.'

As the kettle boiled, Gail gave me a final pat on the head before she rose and poured boiling water on the bags.

'Tea's ready, love,' she called, reaching for a biscuit and delicately biting around the edges.

'That's a sight for sore eyes,' Simon chuckled, greedily helping himself to a handful of biscuits just as Gail slapped his hand.

'Oi! Don't eat them all.'

'Oh, leave off, I'm starving,' he said, his mouth full of custard creams sending crumbs everywhere. Taking his tea, Simon walked through to the living room, with Gail and me following. As he sank back on the sofa, Simon let out a huge sigh. 'It's nice to sit down for five minutes.'

'Tell me about it,' Gail agreed, sinking onto the sofa beside him and leaning in for a cuddle. Gazing down at me, she patted her lap. 'Come on, Perce, I want a cuddle. Jenny wants a full progress report on what you've been up to.'

Simon sipped his tea. 'That's true. You're all our Jen's talked about. She's really missing you. In fact, I've been wondering if we shouldn't take you to see her.'

'What do you mean?' Gail asked, her brow furrowed with concern. 'You know dogs aren't allowed in the hospital.'

'I know.' Simon nodded. 'But he's only little. We could sneak him inside somehow, when we pop back in a bit.'

'Simon! That's stupid! We'll get caught!' Gail gasped.

'Oh, we won't. And if we do, we'll just leave. Come on, it'll cheer Jenny up and we won't stay long, so there's no chance of us getting in trouble.'

My heart raced as I watched Gail's face for any hint of a decision. The idea of seeing Jenny, even if it was just for a few minutes, was so exciting and I willed her to say yes.

'Go on then.' She smiled. 'I'll get my bag.'

As Gail got to her feet and walked up the stairs, I met Simon's gaze. He gave me a huge smile and tickled me behind the ears.

'See, Percy, all the family should visit a loved one when they're sick. I don't see why you should get out of it just cos you're a dog,' he chuckled. 'You're one of us now, you know.'

I craned my head into his hands and felt a pang of affection for Simon. Was it possible that amongst all the chaos he had learned to love me? Was I finally safe from being returned to the tails of the forgotten?

17

I wrinkled my nose and did my best not to sneeze. I had been hidden in Simon's jacket for at least ten minutes now and the darkness and old tissues stuffed inside his pockets were playing havoc with my eyes. Simon had promised he would only hide me for a few minutes while we made our way from the car park to Jenny's room, but with barely any room to breathe, it was beginning to feel like ever so much longer.

We had arrived at the hospital in darkness, but from my position on the back seat, I could already tell the hospital looked huge. Lights lit up every window and, despite the fact it was early evening, the place was a hive of activity with people coming and going through the main entrance.

Once we had parked, Simon had gently lifted me out of my carrier and bundled me up inside his parka.

Gail let out a squeal of delight. 'You look six months pregnant.'

'I do not!' Simon protested. 'I may look as if I've had one too many pies, but Percy here's only little.'

'That's right,' I barked in agreement.

'Okay, no more barking from you,' he whispered, patting my body through the fabric of his jacket. 'It's not for long and it will all be worth it when you see Jenny.'

I snuggled against the warmth of Simon's body and listened to the sound of his heart beating. It sounded strong and I found the steady beat comforting in the pitch black. As Simon set off across the car park, I jolted against him, the weight of his hand resting against my back ensuring I did not slip down and out of his jacket.

Once inside, the smells were an assault on my nostrils. The heavy scent of lemons, combined with something that smelt like the toilet cleaner Gail and Simon used in the loo, hit my senses hard, and my eyes began to water as I did my best to choke back a sneeze. I caught snatches of conversations as we continued walking. Some were laughing, some were crying, some sounded as if they were carrying an army of worry on their shoulders as they fretted over loved ones who were being cared for inside.

Despite the warmth of Simon's body heat, I shuddered. There was so much sadness here, all I could focus on was seeing Jenny and I began to wonder if we would ever reach her side. Eventually, the sounds of chatter drifted away as we turned a corner and I felt my mood lift. This time I heard the sounds of children laughing while adult voices told them jokes. Elsewhere, I caught the strains of pop music and, as we slowed down, I felt Simon push open a door, where the sound of One Direction blasted out of the room. Finally, we had found Jenny.

'Dad! Mum!' I heard a familiar voice exclaim. 'I wasn't expecting you until later.'

'Well, we thought we'd come a bit earlier,' Simon explained. 'We've got a surprise for you.'

'A surprise?' Jenny giggled. 'What is it?'

'Ta dah!' Simon announced, unzipping his jacket. As he set me gingerly down on something soft that felt like a bed, I blinked rapidly, adjusting to the sudden burst of bright light.

'Percy!' Jenny exclaimed.

'Ssssh,' Gail hissed, as she rested a comforting hand on my back. 'He's not supposed to be here.'

As my eyes got used to the bright light, I looked at Jenny and felt a pang of love for the little girl. Even though she had what looked like a million different wires coming out of her body and was surrounded by lots of beeping machines, she looked well. Her face had colour and her big, beaming smile made me realise just how much I had missed her.

'Hello,' I whined, shuffling gently towards her across the bed. 'How are you?'

I rested my head against Jenny's tummy and breathed in the scent of her. It felt so good to be around my favourite little girl once more and, as I felt her soft palm against my fur, I breathed a sigh of relief. For just a few minutes, everything in my world felt right again.

'I can't believe you're here, Percy,' Jenny crooned, shock and wonder etched across her face. 'I've missed you so much.'

'And he's missed you, love.' Gail smiled, joining me on Jenny's bed and sitting next to me. 'Just seeing the two of you together is so wonderful.'

I looked across at Gail and saw there were tears in her eyes. Gently, she ran her hands along my fur and planted a kiss on Jenny's cheek.

'How are you doing today sweetheart?'

'I'm fine, Mum. The doctors say they should have my test results back soon so I'm a bit worried about what they're going to say,' Jenny replied honestly. 'But having Percy here is just wonderful. I wasn't sure when I'd see him again.'

'Well, we got the feeling Percy was missing

you as much as you were missing him,' Simon explained.

'Awww, is that true, Perce?' Jenny asked, leaning over and covering my face with kisses. 'Have you missed me?'

'More than you'll ever know,' I yelped quietly.

'You're the best dog in the world. Thank you for being brave enough to come here,' she whispered into my fur, before raising her head and addressing her parents: 'What made you think to bring him? You know the nurses will go spare if they catch him.'

'Ah well, you know me and your mother, Jen,' Simon chuckled. 'We'll take anyone on if it means we can do what's right.'

'Oh, yeah.' Jenny chuckled wryly. 'Is that why you're loitering by the door, Dad, to check nobody's coming.'

'Hey! There's nothing wrong with being prepared, young lady,' Simon quipped easily.

Glancing at my family, I had to admit I felt a burst of pleasure I had some small paw in bringing them all together in this way. I much preferred it when they got on, if only they could see that constant rowing was not the answer.

'Quick!' Simon hissed. 'Hide Percy, doctors are coming this way.'

'Where shall I put him?' Gail wailed,

glancing around the room in desperation.

'Put him under the bed, Mum,' Jenny suggested. 'Nobody will look there.'

Hurriedly, Gail grabbed me by my tummy and placed me gently on the floor under the bed. 'Ssssh,' she whispered, smiling as she placed a finger to her lips.

From my vantage point, I was able to get a good look at some of Jenny's room. It was amazing how much it seemed like her bedroom back at home. A One Direction poster was tacked to the wall next to a little corner sink, while a string of fairy lights hung from the mirror. All in all, it looked quite homely, and I was just about to crane my neck to see the rest of it when the sound of a door being pushed open sent me scampering back underneath the bed.

'Jenny, hello there, how are you doing today?' I heard a man say.

'Good, thanks, Doctor Mike,' Jenny replied.

'And Gail and Simon, good to see you today. How are you both?' Doctor Mike asked.

'We're fine,' Gail replied. 'We're wondering if there's any news. Jenny mentioned that you might have her test results today.'

There was a brief pause as I watched Doctor Mike tap his trainer-clad feet.

'Yes, we do have some news. And I'm glad you're here as I was about to ring you both and ask you to come in,' he said, his voice grave.

'What is it, Doc?' Simon asked. 'This sounds serious.'

There was another brief pause before Doctor Mike spoke again. 'It is serious, but I want you to see it as good news, as we've finally got some answers and a clear treatment path.'

'What does that mean?' Gail asked, her voice shaking.

'It means we've run a number of tests, as you know, Jenny,' Doctor Mike explained.

'I know that, Doctor Mike,' Jenny said, laughing. 'You've stuck so many needles in me, I feel like a pin cushion!'

A lump formed in my throat at the sound of my favourite little girl doing her best to be so brave. Whatever this doctor had to tell her, it did not sound good, but Jenny had so much experience of hospitals she was ready to take this in her stride. I already felt so proud of her and I had no idea what the doctor wanted to tell her yet.

'I'm sorry about that, Jenny.' Doctor Mike gave a little laugh. 'But what can I tell you? Our nurses need someone to practise on and you have such good veins and are an old pro now I let them all have a go on you.'

'Ha ha!' Jenny giggled.

'Which leads me on to your results,' Doctor Mike continued, 'but actually, just a minute, can anyone else smell something like dog in here?'

I froze in shock. Was Doctor Mike talking about me? I shuffled my paws in outrage. I was a very clean dog, thank you very much. In fact, Peg was always talking about my sweet smell. How dare this doctor say there was a smell of dog in the room.

'I can't say I can smell anything,' Simon said, his voice rising an octave as he denied my existence.

'Me neither.' Gail laughed, slightly manically. 'Perhaps you've been on your feet too long, Doctor Mike. You know how some people start seeing things — maybe you're smelling things.'

Doctor Mike sighed. 'You could be right. I was on call last night and didn't manage to get a lot of sleep. I'm clearly going mad. Anyway, Jenny, back to you. As I said, I want you to try to view these results in a positive way.'

'Which is?' Simon said impatiently.

'Which is that Jenny's condition has now become very serious,' Doctor Mike said. 'As you know, we've been trying to find a solution for some time and have tried a pacemaker along with various drugs. Yet, Jenny's collapse the other day, along with the results from her latest blood work and heart tests, show that her condition is deteriorating.'

'How badly?' Gail asked quickly.

'Badly enough that we need to operate tomorrow and insert a powerful blood pump that will help keep her heart beating. I'm afraid Jenny's best chance now is through a heart donor, but this pump will keep her alive until we can find one,' Doctor Mike said.

'A heart donor? So that means a transplant?' Simon gasped.

'That's right,' Doctor Mike confirmed. 'We'll keep Jenny here for a few weeks until she's recovered from the operation, but the pump will enable her to go home if we haven't found a donor by then.'

Simon groaned and pinched the bridge of his nose between his fingers. 'There must be some other way, some other solution.'

'Dad!' Jenny hissed. 'Doctor Mike knows what he's talking about. We've been seeing him for years.'

'I know he does, love, but I can't believe a transplant is the only solution. What do you think, Gail?'

'I don't know,' Gail admitted, her voice low. 'I'm a bit shocked, love.'

'Mummy, please,' Jenny begged. 'Doctor Mike knows us better than anyone. I want this if it means I can be like everyone else.'

'But, sweetheart, you're not like everyone else. You're special and me and your dad love you for it,' Gail replied, her voice now thick with emotion.

I felt the bed above me shift as there was a pause in conversation and I wondered if Gail was hugging her daughter tightly in her arms.

'Look, I know you're all scared, and you should be. I wouldn't be suggesting this if I thought there was another way,' Doctor Mike said, breaking the silence. 'Inserting the pump is a big operation and the transplant is huge. I wouldn't be doing my job properly if I didn't make you aware of all the risks. But the benefits for Jenny could be wonderful. This is a chance for her to have a normal life, be like other children.'

'Did you hear that, Mum, Dad?' Jenny said, her voice full of enthusiasm. 'I could be just like other children. Surely we have to give this a try.'

'It's all a lot to take in, love,' Gail said quietly. 'I know what you're saying and you know all we want is for you to be happy above all else.'

'Your mum's right,' Simon said. 'We just want to make sure that this is the best chance of you being happy.'

'But it is right,' Jenny pointed out. 'If it wasn't, Doctor Mike wouldn't have said it. And like he said, I can be normal again. How great would that be?'

Bless Jenny. How typical of her to be so full of courage and I thought how many humans could stand to learn a thing or two from this little girl. Before I could help myself I let out a bark of appreciation. 'Well done, Jenny. You're so brave,' I woofed.

'What the hell was that?' Doctor Mike gasped, his trainers stepping back from the bed.

'Er, computer game,' Simon babbled. 'The noises they make these days are all so realistic.'

'That wasn't a bloody computer game, Simon. Come on, don't take me for a fool. I knew something wasn't right. You've got a bloody dog in here, haven't you?' Doctor Mike hissed.

'Hey!' Jenny protested. 'Percy is not a bloody dog, he's the best dog in the world and my best friend. Come on, Percy, out you come.'

I knew there was no point hiding any more. The dog was out of the bag, so to speak. Gingerly, I placed one paw in front of the other until I emerged from under the bed and out into plain view. Looking around me I saw Gail and Simon's terrified faces, while the man I assumed was Doctor Mike glared right at me. He looked about the same age as Gail and Simon, and with his dark hair, beard and big green eyes, I thought he would look quite friendly if he did not look so angry.

Something about his expression made me feel a flush of fear. I knew I was not supposed to be here, but that was no reason to look at me as if I was something the cat had dragged in. A fact Jenny was quick to point out.

'You told me I should focus on things that make me happy, that being positive was good for recovery,' she said bravely. 'Well, Percy makes me happy, so don't look at him like that, it's not his fault.'

Doctor Mike glanced at the little girl, then back at me, his expression softening. Sensing his mood thawing in the face of Jenny's logic, I thought of the trick Jenny had taught me recently and without prompting, raised my paw to cover my eyes then lowered it again.

'Peek-a-boo,' I barked.

Just as I hoped, my trick had the desired effect: Doctor Mike burst out laughing and bent down to ruffle my ears.

'Sorry, Percy is it?'

'Yes,' I woofed in reply.

'Jenny's right, you're lovely, but you can't

be here, I'm afraid. This is a hospital.' Giving me a final pat on the head, he got to his feet and folded his arms. 'Guys, you're going to have to take him home now.'

'Just a few more minutes please,' Jenny begged, her face crumpling. 'He's only just got here.'

'Yes,' I barked. 'I've only just got here.'

But Doctor Mike shook his head. 'I'm sorry. If Nurse Brenda catches you with a dog in here, she'll kill you, closely followed by me.'

Gail lifted me up. She held me close and kissed the top of my head before holding me out towards Jenny to cuddle and say goodbye.

'Bye, Percy,' Jenny wept. 'It was nice to see you.'

'And you,' I yelped, licking her nose. 'I'll come back, just wait and see. You won't have to wait long, these doctors don't know anything.'

'Come on then, Percy, let me take you home,' Gail said gently.

'Why don't you both go and make sure Percy's okay,' Jenny said. 'I'm really tired. I just want to watch telly and go to sleep so I'm ready for tomorrow.'

'I'm not sure, sweetheart. It won't take long to pop back in,' Gail protested.

'But, Mum, I just want to nap. Honestly,

I'll see you before my surgery in the morning.'

I looked up at Gail. She seemed far from convinced, but Jenny did appear pale and tired. Perhaps a sleep would be the best thing for her. Doctor Mike seemed to read my mind.

'Jenny's fine,' Doctor Mike promised. 'The girls in the rooms along the corridor are organising a pamper party, anyway, and I believe nail varnish is involved so if Jenny wants company to take her mind off tomorrow, I think they're going to offer a better prospect than you two worrying over her all night.'

'That true, Jen?' Simon asked, glancing fondly at his daughter.

'Kind of,' Jenny admitted reluctantly. 'And besides, Nan and Granddad said they'd pop in later before they checked into their hotel. I'll be okay.'

Simon shook his head and kissed Jenny on her forehead. 'Then we'll see you bright and early in the morning and, in the meantime, we'll all sleep on what Doctor Mike has told us, okay?'

'Okay,' she agreed. 'But no worrying, okay?'

'No worrying.' Gail smiled, bending down to kiss Jenny goodbye and giving me a final opportunity to lick her cheek goodbye.

'Bye, Percy. I love you,' Jenny whispered.

'Love you too,' I barked.

'Okay out! Now!' Doctor Mike ordered, ushering us out of the room. 'And, Percy, it was very nice to meet you, but please don't take this the wrong way when I say I hope I won't see you again.'

'We'll see,' I barked mutinously, as I allowed Simon to bundle me back into his coat and out into the cold night air.

By the time we reached the car and Gail had safely settled me into the dog carrier, I had to admit I could do with a nap myself. All the excitement of seeing Jenny and getting caught by Doctor Mike, not to mention dealing with her heartbreaking news meant I was exhausted. Stretching out in the confines of my carrier, I shut my eyes. I promised myself it would only be for five minutes, but when I opened them again we had just arrived home.

'Here already,' I barked, slowly blinking my eyes awake.

'Come on then,' Gail coaxed, freeing me from my cage and helping me to the floor.

As I trotted along behind them, I sensed a tension between Gail and Simon once more and wondered what I had missed while I had been asleep.

'All I was trying to say was that it was obviously a bad idea,' Gail said to Simon's retreating back as she shut the front door behind her. 'We know dogs aren't allowed in hospital and we need everyone on our side if Jenny's going to undergo a heart transplant.'

'You're not saying that you think Jenny's going to get looked after any less because we brought a dog into the hospital?' Simon said, turning to face Gail and rolling his eyes.

Shivering, at the thought of yet another row brewing, I trotted into the kitchen and headed for my bed, curling up tightly into a ball and hoping my family would change the subject.

'I don't know what I'm saying, I just know that I should never have let you talk me into bringing Percy to the hospital,' Gail said, pushing past Simon in the corridor and walking into the kitchen.

'So is this yet another thing you're blaming me for?' Simon blasted.

'And what else am I blaming you for?' Gail shot back.

'You know what,' Simon replied quietly.

'The note you mean,' Gail fired, as I opened my eyes and saw her resting against the kitchen sink, her eyes twisted with fury. 'You're still upset that I'm angry about the note you left me, explaining our daughter was

251

in hospital. Is that what you mean?'

'Not this again, Gail, please! It was just one of those things, it could easily have happened if you'd been here and I'd gone out.' Simon sighed.

'But it didn't,' Gail snarled, 'it happened when I was out, and what hurts the most is you left a note on the fridge for me to find! You didn't call me or even text me to tell me to come home straight away. No, you left me a note on the fridge as if you'd popped out for a loaf of bread. What were you thinking? How could you do that to me? To Jenny? You know how much she would have wanted me to ride in the ambulance with her.'

Suddenly Simon quickly walked towards his wife, his face flushed with anger. 'We've been through this a hundred times, Gail. How many times do you want me to apologise? I didn't think, I panicked, everything was happening so fast. When I found our daughter upstairs collapsed in a heap, all I could think about was her, so when I saw the notepad, I reached for it and scribbled a note before we left, I'm sorry.'

Gail shook her head. 'I know you're sorry, Simon. And I'm sorry I keep bringing it up. I guess I just wonder if maybe it was a mistake to have taken her out the day before. Maybe that triggered something that caused her heart to fail.'

'No! Gail, how can you think that?' Simon said more gently as he took another step towards his wife and tenderly lifted her chin upwards.

'Because it's true,' Gail replied fiercely. 'I know the doctors say that wasn't the problem, that she might have become this sick anyway, but I know my daughter. I know that she wasn't strong enough to have coped with a day out, but I listened to you and let us get carried away with it when I should have said no to you and now she's facing surgery tomorrow and a bloody heart transplant to boot.'

I gulped nervously as I watched Simon get to his feet and back away from his wife as though he had been burned with a hot iron.

'So that's yet another thing you think is my fault. You think that if I hadn't taken us all for a family day out, Jenny would be okay?'

'I didn't say that.'

'You didn't have to,' he snapped. 'Oh my God! I can't believe this, Gail. You actually think I'm the one responsible, just admit it.'

Gail's eyes narrowed. 'All right, I do think it's your fault. You've been pestering me for months to go on holiday and I said yes to the day out because I felt sorry for you because I always said no. I knew our daughter wasn't strong enough to go anywhere but you kept on and on, and so when you suggested a family day out, I said yes when what I really should have said is no! So yes, in short, Simon, I do think this is your fault.'

There was a deathly silence as Gail glowered at Simon, all the resentment, anger and worry she had been holding on to for the past few months finally out in the open. As for Simon, I saw he had gone very white as his eyes flickered in surprise and shock.

'Well, you know what, Gail,' he said, shakily, 'I'm glad you've finally admitted how you really feel. You kept telling me there was nothing wrong, but I knew the truth. I thought I was going mad, or imagining things, but I know you too well, and I know that I can't carry on like this.'

'What do you mean?' Gail asked quickly.

Simon looked her squarely in the eye. 'For months now, I've been treading on eggshells for Jenny's sake, pretending our marriage was fine, that there was nothing a bit of time together wouldn't solve,' he said quietly, as Gail's eyes brimmed with tears. 'But I was kidding myself, Gail. All we ever do is row and I've had enough. I think we have to admit we're over. I don't honestly think there's anything left between us any more and hasn't been for a long time.'

'That's not true,' Gail gasped. 'How can you talk like this when Jenny's in hospital? The last thing she needs is to be worrying about us.'

'Which is exactly why I think we should end things, Gail. Our daughter's been worrying herself sick about you and me for a long time now and it's not fair to her. We've both tried, blimey you even brought poor Percy into the house to try to fix things, but we're done, Gail. I don't want to live this way any more, life's too short, Jenny's taught me that,' Simon said, raising his voice.

Gail shook her head. 'I know I'm cross with you, Simon, but I can't believe you want to throw away our marriage, not when we need each other the most.'

'But we're not doing each other any good, Gail,' he said, shaking his head sadly. 'It's time to face facts. Our marriage was over a long time ago.'

'Is there someone else? Is that it?' Gail demanded, as Simon walked past his wife towards the stairs.

As the words hung in the air, he turned slowly. 'Of course there's nobody else. How could you think that? At the very least, we just need some time apart, Gail. Surely you can't want things to go on like this?'

A chill coursed through my body. This was all so sudden — was Sally the reason Simon suddenly wanted to leave? After all Gail and Simon always rowed, why had he suddenly had enough? Simon did not wait for an answer as he turned to walk up the stairs.

'I want more from life than daily rows, Gail,' he called, his voice floating angrily from the hallway. 'You should too.'

I saw Gail sink to the kitchen floor, shaking violently, as the reality of the situation hit home, and raced to her side.

'It's all going to be okay,' I whined, licking her face and absorbing the salty tears. 'He doesn't mean it, it's just the shock.'

Gail raised her hands to my head, and covered my. face with kisses. 'Oh, Perce, this has been coming for a long time. I just can't quite believe this is happening, especially now.'

I looked into her eyes and saw that all traces of hope had gone. Gail looked utterly exhausted and, as I rested my paw on her, I tried to convey that same sense of reassurance and love we had offered one another when we had first met at the tails of the forgotten, before tearing myself from her side and pounding up the stairs to find Simon.

I could not let my family tear themselves apart without trying to stop them. Javier had never fought to keep us all together, and I certainly was not intending to follow his lead. I was sure there was something I could do. I tried the man cave first, and then, finding that empty, the family bedroom. Pushing open the door with my nose, I could not believe my eyes. My owner was packing what looked like all his belongings into a suitcase. Clothes, shoes, toiletries, all were going in at breakneck speed. I looked at him in horror — was this really it? To think that all the time I had worried about my family becoming so sick of me they would return me to the tails of the forgotten after Christmas, it had never occurred to me that one of my family would leave.

18

Quick as a flash, I jumped onto the bed and padded across the duvet towards Simon's open suitcase. Hopping inside, while my owner was facing the wardrobe, pulling shirts off hangers, I started flinging his clothes to the ground with my mouth. Out went the wash bag, then the shirts and sweaters, all over the bed and the floor. Next were the jeans — larger and heavier than his other clothes, I tugged them out carefully, not wanting to rip them, but determined to get them out of the case all the same. As the denim hit the floor with a loud thud, Simon turned back to the bed, armed with clothes and a look of disbelief across his features.

'Percy!' He gasped. 'What are you doing?'

'Trying to convince you to stay,' I woofed in reply, reaching for another pair of jeans with my teeth, ready to fling them to the ground.

Seeing what I was about to do, Simon raced towards me. 'Percy, no! Don't do that, please.'

Bending down to pick up his belongings, he dumped them on the bed and looked at me still sat in his suitcase wearing a dogged expression. Something about the way I looked at him must have caused something to stir, as his face softened and he leaned over to ruffle my ears as he usually did.

'I know this is hard for you mate, but just because I'm leaving doesn't mean things will change between us,' he explained, gently. 'I love you buddy, that doesn't go away overnight.'

'Then why are you leaving?' I barked more softly, leaning my head in towards his palm for a stroke. 'Why aren't you staying and fighting for your marriage, for Jenny or for me?'

Scooping me out of the suitcase, he let out a huge sigh as he rested me on his lap and held my face between his hands.

'I know you won't understand why I have to leave Perce. But the truth is, all this fighting isn't doing me or Gail any good. We don't talk, we argue, all the time and it's wearing me out. Worst of all I know it's wearing Gail, you and Jenny out too, and that's not fair.'

'I don't mind,' I barked, insistently. 'You can fix this, I know you can.'

'I can't live here at the moment, I hope you can try and understand.' Simon kissed my head and set me on the floor.

Moving back towards his suitcase, he started repacking; bending down to pick up all his belongings I had just flung across the floor. Just then, I heard the sound of footsteps treading softly on the stairs. Knowing it was Gail, I let out a little bark of welcome before she appeared, leaning on the door jamb, arms shoved sheepishly into her jeans pockets. I watched her survey her husband picking his items up from all over the floor and despite her sadness she managed to raise a little smile as she realised what I had done.

'Where will you go?'

Simon shrugged. 'A mate's, my mum's, I'm not sure. I'll let you know.'

'Will you?' she spat. 'Or will you leave me a note on the fridge?'

Arms full of clothes, Simon turned to Gail, his face a curious mix of anger and sadness. I wanted to turn away or better yet hide in the other room. I hated seeing Gail and Simon fight like this, but more than anything I felt I owed it to them to be there, offer myself as some sort of security blanket they could pick up and stroke or cuddle if the going got a bit rough.

'And that sort of comment is exactly why we need to separate,' he hissed. 'I'm not getting into this again, Gail. Our daughter's dealing with major surgery in the morning and this petty arguing is the last thing either of us should be engaging in.'

With that, he turned back to his case, flung the last of his clothes inside and zipped up the lid. 'Bye mate, I'll see you soon,' he said, bending down to kiss my forehead once more.

Turning back to the bed, he picked up his case, pushed past Gail and ran down the stairs and into the hallway, where I heard the sounds of him rooting through the coat rack trying to find his jacket. Panic flooded through me as I caught Gail's resigned expression and realised she was not about to try and stop him.

I jumped off the bed and raced downstairs, still full of fight. Then it hit me like a poorly aimed tennis ball that I just knew what to do. Reaching the hallway, I saw Simon had gone into the downstairs loo, so I pounded towards the kitchen and spotted the hanger where the keys were kept. Seeing Simon's van keys I jumped onto the bin, then the worktop and walked across it, taking care not to slip. I grabbed the keys with my mouth before quickly walking back along the surface and jumping to the floor, where I hid the keys behind the bin.

Ha! I thought to myself as I heard the sounds of the loo flush. Simon would be going nowhere fast without transport and, maybe once he realised he was grounded, he would sit down and have a proper talk with Gail about their future, sorting this mess out once and for all. Padding nonchalantly into the living room, I lay down on the sheepskin rug and sighed happily at my plan.

Sure enough, as Simon emerged from the toilet, I caught a glimpse of him walking into the kitchen, and the familiar rattle as he rifled through the keys on the hanger.

'Gail, where are my keys? Have you seen them?'

'Your van keys? What would I want with your van keys?' she asked, thundering into the kitchen. 'They'll be wherever you left them, I expect.'

'And I left them here, as I always do,' Simon snarled, jabbing at the hanger.

'Then that's where they will be,' Gail replied, the exasperation clear in her tone.

'But they're not. Have you moved them?'

'Of course not,' Gail gasped. 'Why would I move them?'

'I don't know, maybe you're trying to stop me leaving.'

'Please, Simon, if you want to go, then go, I won't stop you, and I certainly haven't taken your keys,' Gail said flatly. 'Funny though, isn't it? You can't even get out of the house without asking me for help. Quite how you'll manage in the real world without me is anyone's guess.'

There was a pause and I lifted my head to try to hear what came next.

'Well, we'll see about that,' Simon replied. 'I don't need keys. In case you'd forgotten, we don't live in Devon any more and in London there's a little thing called the Tube — I'll take that instead.'

'Fine,' Gail replied.

'Fine,' Simon shot back, walking back out into the hallway.

Panic coursed through me, and I felt my fur stand up on end as I got to my feet and padded out into the hallway just in time to see Simon open the front door and head out into the dark night. This was not a part of the plan. I mentally kicked myself for not thinking about the Tube or the fact Simon would take it. I looked at Gail, who had walked into the hall.

'Are you okay?' I barked, trotting over to her so she could pick me up.

'Looks like it's just you and me now then,' she said, hugging me tightly around my middle.

I licked her ear in return and together we wandered back into the kitchen. I snuggled into her chest to offer my support as we stood looking out into the garden trying to come to terms with everything that had happened. My mind was a blur, so many things had changed in the past few months from being abandoned and left at the tails of the forgotten to falling in love with a new family. Now everything felt as if it were falling apart with one member in hospital and another who had walked out. I had done such a good job of putting my own feelings to one side, but now Simon had officially left I felt cloaked in sadness. I thought back to that day Gail and I had met, and realised that I had been right, sometimes things were too good to be true. I looked up at Gail, her eyes shining with tears.

'I'm sorry, Percy,' she whispered, 'I didn't mean to lose Simon. I bet you wish I'd never adopted you that day.'

A pang of guilt washed over me as I realised she had yet again tapped into my thoughts.

'Of course not,' I barked reassuringly. 'I love you, Gail, I've always been glad you and I have found each other.'

And it was true. Despite everything, I adored Gail and her family. I just wished that I could have kept my promise and brought her family together. I rested my head against her chest again and listened to Gail's slow, steady heartbeat. We stood staring at the garden for what felt like an eternity before Gail eventually broke the silence.

'So, Percy, want to help me look for Simon's keys?'

A chill crept down my spine. Was Gail onto me? I let out a low, nervous whine. 'Okay.'

'He's such a stupid, stubborn man, Percy. He's always losing his keys and I'm sure I saw them hanging on the rack when I put my own up there earlier,' she said, moaning as we walked back inside.

I said nothing and instead tried to think on my paws. Just what was the best way forward? The last thing I wanted was for Simon to leave, yet I also did not want Gail to get the blame for something I had done. Perhaps it was time to backtrack and think of a new plan that would bring my owners together.

Instead, I merely followed Gail around the kitchen, offering her support as she turned the house upside down trying to find the things.

'For heaven's sake, they must be here somewhere,' she grumbled, pulling yet another cushion off the sofa.

I could stand it no longer and instead trotted into the kitchen and barked by the bin, hoping she would follow me for a change. Of course I kept my bark casual, less of a 'here they are, here they are' woof and more of a 'why don't you try the bin area' kind of bark.

Eventually, it worked as Gail appeared just a few seconds later and started poking around in cupboards and behind the coffee maker. Seeing me by the rubbish, she stopped and stared, and then as if a light bulb went off she pulled the bin out and reached down.

'Found them,' she said, grinning triumphantly. 'I knew the stupid man would have mislaid them. As if I would take his keys Percy. Just how desperate does he think I am?'

'Quite,' I whined again as she bent down to affectionately tickle my ears.

'All this isn't fair on you, boy,' she said gently. 'But I promise I'll sort this out. Me and Simon love you and we love Jenny. There is no way on this earth I will ever allow you to go back to the shelter. No matter what the future holds, once Jenny is home we will all lead a normal life, and will be happy again, even if Simon and I aren't together, I promise.'

'Okay,' I barked again, unsure of what else to say.

Part of me was ecstatic to hear once and for all that I would never return to the tails of the forgotten, but it sounded as though Gail was on the verge of giving up, which seemed wrong somehow.

If I was honest, I was exhausted and it was not just the events of the evening that had worn me out. For the past few weeks I felt as though I had been treading on eggshells around my family, terrified that they would never find a way to solve their problems and in turn send me back to the shelter.

Now I felt as though I had to do something to save my family, but what? My interventions so far had been far from pawesome and I was unsure what to do next.

For now, I thought the best thing to do was nothing. As I followed Gail into the living room and curled up on her lap, I wondered if the time had come to take a break and let my family sort out their own problems. After all, I was just a pug, what more could I do?

19

My tummy growled loudly, as if it belonged to a lion, but I ignored the sounds of my body begging for food, I was simply too worked up to eat. Since Simon had left a few days earlier, my appetite had disappeared with him and I could no longer face my favourite bowl of kibble or even a juicy bone. I knew my owners were worried about me as Simon often brought me treats, like a large hunk of cheddar to nibble on, when he returned home from the hospital. With Christmas just around the corner, Gail had tried to tempt me with some of the specially made festive doggy goodies that lined the supermarket shelves. But no matter how tasty the morsel on offer, I found it impossible to work up an appetite, preferring to snooze all day and shut out the world.

I ought to have been happier than I was. After all, Jenny's operation to insert the pump that would keep her alive until a donor could be found had been a success and, even if no heart donor was discovered in the near future, she was expected to be well enough to return home in the New Year.

With Christmas now just a week away, I should have felt comforted that Jenny would be home soon, but the strangeness of life had taken a toll, so much so I was gripped by a sadness I found difficult to shake. These days, life had taken on a funny routine. Gail popped by in the mornings to give me breakfast after she had spent the night at the hospital, then Simon would come over to give me dinner.

Gail's mum and dad were still here, and staying at a hotel near Great Ormond Street so they could help out with Jenny and offer support. Sometimes they came with Gail to walk or feed me but, naturally, they could not stay long, as they had to get back to the hospital and so Sally and Peg often came over to walk me instead. But I felt so upset and so alone, I often preferred to stay inside and would successfully put them off by remaining in my bed pretending to be asleep until they got the message. I had become increasingly fond of Peg, but life felt unbearable and I simply did not want to see anyone or do anything.

This morning, however, they had refused to take no for an answer when they had found me napping in my bed. Peg had come over, as she usually did, but rather than give me a gentle lick in my ear, which I found sleepily reassuring, she barked loudly, rousing me from my slumber.

'I've a bone to pick with you! It's time to stop feeling sorry for yourself,' she woofed. 'You're going to the dogs lying here all day doing nothing, it's time to face the world.'

I opened one eye and glared at her before shutting it firmly. Yet Peg was not put off.

'Percy, I'm not going anywhere. Not until you get up, have some fresh air and a run around the park. It'll do you good, I promise,' she woofed again.

This time I opened both my eyes and looked my friend squarely in the eye. Who was she to start bossing me around? I was about to open my mouth and say as much when I caught her expression. Despite the tough exterior, I saw a hint of worry in her brown eyes, and a pang of guilt shot through my fur. I did not want her to fret about me as well. Perhaps she was right, maybe a walk around the park and a chew on a tennis ball would make the world seem a brighter place.

'Okay,' I barked wearily, 'give me a minute.'

Getting to my feet, I watched Peg recoil as I gave myself a little shake.

'Blimey, Perce!' she barked, screwing up her nose. 'You might want to have a little wash in the duck pond while we're up at the park.'

'Leave me alone,' I yapped. 'I just need some fresh air, that's all.'

'Fair enough, but at least you've admitted you need to get out of the house,' she woofed smugly.

Realising I had been had, I got to my feet and let Sally clip on my lead and together with Peg trotted along the more than familiar route towards the park. Feeling the cold morning air along my fur, I realised Peg was right, I had needed to stop moping, and it felt good to bump into all the dogs and bark quiet good mornings and nice to see yous.

By the time we reached the park, I felt more like my old self and, as Sally patted us goodbye and went in search of a coffee, I joined Peg in a scamper towards the dog track. My heart soared as I caught sight of Bugsy, Heather and Jake, barking away together by the tree. Just the sight of them made me pick up my pace and I let my paws scamper over the cold earth to reach them faster, overtaking Peg in the process.

'Percy!' Heather woofed delightedly, as she saw me approach. 'We've missed you! Come and sit down.'

'Good to see you, old chap,' Jake barked in agreement. 'Place hasn't been the same without you.'

'Thanks, guys,' I yapped in reply, choosing

to sit next to Heather, who gave me an affectionate lick on the ear.

Bugsy said nothing, preferring instead to just look at me, his big eyes fixed on me, making me feel slightly uncomfortable.

'Are you okay, Bugsy?' I asked quietly.

The Border collie nodded, then suddenly rushed towards me, sending poor Peg, who had just joined us, tumbling over. As he reached me, he placed both his paws around my neck and nuzzled his head against mine, causing Jake to shoot me a look of concern.

'Easy there, Bugsy, old boy. No need for any excitement,' Jake barked.

Bugsy broke away, stepped back and looked at me. 'I'm sorry. I've just really, really, really, really missed you, Percy, and I've been so worried about you, and Peg said you weren't eating and you wouldn't come to the dog park and you didn't want to see us and I've just been really, really, really worried.'

Exhausted by his speech, he flopped to the floor by my feet, while I looked at him affectionately. Good old Bugsy, it was nice to know some things had stayed the same and I had to admit that his little speech had been just what I needed to hear.

'Thanks, Bugsy,' I barked earnestly, 'I've missed you all, too; hadn't realised quite how much until now.' I looked around them all with affection, and turned to Peg gratefully, silently thanking her for having the good sense to get me out of the house. 'So what's been happening while I've been away?'

'Not a lot,' replied Peg, who was now back on her paws and shaking herself free of mud. 'I hope you don't mind, Percy, but I filled everyone in on Simon leaving, but it does mean you've been the talk of the park.'

'Oh, no, really?' I yapped in dismay.

Heather saw my distress and licked my ear once more. 'It's a nice thing, promise. We were worried about you. You're normally so cheerful and happy that it was terrible knowing you were hurting so much. If Peg hadn't brought you out today, we were all set to go round to yours and drag you out.'

'Heather, it wouldn't have come to that,' I woofed. 'I'd have appeared eventually. You can't keep an old dog down.'

'But you're not an old dog,' Jake barked in protest, shaking his hips to guard against the cold. 'You're very much a young dog, and that's why we were so worried. Not good for a chap to be alone like that.'

I hung my head in shame. First Peg, Gail and Simon, and now the rest of my friends, had been worrying over me. I hadn't meant to cause anyone so much distress and felt guilty for doing so.

'Don't worry, Perce,' Peg yapped, resting her paw on mine, 'we all go through bad times every now and again. We just didn't want you to feel alone.'

'I don't,' I replied, realising it was true as I looked around my friends. 'I'm just grateful you all cared so much.'

'So how have things been?' Jake asked softly.

I barked gruffly to clear my throat. 'Well, I think you know. Simon's left, Jenny's had an operation that's gone well, but she's still in hospital, waiting for a heart transplant, and Gail's muddling through.'

'Are you seeing much of her?' Heather barked.

I shook my head. 'She pops in during the morning, and Simon comes over in the evening to feed me, but I must confess I haven't been eating much.'

'Percy!' Heather admonished. 'You've got to keep your strength up, isn't that right, Peg?'

'I'm sick of telling him,' Peg replied. 'I've tried every day to get him to eat, but apart from a few mouthfuls, he's barely managed a thing, I — '

'Okay, okay, ladies, enough, I promise to eat, okay?' I barked with an affectionate shake of the head.

Jake caught my eye and rolled his eyes. No doubt he had suffered at the paws of these women for years and shared my pain. Besides, just being here amongst my pals was making me feel better. I was already feeling the stirrings of hunger for the first time in days. I turned to look around me. There was something comforting about the park, it felt like a constant. Yes, the trees were now bare, and the ground was more like mulch, but it felt a bit like home if that were possible.

'So any idea if this separation between Simon and Gail is a temporary thing or if they'll get back together?' Jake barked, getting to the heart of the matter. 'Does Gail want Simon back?'

'She's not sure,' I yapped, wearily. 'They both say they don't know what they want, that they still love each other, as well as me and Jenny, and will do what's best for us. They just don't want to live together and keep rowing.'

'Oh, lovey, it's hard when your family separates,' Heather barked knowingly. 'And tougher for us doggies, who get caught in the crossfire. When my lot split, I did everything I could to get them back together, but nothing worked and I realised the best thing I could do was be there for them when they needed me.'

275

'That's what I've been trying to do,' I woofed, 'but I feel so helpless. I don't even know where Simon is. Every time Gail asks him where he's staying, he just says round at a mate's house. How can I be there for them both when I don't even know where one of them is living?'

I glanced at my friends mournfully. I hated all this. Despite agreeing with Heather about being there for my family, I desperately wanted to make things right between them all. There was such a lot of love left in that family — our day out had proven that. It didn't seem right to do nothing. I looked at Peg, hoping she would have some words of wisdom, but instead she focused her gaze on the floor.

'Peg?' I barked quietly. 'Are you all right?'

'Fine,' she replied. 'Just, er, looking at this grass. Patchy, isn't it?'

'Since when have you been interested in grass?' Heather demanded. 'If something's on your mind then tell us. We're your pals, we're here to help.'

'I don't want to,' she yapped in despair.

Something told me Peg had something to say I would dislike and she was clearly distraught about it. Whatever it was, I was man enough to take it.

'Come on, Peg,' I barked brusquely, 'out

with it. There's no point hiding things.'

Peg gave me a sideways glance, then took a deep breath. 'Percy, I know where Simon's been staying. I know where you can find him.'

'Where?' I demanded.

'At Sally's,' she woofed gently.

'What? There has to be a mistake?' I barked loudly.

Peg looked again at the floor. 'Sorry, Percy, but there's no mistake. I've been getting up in the morning and finding him asleep on our sofa.'

'But why would he stay with you when his mum is just around the corner?' I asked desperately. 'It doesn't make any sense.'

'Unless they're going out together now,' Bugsy barked eagerly. 'Johnny slept on Bella's sofa before they got married, and he moved in with her and her mum, he told me. But it wasn't for very long — Johnny said it would be more comfortable to sleep on a bed of nails than Bella's mum's sofa, so they'd better get somewhere together and now they're married.'

'Shut up, Bugsy,' Peg barked crossly.

'Yes, do be quiet, old boy. Comments like that aren't all that helpful,' Jake agreed.

I looked at Bugsy in dismay. 'You think Sally and Simon are dating? You think they're getting married?'

'No,' Peg barked quickly, 'I don't think that. At least not yet anyway.'

'Not yet?' I replied echoing her bark. 'Just what has been going on, Peg?'

Peg paused, seemingly unsure where to begin. 'Simon turned up last week with a suitcase after he left yours. Sally was very shocked to see him, but said that of course he could stay. Since then he's been on our settee and Sally either cooks him a meal or they get a takeaway and then they watch television.'

'Are they romantic with each other?' Heather barked in astonishment.

'I don't know,' Peg whined. 'He's bought her flowers to say thank you a couple of times, and last night he took her out for dinner, leaving me all on my own!'

I felt sick. Was this the reason Simon had left? Had abandoned his family? To be with Sally? Had she finally found the happiness she was looking for? With someone else's family? I shook my head in sadness, trying to make sense of it all. I had always known something was up between the two of them and, much as I liked Sally, I got the feeling she would love nothing more than to be with Simon. They had a shared history, and the fact Simon had lied to Gail about where he had been was further proof that he had been up to no good. I felt a shiver of sadness through my fur as I thought of Gail. How would she take this betrayal? Not only was she having to cope with her daughter in hospital, but now she had to cope with the fact her husband was having an affair. And then there was Jenny. The news her father had left her mother for another woman could send her health spiralling.

'Now, Percy, this really might not be what you think it is. Let's not jump to any conclusions,' Heather barked warningly.

'Heather's right, old chap,' Jake agreed. 'In my experience, two bones plus two bones rarely equals a full square meal. This could all be perfectly innocent.'

'Unless they're in love, like Bella and Johnny,' Bugsy woofed excitedly.

'Be quiet, Bugsy!' Peg growled. 'We've all heard quite enough from you.'

'It's not Bugsy's fault, Peg,' I barked gently, resting my paw on hers to try to get her to calm down. 'He's just telling us what he's seen, that's all.'

'Yeah!' Bugsy barked sulkily. 'I was just saying what I saw.'

I paused, looking thoughtfully at the group. 'I hate to say it, and I know Jake and Heather have a point, but it doesn't look good, does it? And now he's moved in with Sally . . . '

'He hasn't moved in,' Peg barked in protest. 'He's just staying, Percy. But, no, I hate to say it, Sally's very giddy at the moment, and she only ever gets like that when she's in love.'

'Even so, Peg, let's not forget they've known each other a long time. They might just be friends,' Heather barked imploringly.

'Come off it, Heather,' Peg woofed, her wrinkled face screwing up in disgust. 'You know what Sally's been like since she lost the baby. I adore her, but even I have to admit she's man mad, and she's always been sweet on Simon.'

'And then there are the lies Simon told,' I yelped, joining in. 'If they were just friends, why wouldn't he tell Gail the truth about where he was spending his evenings and why hasn't he told her where he's staying now? Why has he told Gail that he's just staying, at a mate's house?'

The others looked downcast, at a loss for words until eventually Jake woofed so quietly at first I struggled to hear him.

'It may be true, old boy,' he finally admitted, looking to Heather for support. 'When you put it that way, the evidence is pretty damning.'

'That's true,' Heather barked, gently. 'It's possible Simon has left Gail for Sally and, in that case, perhaps we ought to do more than just be there for the pair of them, especially with a sick kiddie's life hanging in the balance. She's going to need her mum and dad back together, so perhaps, Percy you're going to have to up your game, as the humans say.'

'How do you mean?' I barked, feeling confused as the leaves on the ground rustled around us.

'I mean — ' Heather smiled, her eyes brightening as she paced around our little group ' — perhaps we ought to do for you what we did for Bugsy.'

'Sorry, Heather,' I barked, shaking my head, 'but I don't think a failed, tuneless attempt at singing children's lullabies is going to help Gail and Simon's marriage.'

'Don't be silly!' Heather woofed. 'I mean, the way we all got together to help Bugsy in a very practical way. It's not enough any more for us to just offer support, we have to come up with a plan.'

'You think?' I barked, feeling more hopeful than I had in days.

'I know!' Heather replied, earnestly. 'We all do.'

Everyone uttered barks of approval as Heather warmed to her theme. 'We need to consider practical ways of helping your family once and for all, and I know just where to start.'

'Where?' I asked.

'By showing Simon that home is where the heart is. It's time he realised just what he's missing,' she woofed knowingly.

20

Not for the first time, I found myself thanking my lucky stars I had been adopted by Gail. Not only had I found a place to call home with the warmest, gentlest woman in the world, but I had also found the nicest and best friends on the planet. For the first time since Simon had left, I felt a glimmer of hope about my future, perhaps things would not be so bad after all. Perhaps with a team behind me, we could find some way of making sense of all this mess.

Before Peg and I had left the dog park, we all agreed to meet at mine later, just before Simon came home to take me out for my evening walk. Heather and Bugsy said they could easily get away with their owners at work all day, while Jake and Peg said it would be easy for them to give Giles and Sally the slip.

Sitting in the kitchen with the smell of stale rubbish that was in desperate need of taking outside, I cocked my head at the sound of a dog barking. Was it Heather? The sound of the agreed three short barks followed by a long one told me that it was, and I pushed my head through the cat flap and replied with two long woofs. Soon enough, my faithful tribe of Heather, Bugsy and Peg appeared, swiftly followed by Jake bringing up the rear.

'You made it!' I woofed as they all stood before me, all out of breath apart from Bugsy.

'Was there ever any doubt?' Peg asked affectionately.

I shook my head, and gave them each a lick of thanks, before leading the way back into the house through the cat flap.

'Percy! We can't fit through that!' Heather barked in fear. 'Isn't there another way inside?'

'Oh, goodness, I hadn't thought of that,' I replied anxiously. 'I'm so used to slipping in and out like a cat, I forgot about you larger dogs.'

'Well, I have a sizeably larger behind than you do,' Jake woofed, 'and Heather's is even larger!'

'Thank you, Jake!' Heather scolded. 'There's no need to talk about the size of my bottom. It was once voted best in show at Scrufts! And anyway, I think you'll find it's my hips.'

'If you say so,' Jake yapped, his tongue lolling cheekily. 'But I meant no offence, my dear.'

Heather said nothing and instead shot Jake

a hard stare as she turned to Percy. 'What about a back door or side door, lovey, is that open?'

I shook my head. 'Gail and Simon always lock the sliding garden doors with a key. Other than that, there's a side door in the kitchen with a funny handle that goes up and down. I've never worked out how they do it, but even if I could, there's no way I could reach.'

'Can you show me?' Heather asked.

'Course, but I'm not sure what good it will do,' I woofed mournfully.

I pushed my way through the cat flap, with Peg close behind, and made my way through the kitchen and out to the back door, where I found Heather and the others waiting for me.

'It's there,' I barked, gesturing with my nose the large plastic handle.

'Thanks, Perce,' she replied with two short barks, before turning to the others and clearly having what looked like a conflab. 'Step back from the door, Percy,' she barked authoritatively, 'Bugsy has a plan.'

Worried about what Bugsy might be about to do next, I did as I was told and waited. Sure enough, Bugsy made his way towards the door, got onto his hind legs and started using his black button nose to jiggle the door handle up, then down, then up again. With one final jiggle down, he pushed the door open, sending himself and a stream of cold air crashing into the kitchen.

'Well done, Bugsy!' Heather and Jake barked admiringly, as they followed him inside.

'Yes, that's really quite some trick you've got there,' Peg woofed in appreciation. 'Where did you learn how to do that?'

Bugsy coloured underneath his black and white markings, and woofed to calm everyone down. 'I just saw a dog do it on television once and thought I'd try myself, Peg. Honestly it was nothing,' he barked bashfully.

'So this is your pad?' Jake woofed approvingly, as he took in his surroundings. 'Very nice it is too, old boy.'

'Thanks,' I barked in reply as I showed them my bed. 'Look at all these lovely blankets Gail made for me.'

'Goodness,' Heather exclaimed, 'the work she's put into them all, they're beautiful.'

'He's thoroughly spoiled, is our Percy!' Peg teased.

'Nonsense, he's just well loved, as we all deserve to be,' Jake yapped knowingly. 'Now then, how about we get started on Operation Family?'

'Good idea, Jake, there's just one thing before we start,' Heather barked, turning to

Bugsy. 'You did ever so well getting that door open for us, lovey, but do you think you could shut it now only it's darned freezing.'

'Yes, Heather, sorry, Heather,' Bugsy woofed, scampering across to the back door and doing his funny nose trick. I couldn't tear my eyes away — that was something I would have to ask Bugsy how to do myself.

With the door shut, I turned to the others who were all huddled together by my bed expectantly.

'Where should we start?' I barked.

'I don't know, old boy,' Jake replied. 'I thought you might have come up with a plan yourself.'

'No,' I replied horrified, 'I haven't got a clue.'

'Don't worry, Percy,' Heather soothed. 'Let's start by taking a walk around the house and seeing if anything jumps out. How long do we have before Simon comes home?'

I looked outside and saw it was just beginning to get dark. 'Just under an hour, I think.'

'Perfect, Percy,' Heather barked. 'That should give us more than enough time to work something out. Show us the way and let's see if inspiration strikes.'

As I led the dogs around my home, I tried to see things through their eyes. I admired the beautiful soft furnishings Gail had chosen, the family photographs that lined the walls, the books on the shelves and the ornaments the family had picked up on various holidays abroad. Admiring one blue, slightly misshapen bowl that Gail and Simon had brought back from a holiday in Morocco, once, I remembered how they told me they had fallen in love with it, but had been terrible at haggling the price down and had failed to inspect it properly as they handed over more money than they should have done.

'Later, when they got back to their hotel, Simon had been disgusted to find the bowl had a huge crack in it, and was only good as decoration,' I barked, as I finished telling my pals the story. 'Gail had laughed and said there was a lesson in there somewhere and now she likes to display the bowl around the house, as a sign of the happy time they had shared.'

'That's it,' Heather barked as I finished, 'that's how we'll get Simon to realise what he's been missing.'

'With a bowl?' I woofed doubtfully. 'I'm not sure that'll do it, Heather.'

'No! Don't be silly,' she yapped, gesturing to the photos on the wall. 'With all these, and more besides. We'll make him remember the blissful times he, Gail and Jenny have shared and get him to really think about what he's throwing away.'

'That's a good idea, Heather,' Peg agreed. 'And on the plus side, that's something Sally can't compete with. She may have a shared history with Simon, but she doesn't have a lifetime of special memories like Gail does.'

Looking at the girls, I felt excited. The plan was brilliant. The only trouble was how were we going to get all these photos down from the walls without breaking them?

'Well, Bugsy's clearly demonstrated a natural talent for that, don't you think?' Heather barked when I shared my doubts. She turned to the Border collie. 'What do you think, Bugsy?'

He looked around the walls and inched his way up the stairs, clearly deep in thought.

'No problem,' he barked casually, inching his nose towards a particularly lovely photo of Gail and Simon with Jenny on a beach somewhere, smiling widely into the camera.

As it dropped to the floor with a soft thud, I stood back and marvelled as the Border collie padded up the stairs and expertly nudged another family portrait to the ground. Bugsy really did have a natural talent for something, though I was unsure how to describe it. All I could do was hope he never ended up at the tails of the forgotten, because if he fell into the wrong owners I could see he could be encouraged to be an excellent burglar.

I gathered the photos into my mouth and carried them gingerly into the living room. The place was a hive of activity. Jake was carefully collecting photos from the tops of tables and sideboards while Heather was giving instructions. As for Peg, she was artfully arranging each photo to form a large heart shape.

'Where shall I put these?' I asked, setting the photos down on the floor.

'Pop them over to Peg,' Heather instructed. 'She's doing a marvellous job making that heart. I thought we could put that large photo of Gail and Simon over there in the middle, it's such a good one.'

I looked over to where Heather was gesturing and saw she meant the photo of Gail and Simon's engagement. It was sad that Gail had such high hopes when she found that photo with the way things were now.

'Excellent idea,' I barked, taking it over to Peg, who was busy arranging the rest of the photos Bugsy had collected.

As Peg pushed the photos together to complete the design, she placed the engagement photo in the centre and we all stood back to admire her handiwork. There were so many photos she had managed to create a heart that covered almost the entire living-room floor. With the Christmas tree in the corner, the scene looked breathtaking.

'It's beautiful,' I told her, my bark thick with sentiment.

'Do you really think so?' she asked quietly.

'I do. You're so clever, Peg.'

Jake padded across the floor to join me. 'Well, if that doesn't tug at his heart strings, nothing will, old boy.'

'He's right,' Heather marvelled, 'it's a work of art.' She looked out of the window and noticed the darkening night sky. 'And I think it's time we were off. Simon will be home in a minute, Percy.'

I looked at each of them in gratitude. 'I don't know what to say.'

'You don't have to say anything, Percy,' Peg woofed, nibbling my ear as she walked into the kitchen and headed for the side door. 'You'd do the same for any of us.'

As the rest of them passed me to join Peg in the kitchen, I gave them each a pat or a lick to let them know just how much their kindness meant to me.

'Go on then, Bugsy, do your magic again,' Heather coaxed.

'Okay! I'm much faster from the inside

than the outside,' he replied eagerly.

True to his word, I watched him jiggle the door open in seconds, just as I heard the front door opening. 'Simon! Go!'

My friends needed no further encouragement and raced down the passageway, away from danger leaving me to wrestle with the door.

'See you later, Percy. Can't wait to hear how it goes,' Heather barked, as she trailed after the others.

'Thanks, Heather,' I replied, following her outside. Quick as a flash, I pushed the door shut then raced through the cat flap just as I heard Simon calling my name.

'Hello, boy,' he said, with a smile, as he walked into the kitchen and flicked the light switch on. 'Have you been running up and down the house? You're panting.'

'Er, no, nothing like that,' I barked, trying to still my beating heart.

I walked down the hallway to try to encourage Simon into the living room when I heard the familiar clink of a beer being opened.

'Be right with you, buddy,' he called. 'Give me a few minutes to sit down and sup this beer, then we'll nip out for a walk before I get back up to the hospital.'

'No problem,' I barked urgently, 'but you

might be more comfortable in the living room.'

Thankfully, Simon got the hint and followed me. Keen to gauge his reaction, I stood in the middle right by Peg's heart and anxiously watched his response. Just as I hoped, his jaw dropped and his eyes widened in surprise.

'Where did this come from?' he gasped, resting his beer on the coffee table and walking towards me.

Looking at the amazement on his face, it suddenly occurred to me that perhaps my plan to stir my family's memories of happier times would be more effective if they each thought the other was responsible for the photo heart.

'However would Gail have had the time to do this?' he continued breathily. 'She's barely left the hospital over the last couple of days. I'm amazed she managed to get the Christmas tree up.'

As Simon bent down to examine the heart, he began doing just what I had hoped; picking up the photos, stroking the frames and marvelling at times gone by. When his eyes came to rest in the middle, he saw the engagement photo, picked it up and clutched it to his chest.

Smiling as he turned to me, Simon said,

'Do you know, Percy? I can remember this day as if it were yesterday. I'd spent months planning to ask Gail to marry me. I thought a winter picnic would be a memory she would treasure for ever, but when the day arrived, and the snow started to fall, I almost didn't go through with it. Instead, I was going to suggest we went to the pictures as normal.' His eyes moistened at the memory. 'But, I knew nothing like that would ever put Gail off, she would carry on with her plan regardless, which was just one of the reasons I wanted to marry her, Percy. She was always so determined and strong, I knew she was the girl for me the moment we met. I wanted Gail every second of the day. When we learned she was expecting Jenny, well, I thought I'd won the lottery.'

As Simon's eyes filled with tears, he wiped them away with the back of his hand and stared back at the photo again. 'I wish it could be like that again. I'd like to get in a time machine, life was so simple then, but now, well, now everything's changed. I don't know where that girl in the photo is any more.'

'She's still here,' I reasoned, yapping excitedly in his ear, trying to get Simon to see sense. 'She still loves you, you still love her, surely that's all that matters.'

Simon smiled affectionately at me and put the photo back down. 'But instead, life has a funny habit of kicking you when you're down.' He shook his head sadly as he got to his feet, and wiped his still moist eyes. 'All I ever wanted was to be a family man, wife, kid, that was enough. But never in a million years did I think Jenny would get so sick, and never did I think Gail and I would turn on each other. I love them with all my heart but, now, Gail and I are looking at divorce, and Jenny, well, if we can't find a donor for Jenny, I don't know what will happen. I feel like a little boy who's hiding behind the sofa during the scary bits of *Doctor Who*. I'm too frightened to face up to what might happen.'

Simon sat down on the sofa, reached for his beer and took a big gulp of the amber liquid. As it trickled down his throat, I jumped up onto his lap and rested my head against his chest. I reached out a paw and let it rest on his arm, while he gently held it.

'Oh, Percy, this is such a mess,' Simon said quietly, resting his forehead gently against mine. 'I can't believe the effort Gail has gone to, but a few photos won't solve our problems. I thought she understood that. No, it's best we stay apart, too much has happened.'

'No, it hasn't,' I whined. 'It's obvious how

much you love Gail. Make it up now, before it's too late.'

Simon pulled his face back and looked into my eyes. 'Sorry, mate,' he said, chuckling a little, shaking his head. 'It's not like you can understand a word I'm saying. But I do know one word you understand, and that's walk. Am I right boy?'

As Simon stood up and walked towards the door, I followed him with a heavy heart. My friends would be expecting a full progress report, and I hated the idea of telling them our plan appeared to have failed.

Reluctantly, I walked with Simon to the park, dragging my paws along the frosty pavement, the sight of twinkling Christmas lights in the windows of homes doing nothing to boost my mood. Spotting my pals' expectant faces at the dog park did not make the task any easier. Despite the darkness I could see their eyes were agog as they stood around me waiting to hear how it had gone.

'It didn't work,' I howled, in despair. 'Simon says it's best he and Gail stay separated at the moment.'

Heather crinkled her eyes with concern. 'Come on, lovey, it can't be that bad. What did he say exactly?'

'Just that he still loved Gail, that he loved me and Jenny of course, but right now he and

Gail shouldn't be together, even though they had a lifetime of happy memories,' I woofed, sadly. 'It was all a waste of time.'

'Don't say that,' Peg barked sharply. 'You got him thinking that's the main thing.'

I looked across at my owner who was standing by the gate and appeared to be deep in conversation with Sally. She had her hand on his shoulder and was squeezing it as he chatted. I growled in spite of myself, it should be Gail he was turning to, not some old crush from school.

'Peg's right,' Heather barked, giving me a gentle nudge to encourage my attention back to the group. 'Today was just the first plan of many, we've got to keep going, Percy.'

'How do you mean?' I woofed, curiously.

'Well, you didn't think a few photos strewn around the room would be all it would take to send Simon home did you?' Heather yapped, her bark thick with laughter.

'Well, I . . . ' I began.

'Oh, Percy, it's not that simple with relationships,' Heather interrupted. 'This is going to take time; it's just phase one if you like.'

'Certainly is, old boy,' Jake agreed as he leaned in towards me. 'And I think to get results we're going to have to think big.'

21

As the bus rattled around the corner, I held my breath, terrified I would end up sprawled across the gangway. Thankfully, we turned safely into the road and, as we carried along the street at a slower speed, I found myself questioning just the sense in my latest plan.

When Simon dropped me home after our trip to the park, he had called Gail and told her I had seemed glum during our trip to the park and needed a bit of TLC, whatever that was. He suggested he stay with Jenny that night so I could have some time with Gail. I was elated when I learned she was going to come back just for me and, after Simon left, I thought long and hard about what Jake had said. He was right, I did need to start thinking big, and not give up at the first hurdle, but where to start? I needed to confide in Jenny. I missed her desperately and despite my disastrous visit to the hospital, I felt like I had to see her now, regardless of the consequences. She always gave me the best cuddles and tummy tickles, plus her warm smile, which was the spitting image of her mother's, always made me feel good inside.

I had paced up and down the living room, waiting for Gail to return, wondering if Jenny was missing me as much as I was missing her. Hopping up onto the windowsill and watching passers-by walking home carrying huge work bags, an idea had struck me. Gail always carried a massive leather bag to and from the hospital, it was easily large enough for me to climb into, meaning there was no reason for me not to sneak inside and visit the little girl. I had been told in no uncertain terms courtesy of Doctor Mike that dogs were not allowed inside the hospital, but I was so tiny I was sure nobody would notice and when they did, Jenny would be delighted to see me, and Gail would be so surprised that I thought I would be able to at least hug my favourite little girl before I was whisked away. If things went really well, then perhaps Jenny would give me some idea of how her mum and dad were doing when I was not around, which might give me an idea of how to get them back together.

After breakfast earlier this morning, I had dived into Gail's bag as she brushed her teeth in readiness for the hospital and wasted no time putting my plan into action. The bag itself was surprisingly roomy and smelt comfortingly of Gail combined with a curious scent of leather and peppermints. It was the perfect travelling vehicle, at least for a short while, and to make sure I remained unseen, I hid under one of Gail's scarves, but the bus had come as something of a surprise. It was such a bone rattler, I felt as if I were being shaken about like one of Simon's homemade cocktails.

Minutes later, the bus came to an abrupt halt, and I felt myself lifted into the air as Gail picked the bag up and walked along the gangway to step off. As the wind whipped across the top of my head, I was unable to resist peeking out of Gail's bag to get my bearings. With a start, I realised we were next to a busy road, with cars, buses and taxis whooshing by. Overhead stood what appeared to be a massive children's climbing frame, with men in orange hats and fluorescent yellow vests climbing up and down, shouting and making lots of noise and mess. As one whistled at Gail, I felt her speed up. She muttered something that did not sound very nice under her breath. I hid back in the bag again, worried the men might notice me, or worse start whistling at me. When I saw that we had now reached a large building, I was sure this must be the hospital and felt a rush of thankfulness we were approaching safety.

It all looked so different in the day. People in uniforms were rushing around everywhere.

Some were chatting, carrying or helping other humans out of large vehicles. Others were in a hurry, shouting and calling to others as they dashed towards a large bay filled with what I guessed was an ambulance due to the flashing lights and loud siren. I shuddered at the sight of it as I realised that must have been how Jenny arrived here. Craning my neck to take in the sight of the poor soul being helped out of the van, I felt a pang of longing for my favourite little girl. I ached to see her and, as I looked up at the building before me, realised it would only be a few minutes before we would be reunited.

'Excuse me!' I heard a woman's voice shout loudly. 'You can't bring a dog in here. It's not sanitary.'

I looked at the woman, who was gesturing at Gail, her face pinched in disgust. With a black-and-white-spotted suit, and hair piled on top of her head, she looked like Cruella de Vil and I shuddered.

'What dog? What are you talking about? I'm in a rush to see my daughter, if you don't mind!' Gail snapped.

'Oh, yes,' the woman sneered, hands on hips and eyebrows raised. 'Then what's that, the latest handbag accessory? Leave it outside now.'

With that, the horrible woman turned on

her heel and walked back inside, leaving me struggling for breath in the face of her overpowering perfume. I turned my head to look at Gail and she gasped, her face a picture of horror as I licked the hand holding her bag.

'Percy! How on earth did you get in my bag?'

Sensing trouble, I widened my eyes and wrinkled my face in the way I knew she always adored. 'I just wanted to see Jenny,' I whined. 'I didn't mean to be bad.'

Clearly still in shock, Gail walked over to a nearby bench and sat down. She pulled me out of her bag, rested me on her lap and ran her fingers through my fur.

'You know you're not allowed in here. Look what happened the last time,' she said, running her fingers through my fur. 'How did you manage to stay quiet for so long? I didn't hear a peep, and my bag didn't feel that much heavier either.'

'I just wanted to see Jenny,' I whined again. 'I knew dogs weren't allowed, but I thought if I sneaked in and surprised you then it would be too late.'

'Oh, Percy, I don't know what to say. You're full of surprises, a bit like Simon,' she marvelled, her face softening as she ran her eyes over my face. 'When I saw those photos arranged in a heart last night, I was so shocked. I felt as if he was trying to tell me that he still loved me, and that we'll find a way through all of this. I didn't know he cared so much.'

To my surprise, Gail's eyes filled with tears and, as she looked around the hospital grounds helplessly, guilt washed over me. The last thing I had intended was to make her life difficult. I was beginning to see how this plan had not been one of my finest. I had been blinkered in my determination to see Jenny and now it looked like I was going to have to sit outside in this noisy, glorified car park all day.

'Can't you pretend you didn't see me, and go into the hospital with me hidden in your bag? If it hadn't been for that old trout, you never would have seen me anyway,' I barked in annoyance.

'Bloody hell, Percy!' Gail scolded in frustration. 'If it wasn't for that old cow, I never would have known you were here. Whether I should be thankful for that, I'm not sure, but Mum will be here in a minute and I can get her to take you back, but in the meantime I've got an idea. I know how much you want to see Jenny, and I think I know how I can make that happen.'

My heart sang with joy, as I gave Gail a lick

of appreciation. I knew she would have the answer.

'Obviously, you can't go inside, but if Mohammed can't get to the mountain, then the mountain will have to go to Mohammed. What do you think?'

'Whatever you say,' I barked, covering her face in tiny excited licks. 'Get this Mohammed fellow down here immediately if he's my doggy passport to Jenny.'

'Mind, Perce,' she chuckled, 'you're ruining my mascara! But you're welcome. I should have thought of it sooner. Look, there's Mum, let me explain it all to her.'

As Gail stood up and waved to Doreen, she set me on the bench and waited for her mum.

'How was the hotel last night?' Gail asked, kissing her mum on each cheek.

'Very nice.' Doreen smiled. 'I've told your father I'd see him here in a while. He was busy at the breakfast buffet when I left. You know what he's like, can't resist filling up until he makes himself pig sick, or should that be pug sick,' she said, chuckling wryly as she caught sight of me in Gail's arms.

'Speaking of pugs we have a little problem of our own,' Gail replied.

Seeing Doreen grin at the sight of me, I decided to play 'peek-a-boo', raising and lowering my paw, until she gave in and kissed me on each cheek as well.

'So what's Trouble doing here?' Doreen asked. 'Were you going to stick a bonnet on Percy and pretend he was Jenny's baby sister?'

What a brilliant idea! Perhaps it was time to start including Doreen in our plans to get Simon and Gail back together.

'No, Mum.' Gail laughed. 'This little monkey snuck into my bag to see Jenny but the mean old bag at reception caught him and had a go at me, when I knew nothing about his antics.'

'She misses nothing that one.' Doreen sniffed. 'And as for Percy, you know butter wouldn't melt, I'm surprised he didn't do something like this sooner, so what's your plan, Einstein?'

'Well, I hoped you might take him home if that's okay?' Gail asked. 'But before you do, can you mind him for a few minutes out here while I go and get Jen?'

'Course I can.' Doreen grinned, sitting on the bench and settling me on her lap. 'That old bag better not say anything to me or I'll give her something to whinge about, isn't that right, Percy?'

'Too right,' I barked in agreement. I liked Doreen, you knew where you were with her.

'Give me five minutes,' Gail said, rushing inside.

As we waited, I trained my eyes on the sliding doors that people went in and out of, hoping that the next time they opened my favourite little girl would appear. Doreen knew how desperate I was to see Jenny, and she filled me in on how well Jenny was doing, and how everyone was doing their best to stay positive, even though they had all braced themselves for a long wait for a donor heart.

Finally, after what felt like a lifetime, Jenny appeared and I hopped up and down on Doreen's lap trying to get a better look at her. Her appearance shocked me to the core of my furry soul. Not only was she greyer and thinner than she had been just a few days ago, but her face was utterly joyless. Dressed in a hospital gown beneath a big, blue wool coat and scarf I could just about make out the wires under her gown. My heart went out to her, she looked desperate for a cuddle and I refused to wait a minute longer to give her what I knew she needed.

Hopping onto the ground, I ignored Doreen's screech to watch out for cars, and scampered across the grounds at breakneck speed to see her. I knew that the moment we were reunited everything would be so much better and I was desperate to tell her so.

'Jenny! Jenny! Hello! It's me, Percy,' I barked excitedly, narrowly missing a nurse pushing an elderly man in a wheelchair. 'I've missed you so much.'

As Jenny saw me, her face broke into a delighted smile and she now looked like the little girl I knew and loved.

'Oh, Percy, it's so good to see you,' she gasped.

I didn't wait for an invitation and, as I reached her wheelchair that Gail had parked outside the entrance, I hopped up onto her lap immediately.

'Careful, Percy,' Gail warned gently, placing a protective hand on her daughter's shoulder.

'Sorry,' I barked up at Gail. The last thing I wanted to do was hurt Jenny.

Knowing I didn't mean any harm, Gail rewarded me with a megawatt smile, and helped me settle onto Jenny's lap.

Once I was settled, I noticed she smelt of disinfectant and lemons, just like the place inside, and as Jenny raked her fingers through my fur I shivered in delight at her touch. It felt like ages since we had enjoyed some time together, and now, here I was with my two favourite women and I was unbelievably happy. Gingerly, I got onto my hind paws and covered Jenny's face in delicate little licks, keen to show her just how much I loved her.

'You're the best medicine in the world,' she

whispered, scooping my face between her palms and covering it in butterfly kisses.

Pulling away, to drink in the sight of her, I was touched and horrified to see Jenny had tears in her eyes. Carefully, I remained balanced on my hind legs and reached my paw up to her face to gently wipe the moisture from her eyes.

'I'm so happy to see you,' I whined. 'Don't cry, you'll be home soon and we can play and go for walks and curl up on the sofa all the time. You can teach me all the tricks you want to as well.'

'I'm so happy to see you too,' she wept, burrowing her face into my fur. 'I can't believe you're really here.'

With that, she ran her hands across my body urgently, as if to check she wasn't dreaming then planted another kiss on my forehead. Cheekily, I lay on my back, and exposed my tummy, determined to make the most of my visit and get a belly tickle.

Jenny took one look at me with my paws in the air and burst out laughing, before she gave in and ran her fingers through my soft underbelly. I smiled broadly as I lay upside down, legs akimbo, and gave in to the sheer pleasure of it all. Once Jenny's laughter had subsided, I turned over and settled back on her lap, happy to just enjoy the pleasure of her company.

'So how have things been at home?' Jenny asked, as the cool breeze whipped through her hair.

'Fine,' I yapped, 'nothing to report.'

Of course I had planned to confide in Jenny, but seeing just how ill she looked made me think better of it.

'And Peg?' she quizzed. 'Mum says you two are in lurve!'

I turned to Gail, and saw she was trying not to laugh. 'Sorry, Percy, but you two are so sweet, we love imagining you two having little pug babies one day, don't we, Jen?'

'Yep! We've even picked out names,' Jenny giggled warmly. 'If you have a girl you should call her Penny and if it's a boy I really, really want you to call him Pogo.'

I wrinkled my wrinkles in revulsion. Pogo? What sort of a name was that? When could a man get a bit of peace? Peg and I were just friends. What was it with these women? Keen to change the subject, I turned back to Jenny.

'Peg is perfect,' I woofed, 'but I want to hear about you. How are you? These wires look scary.'

Jenny smiled at my concern and tickled my ear. 'I'm so bored of hospital food, Perce, and I think Mum needs a proper night's sleep. I keep telling her that I'm fine, that she and

Dad ought to enjoy some time together, especially with Nan and Granddad here.'

I felt a prickle of alarm course through my fur. Was Jenny unaware her parents had separated? I looked up at Gail and Doreen for confirmation, but while Doreen looked everywhere, but at me, Gail's face was blank.

'I just can't wait to get home,' she finished.

'But it won't be long, love,' Gail said, reassuringly. 'The transplant team has put you on the urgent list, and are hopeful they'll have a heart for you soon. We have to stay positive, and in the meantime, Percy's doing an excellent job of looking after the house, while me and your dad are here with you.'

'Poor old Percy,' Jenny said, sticking her bottom lip out in sadness. 'It's not fair you're on your own so much. I bet you feel like you've been abandoned again.'

'It's not too bad,' I whimpered, tenderly placing my head against her chest to try to keep her warm.

'I can't wait for the day we're all together again, it's the only thing that's keeping me going,' she said, resting her head on top of mine. 'I've asked Mum to make sure that she stays with you the last couple of days before Christmas. I want you to wake up with Mum and Dad all together before they come and see me. It's important to me your first

Christmas with us is a happy one Percy.'

I whined again in pleasure. Jenny was so sweet to think about me when she should be worrying about herself. But I had to admit, the fact that she was thinking of me made me feel more secure. Even though the family was facing difficult times, I felt more sure with each passing day that I would not end up back at the tails of the forgotten.

'Besides, Grandma's promised to stay with me, haven't you, Grandma?' Jenny continued.

'I have,' Doreen replied. 'To be honest, I'd stay with you every night, sweetheart, it'd give me a break from your grandfather's snoring.'

Jenny and Gail laughed as I felt a pang of gratitude towards the little girl. I gave her face another lick, and nestled snugly against her chest. As I listened to the sound of the pump making Jenny's heart perform those vital beats to keep her alive, I thought how funny it was that she had more love pumping through her broken heart, than some with perfect hearts ever expressed in a lifetime.

'I think it is time we were getting you back inside, sweetheart,' Gail said, softly as she looked up at the grey clouds overhead.

'Oh, Mum! Jenny protested. 'Percy's just got here, can't I stay out a bit longer?'

'It's about to rain and you're freezing cold,' Gail cried. 'Look at your fingers, they're as blue as your coat.'

'Don't over-exaggerate,' Jenny said, rolling her eyes, before she bent down to kiss my forehead once more.

'It's fine,' I told her. 'You go inside, I'll come back and see you soon.'

Doreen gently lifted me from Jenny's lap, and placed me on the floor then Gail bent down and kissed my head.

'Thanks for everything you've done,' she whispered in my ear. 'You've made Jenny's day, and mine.'

'I'll come back later when I've got this one settled,' Doreen called to her daughter as Gail and Jenny waved me goodbye.

'Bye, Percy,' Jenny called. 'I love you.'

'I love you too,' I barked urgently. 'Don't worry about a thing.'

After watching Jenny return inside, Doreen scooped me up in her arms and together we walked back towards the Underground station. Nestled inside my grandma's coat, I had never felt so worried. Jenny clearly needed the warmth and stability of her family to get her through the hard and difficult operation that lay ahead. If she discovered her parents were not only lying to her, but had separated as well, then heaven only knows what that could do to her health. It had become more important than ever to make sure Gail and Simon had a happy ending.

Once Doreen and I boarded the Tube back home, I made a silent vow not just to think big, but to think like I had never thought before. There was every chance a little girl's life depended on it and I refused to let her down.

22

As I opened my eyes on Christmas Eve morning, I had to admit I felt sad. There was no reason for it, after all, just as Jenny had promised, Gail and I had spent the night at home together in her big comfortable double bed, curled up like a pair of old socks. It should have been a nice evening as we went for a big walk in the park and then watched my favourite movie, *The Lady and the Tramp*.

But waking early this morning and padding downstairs with only the twinkling lights of the Christmas tree to show me the way, a stab of guilt gnawed away at me. Jenny had sent her mother home, believing that her parents would be waking up together showering me with love, during my first Christmas with them. Instead, Simon was at Sally's, leaving me and Gail alone. I hated being part of a lie, even a white one.

Jake had told me at the park last night that Christmas was a hotbed for family rows, explaining more couples separated over the holidays than at any other time of the year. I shuddered at the thought; things had gone from bad to worse between Gail and Simon with them hardly able to exchange a civil word to each other. The thought of things becoming even worse was unbearable.

Walking into the kitchen as dawn began to break, I stared out of the window and wondered what Jenny would be doing now. Would she be fast asleep with Doreen beside her or would she be awake reading her book, listening to her iPod or just thinking about this Christmas and all it would bring. I hoped she would find something to give her comfort. She was only twelve, which although was ancient in dog years, was no age at all for a human.

Hearing footsteps on the stairs, I scampered to the bottom of them and barked a cheery good morning to Gail.

'What are you doing up, boy?'

'Couldn't sleep,' I replied, taking in her mussed-up hair and barely awake eyes.

As Gail walked blearily towards the kitchen, she crossed her arms over her body in a bid to keep warm and flicked the kettle on. Opening the cupboard door, she reached for a mug and threw a tea bag into it, before giving me a warm smile.

'I expect you need a wee,' she guessed correctly, sliding open the back door.

Once back inside, I found she had already

prepared my breakfast, and to top it all off there was a large juicy bone for me to devour later.

'What's this for?' I barked, looking up at her curiously.

'This is your Day Before Christmas, Christmas present,' Gail explained, taking her first sip of tea. 'You've been so patient these last few weeks, I wanted to get you something to say thank you. I thought you might enjoy this lovely bone today, then we'll see what Santa's brought you tomorrow.'

I sniffed it greedily, my depressed feelings forgotten as I marvelled at the sheer size of the treat. The chew was absolutely massive and I was excited to get stuck into it later. My tummy gurgled appreciatively; I seemed to have regained my appetite since I had seen Jenny again, and I knew this would only help encourage me to keep on eating while she was away. Turning to Gail, I barked my thanks, then climbed up onto her lap to truly show my appreciation.

'You're welcome, gorgeous boy.' She grinned, taking another gulp of tea before kissing my head. 'I'm going to make sure you have a wonderful first Christmas with us no matter what.'

Basking in the attention before she went to the hospital, I craned my head upwards, keen for more kisses from Gail, when the sound of a phone ringing from her handbag in the hallway punctured our happy moment.

'Who on earth is this? It's only just after six. Oh God, what if something's happened to Jenny,' she gasped, getting to her feet and rushing to answer the phone.

At the mention of Jenny's name, I shook with fear, and followed Gail out into the hallway. As she found her mobile and pressed answer, I stood next to her, my fur against her bare legs, hoping we could offer each other comfort, no matter who was on the other end of that call.

Holding the phone to her ear, Gail just stood there, listening to whoever was on the other end. I tried to make out a voice, or even a cough, anything that would give me the faintest clue as to who had called so early, but the caller gave nothing away. Looking up at Gail, I saw that whoever had rung was obviously having a powerful effect. Her face had crumpled and tears were now streaming down her cheeks.

I let out a whine of affection, desperately trying to show Gail I was there for her.

'Thank you, yes, thank you,' she said finally, her voice grave. 'I'll be there immediately.'

As she ended the call, I looked back up at

her and barked frantically. 'Who was that? Come on, what was it? If it's awful, we'll get through it together, I promise. You don't have to face anything alone.'

Gail said nothing. Instead, she sank to the floor, still clutching her mobile and put her head in her hands. Wracking great sobs coursed through her body and I watched in terror as she rocked back and forth on her knees weeping.

'My baby girl, my baby girl,' she cried.

I was beside myself now with worry, but knew it would be impossible to get Gail to tell me anything before she was good and ready. Instead, I found a little space between her elbows and knees, then pushed my paw around her arm as I tried to wait patiently.

'It's okay,' I whined. 'Everything will be okay.'

I stayed like that beside her, with my paw wrapped firmly around Gail's arm, until she stopped crying and looked across at me. As she kissed my forehead, I felt her wet cheek brush against my fur and I licked the tears from her face.

Gail smiled as she pulled her face away. 'That was the hospital. It's good news, no it's great news. They've found a donor for Jenny. She's getting her new heart today!'

I could hardly believe it. This was the news we had all hoped for. Finally, my favourite little girl was going to get the heart she needed to live a long and happy life. At Christmas, of all times, talk about the perfect present. Overcome with excitement, I scampered around Gail in little circles, barking at the top of my lungs.

'Jenny's getting a heart, she's going to be saved.'

Gail giggled, ruffling my ears. 'Ssssh, you mad thing, you, you'll wake the neighbours.'

'Sorry,' I barked again, desperately trying to calm down.

As Gail pulled me towards her and wrapped her arms tightly around me, I felt overjoyed something good was finally happening to my family. We stayed together like that, arms and paws entwined, and I felt so safe and comforted I curled and uncurled my tail in pleasure. When I felt Gail pull away, I clung tightly on to her, desperate for a bit more time with her, but as she kissed my head, and tenderly stroked my paws, I knew I had to let her go. She had to get to the hospital and be by Jenny's side. It was unfair for me to keep her.

'Now then, I'll just ring Simon and see if he's heard, then I'll ring Sally and ask her to pop over to see you today,' she said, getting to

319

her feet and pressing another button on her phone.

'Simon? It's me,' she said breathlessly, as I sat at Gail's feet, looking up at her thrilled expression. 'The hospital has just rung. It's Jenny, they've found her a heart.'

As the words left her lips, I heard the sound of a loud shout at the other end, as Simon let out his own human version of a yelp of excitement.

'I know, it's wonderful,' Gail said, excitedly. 'I'm just about to jump in the shower and then I'll meet you there. Can you ask Sally to look after Percy for us today as I don't know if Mum or Dad will have time to come back?'

At the second mention of Sally, my furry ears pricked up. Had Simon come clean and told her he was staying at Peg's or was Gail just expecting him to pick up the phone and find out as she had planned to do? I shook my head in sadness, it was all so confusing and on such a happy day should have been the least of my worries.

Suddenly, I saw Gail's eyes screw up in frustration as she clenched the phone even harder in her hand. 'How can you say that today, Simon, of all days?' she demanded angrily. 'Of course I don't think I have more right to be by my daughter's side, it's just I know I'll take longer to get ready than you, wherever you are, and therefore it makes more sense for you to speak to Sally! I wasn't trying to imply anything.'

As she turned away from me, I saw her shoulders start to shake as Simon shouted down the phone. I couldn't make out what he was saying, but it was clear from the volume of his voice he was far from happy.

'I'm sorry you feel that way, Simon,' she said quietly. 'I don't think we should talk about this any more today. Today is about Jenny, not our marriage. I'll see you at the hospital.'

Watching Gail hang up the phone, I felt a stab of despair. What could Gail and Simon be fighting over now? As Gail walked upstairs into the bathroom and turned the shower on full blast I trotted behind her. But hearing her sobs as the water rained down, I hesitantly turned away. Gail needed time alone, and I needed time to consider how I was going to put my family back together in the same way as a surgeon was reconstructing Jenny's broken heart.

★　★　★

At the dog park a short while later, I felt comforted to find all my friends gathered around me as I told them the latest news about Jenny.

'That's brilliant, Percy! Jenny's going to live!' Bugsy woofed, bounding around me with so much energy he was making my eyes water.

'I'm delighted to hear it, old boy,' barked Jake approvingly, as he shifted the weight in his hips so he was more comfortable. 'You watch, your young friend will make a remarkable recovery now. She'll be like any other normal little girl once all this is over.'

'It's just wonderful, Percy,' Heather agreed, wagging her tail delightedly. 'I can't believe it's happening today of all days either. Jenny deserves nothing less, she's such a sweetheart, I'm glad a donor has been found. Do you have any idea how long she might be in hospital after the surgery?'

'No idea,' I replied, 'Gail hasn't told me, but I expect it will be a long time, I just hope it all goes well.'

Peg sighed and gave me a little prod with her paw. 'Of course it will, misery guts,' she woofed, before turning pleadingly to the others. 'He's been like this all day. It's a happy day — you should be jumping up and down for joy.'

'I am happy,' I replied, my eyes downcast. 'I just wish Gail and Simon were too. They even rowed this morning.'

'I know,' Peg woofed in sympathy. 'I heard Simon in the living room, shouting down the phone. It sounded horrible.'

I said nothing. I had not asked Peg if Simon had stayed over at Sally's last night, somehow I thought it might be better not to know. Yet now Peg had said it, the truth was out there.

'He was staying with you last night then?' I asked quietly.

Peg hesitated before giving the shortest of yaps. 'I'm sorry.'

'Not your fault. But I do wonder how Jenny's going to get better if her mum and dad can't get along for five minutes,' I barked sharply.

'Why don't we put all that to one side for the minute, Perce?' Heather suggested. 'At the moment your little girl is in hospital, undergoing major surgery. Her mum and dad might not be putting on the best of united fronts, but what's to stop us from giving her our support?'

'How do you mean?' I barked curiously.

'I mean, I think we should go to the hospital and wish her well,' Heather suggested.

'That's a lovely idea, Heather,' Peg barked warmly. 'I think she would really like that.'

'I do too,' I woofed, delighted by my supportive friends.

'Shall we sing, Heather?' Bugsy asked enthusiastically. 'We could sing 'Hush Little Baby' again like we did for baby Jasper.'

'I don't think so, old boy,' Jake said, wiggling his hips again. 'It wasn't exactly a resounding success last time.'

'I think it's best we leave the lullabies alone,' Heather barked in agreement. 'Besides, isn't Jenny more of a One Direction girl?'

'I think so,' I woofed, thoughtfully, 'though now they've split up I'm not sure if she's more into Zayn's solo career.'

'Blimey, Perce!' Peg woofed with laughter. 'I didn't know you were so hot on teen music.'

'Well, if you're sharing a house with a pre-teen girl it's all part of the job,' I barked authoritatively.

'I can see that,' Peg replied. 'Our Sal's never moved on from Duran Duran. Anyway, shall we go now? We can all go home, then meet on the corner when we've given our owners the slip and get there before lunch if we hurry.'

'You do know that we're not actually allowed inside the hospital though, don't you?' I barked cautiously as I saw Peg and Bugsy begin to make a move.

'Just as well, lovey,' Heather replied. If Jake here was allowed in a hospital, no doubt he'd start badgering some poor nurse to take a look at his hips.'

'I heard that!' Jake woofed reproachfully. 'And when you reach my age, you'll realise just how painful your hips can be.'

'Yeah, yeah, Granddad,' Heather barked playfully, before turning her attention back to me. 'I think we can just stand outside her window and bark, lovey. Let her know we're there for her.'

I looked at Heather warmly. 'If you're sure?'

'Course, we all want to help don't we?' Heather barked, turning to the others.

As they all yapped supportively together, I felt truly blessed to have friends like these and, as Jenny was about to discover, so was she.

23

Although I had made my way to Great Ormond Street Hospital before, I had not appreciated how much harder it would be as a group. Naturally, because I had made it safely in one piece on the bus, and then returned on the Tube, I felt I knew best how to get there. Yet when we all met at the corner of my street, having successfully given our owners and carers the slip, my friends had other ideas.

'I don't like the Tube,' Peg whined. 'It's noisy, dirty and people always step on my paws.'

'It's the quickest way, old girl,' Jake barked in reason. 'Great Ormond Street is over ten miles from here.'

'That might be true, Jake, but I don't see why we can't take the bus,' she barked again.

Heather laid her paw softly on Peg's. 'Because a driver will never let us all on at once. On the Tube, we've a better chance of sneaking under the barriers and getting on and off without any bother.'

'But Peg's right,' Bugsy barked, his eyes wide with fear. 'The Tube is very scary.

People die on it, and some people push other people onto the tracks, or they fall when they don't mind the gap. I want to mind the gap, and I don't want to die, please don't make me go on the Tube.'

I rolled my eyes in annoyance, my friends were getting on my nerves with these travel plans. Part of me wondered if I was so grouchy because I was tired as I had been unable to sleep properly for days. Something about my expression must have given away my feelings as I felt Peg gently lick my face.

'A bone for them?' Peg barked quizzically, her eyes full of concern.

'What do you mean?' I yapped.

'You know,' she replied, 'a bone for your thoughts. You look as though you haven't heard a bark we've said Percy. Are you all right?'

'Fine,' I yapped. 'I just don't want us to row about how to get to the hospital, I just want to get us to the hospital. I want to see what's happening with Jenny.'

'Fair enough, old boy,' Jake said, giving his hips a signature wiggle. 'Why don't you decide?'

'Well,' I barked, looking at Peg and Bugsy apologetically. 'I think it has to be the Tube. Heather's right, we'll never get on the bus together, at least with the Tube we've more of a chance. When Doreen brought me back on it last time I went to the hospital, it didn't take very long as there was only one train we had to stay on.'

Peg turned to me and cocked her head in sympathy. 'Don't worry, Percy,' she woofed. 'I understand. We'll be fine, won't we, Bugsy?'

I saw Bugsy had rested his head on the floor, and had his paws over his eyes in protest.

'Won't we, Bugsy?' she asked again before giving him a prod with her paw. 'We'll all look after you, there's nothing to be scared of.'

My tongue lolled from my mouth and my shoulders shook with laughter as I looked at my pug friend pushing the bigger dog more aggressively with her paws. Poor old Bugsy was getting what could only be described as henpecked by humans. If I had not been in such a rush to see Jenny, I would almost have felt sorry for him.

'Peg's right,' I barked as I got myself under control. 'We'll all make sure nothing bad happens to you. We'll only be on it five minutes. Now, let's not waste any more time.'

Decision made, we walked to the station around the corner and divided ourselves into two groups. Jake had suggested that would be the best way to get on and off undetected, and so Peg, Heather and I went in one carriage, while Jake and Bugsy went in the other.

As it was Christmas Eve, I expected the train to be filled with last-minute shoppers, travellers and even other animals who were making their way across the country to see loved ones. But surprisingly, the carriage was almost deserted and the three of us were able to slump to the floor of the gangway without worrying too much about people treading on us. The train soon got going and, as we roared through the stations, I comforted Peg, who was clearly finding the floor vibrating beneath us too much to deal with.

'We'll be there in a minute,' I promised over the rattle of the carriage, 'won't be long.'

Sure enough, we reached our stop in minutes and we successfully disembarked without any Tube staff or passengers telling us off. As we reached the top of the station, we crossed the road to the hospital and made our way across the car park.

'Which one's Jenny's room, old thing?' Jake asked as we reached the hospital entrance.

Dread coursed through my fur. I had forgotten that the one and only time I had been inside Jenny's room I had been bundled up underneath a large coat so had not seen the way. I thought hard, I knew we had gone up in a lift, but were there any other details I had missed? I looked helplessly around the hospital grounds and felt a sense of despair wash over me. Great Ormond Street was a big place, how would I ever find Jenny?

'Sorry, everyone,' I barked sorrowfully, 'but I've no idea where to find Jenny.'

'Not to worry, lovey,' Heather barked confidently. 'We can start by following those children over there. They're in wheelchairs and have funny things around their chests. They look like they know where they're heading, so perhaps we'll get lucky.'

Instantly, I felt cheered at Heather's suggestion. Together we followed the group of six children in single file across the car park, taking care to keep a safe distance so as not to draw attention to ourselves. For a hospital, the place looked jolly, I had to admit. The staff in uniforms all seemed to be wearing Santa hats, while tinsel adorned some of the trees outside. Elsewhere, the windows were covered in fairy lights, or had bits of sparkle draping from the blinds, giving the place a real festive feel.

'I feel like a spy,' Bugsy barked. 'I wonder if they would have me in K95? Geddit?' He barked excitedly at his own joke while scampering madly between us all, nearly causing Heather to fall over.

'We geddit,' I woofed quietly. 'K95, human

MI5! Now, for heaven's sake, stop making a fuss, Bugsy! The jokes can wait until later.'

Suitably reprimanded, Bugsy hung his head low, sulking as he stalked in front of me, his paws hitting the pavement with a heavy thwack. As we rounded the corner and watched the children go inside the building, I felt a pang of guilt. It was unfair to have been so hard on him and I was just about to apologise, when something in the corner of my eye caused me to stop and stare.

Huddled together on a nearby bench were Gail and Simon, dressed in thick winter coats to guard against the cold. Their heads were bent low and they looked as if they were deep in conversation.

'We're in the right place,' I woofed eagerly, 'they're here.'

As the others followed my gaze, we hid behind a nearby tree and I watched Gail and Simon clasp one another's hand and felt a surge of hope. For once they appeared not to be arguing and, as Simon wrapped his arms around Gail, I felt a flurry of anticipation. Could they finally work out their differences while Jenny was undergoing surgery?

I continued to watch, hoping against hope that a Christmas miracle was on its way, when I suddenly saw Gail break down in tears as Simon stood up. She held her head in her hands and I looked at Simon — surely he was going to comfort his wife? But instead, he ran his hands through his hair and shouted something that sounded like, 'I've had enough of this,' before walking towards the door and back again to sit on a bench with his back to us.

'Should I go to Gail, do you think?' I barked in distress, turning to the others who, like me had witnessed the scene unfold.

'No, lovey,' Heather barked reassuringly. 'If Gail sees you, she'll be fretting over how to get you home safely, which will only add to her worries. Best to stay here for now.'

'But she's so upset,' I woofed, unable to take my eyes off Gail, who had by now joined Simon on the bench.

'I know she is,' Peg comforted, gently stroking my left paw with her right one. 'But her mum and dad are here, if she needs a cuddle, and we're here if you need one too.'

I licked Heather and Peg's faces gratefully and then turned back to Gail, who was now deep in conversation with Simon, tears obviously pouring down her face. I hated seeing her so upset. If only I could finally get her and Simon to stop arguing and start appreciating each other again, I felt sure half their problems would be over. They needed each other, and Jenny needed them together, of that I was certain.

I thought back to our day out together. Even though it had just been a few weeks, it seemed like a lifetime ago, but then in dog years perhaps it was. Everyone had enjoyed themselves and Jenny and I had loved our time scampering about in the grass. Even things between Gail and Simon seemed nearly perfect. I had watched them closely and been delighted to see them hold hands, laugh and even kiss when they thought Jenny and I were looking elsewhere. It was clear to me those two still loved each other, the heart-shaped photo stunt we had created proved that. But was it possible I could remind them they were better together than apart here in this hospital?

I wracked my brains, and found my poor little head was beginning to ache from all the extra work it was having to do. I thought back to the beautiful photo display Peg had made and looked at her with fondness. She was so talented and creative. It would never have occurred to me to display all those images like that. And, of course, putting the photo of Gail and Simon when they got engaged in the centre had been inspired. It had been the perfect focal point for them to recall happier times and I remembered how they had both picked up that snap with love in their eyes.

Suddenly, I was hit by a stroke of genius. Turning away from my owners and back to face the others, I could hardly wait to share my idea, sure this would undoubtedly save their marriage.

'I've got it,' I barked triumphantly.

'Got what?' Peg woofed, suspiciously.

'I know how we're going to reunite Gail and Simon! Right now! Today!'

Heather looked at me agog. 'Okay, lovey, we're all ears.'

'Do you remember that photo that was taken of Simon and Gail, just after they had got engaged?'

'Yes,' replied Bugsy, 'Peg, put it in the centre of the heart she made. It was really lovely.'

'Yes, it was,' I barked quickly, eager to get to the point. 'Well, it got me thinking that Gail always told me that day was the happiest of her life. She told me how Simon had gone to such trouble to create a picnic and she had been touched at the effort he went to, that when he went down on one knee, she knew he would be the best husband in the world because of the love and thought he had shown her.'

'It's a lovely story,' Jake agreed, 'but what has that got to do with saving their marriage, Percy?'

I paused, looking around the group expectantly savouring the moment I hit them with my big idea. I knew they would love it as much as I did, if only I had come up with it before.

'Why don't we recreate that picnic for them now?' I woofed, delightedly.

'What today? Here? In this hospital?' barked Bugsy, looking confused.

'Yes. Here, in the grounds,' I replied impatiently.

'It's a bit cold, isn't it, Percy?' Jake said, shifting his hips around on the ground as if to make a point.

I barked impatiently. 'Yes, it is a bit cold, but Simon created the picnic for Gail on Christmas Eve when it was snowing. If we do the same thing on Christmas Eve again, they will remember how they promised to love each other all those years ago.'

'It's a lovely idea, Percy,' Heather barked encouragingly. 'But it's not snowing, and where would we get the food from?'

'The snow doesn't matter. It's the fact it's Christmas Eve that's important and we can get food from the supermarket up the road,' I replied.

'But we haven't got any money,' Peg pointed out, not altogether unreasonably.

'That's okay, we'll steal it,' I barked again. I

had an answer for everything.

Bugsy barked reproachfully. 'Theft is wrong, Percy.'

I barked in agreement and looking at my friends' faces knew I had to come up with a solution to encourage them to help me. I turned back to my owners and saw something that gave me a pang of hope. Hanging out of Simon's coat pocket was his wallet and, alongside it, what appeared to be a pair of ten-pound notes. He was famous for stuffing his money in his pocket rather than putting it back in his wallet. What if I managed to snaffle a note from his coat? Chances are if he missed it, then there was every possibility he would assume it would have fallen all by itself.

'Wait here,' I barked softly, suddenly feeling brave.

Holding my breath, I crept slowly towards the bench, ensuring I did not disturb so much as a stray leaf. Nearing the bench, I paused behind a tree and just feet away from my owners glanced across to check whether I had been spotted. Thankfully, their heads were still bent low, their gaze only on each other, so engrossed were they in their conversation. As I got closer, I realised there was so much noise from the ambulances and passers-by behind me, I could not make out a single word they were saying to one another and thought, with an unexpected jolt, that if I could not hear them, they were unlikely to hear me.

Buoyed with confidence, I glanced once more at Simon's pocket and saw that a ten pound note was just waiting to fall out. Glancing back at the others, I saw they were all looking at me with a mixture of awe and horror in their eyes. I raised my left paw, to give them our version of a human thumbs-up, and then picked my moment. Creeping out from behind the tree, I saw there were just centimetres between us and, as I carefully padded towards them, I willed myself not to give into my pug traits and break wind or sneeze. Usually, I was very good at controlling my gassiness, and I prayed to all the gods in doggy heaven that it stayed that away. Now, with the ten pound note close enough to grasp, I glanced up at Gail and Simon and saw they were far too engrossed in yet another row to notice me.

'Blimey, Gail, you don't let up do you?' Simon shouted, as Gail's head remained fixed on her lap. 'Just when will you accept my apology about the note and let us all move on?'

'It's not that simple, Simon, as you well know. I'm hurt.'

Realising this was a row that would run and run, I seized my chance. Heart pounding, I rushed towards Simon, stuck my snout in his open pocket and clamped by jaws around one of the notes. After taking a final look at my owners to check I had not been spotted, I ran away with the grace of a cat burglar towards my pals, never once looking back.

When I rejoined the group, I stuffed the note into my collar and was met with a hero's welcome, as well as a big congratulatory lick from Peg.

'Blimey, Percy!' Peg barked in awe. 'I never knew you had it in you. When did you get so good at thieving?'

'I don't know,' I woofed. 'Must have got a few lessons from Bugsy.'

'You did very well, Percy,' Bugsy yapped solemnly. 'I liked your quick, quiet technique.'

'Thanks, mate,' I barked, my heart still going as fast as a whippet around a race track. 'Did Gail and Simon see me?'

'Not at all, lovey,' Heather barked. 'They're too busy fighting to worry about anything else.'

I turned around, and saw Heather was right. My owners were still arguing as if their lives depended on it. I felt a flush of sadness.

I had to find some way of making them stop this once and for all. For heaven's sake, they were no longer even living under the same roof any more and yet they were still arguing.

'I must say I'm impressed, old chap,' Jake barked, interrupting my thought flow. 'But there's just one thing: where will we hold the picnic, dear boy? A car park is not exactly the most romantic of settings.'

'Fear not, Jake, I have thought of everything. There's a little park nearby,' I barked in explanation. 'Doreen and I walked past it the other day. It's perfect.'

'Well, it seems as though you really have thought this through,' Heather barked admiringly before turning to the others. 'I'm game, if you are?'

Jake exhaled noisily. 'Okay then, Percy, I'm in.'

'Me too,' Peg woofed.

'And me,' Bugsy added.

I looked around my friends gratefully. They were all clearly freezing cold in the December chill. Their fur was standing on end, yet they were still here supporting me, helping me, and I knew I would never forget this day and the kindness they had shown me.

'Come on then,' I barked excitedly, 'let's get this pug picnic started.'

24

As we raced up the hill, towards the supermarket, I felt happier than I had in days. Finally, I had a plan to bring to life and I was determined to pull it off. Scampering past shoppers, commuters, mums and dads, my paws pounded against the cold pavement. Now I had found the perfect strategy I wanted to put it into action immediately. Even though my little heart was throbbing, I refused to slow down and, rounding the corner, I turned my head and saw my pals were lagging behind.

'We're right with you, Percy,' Peg panted, catching my eye.

'But do feel free to go on ahead, dear thing,' Jake yapped, bringing up the rear.

Turning back to the road ahead, I realised I could just about see the store through the gaps in human legs. It was obvious a picnic was the natural way to reunite Gail and Simon. Their engagement had been perfect, and I was sure that recreating the very special feast they had shared all those years ago would remind them of all they stood to lose if they let their marriage rot. Deep in thought, I failed to spot a dog and his owner walking towards me and I collided head first into a bundle of white fur.

'Hey! Watch where you're going,' I woofed angrily.

'That was your fault,' the dog protested, 'you weren't looking where you were going.'

He had a point, but I was in a hurry and in no mood to admit I was in the wrong. Instead, I backed away from the mutt and hastily checked myself for damage. Thankfully my head seemed to be all right, and it was just my pride that was bruised. Raising my face to meet the hound who had caused me to stop in my tracks, I felt a jolt of surprise. 'Boris, mate. Is that you?'

The dog took a step towards me to get a better look at me. 'Percy? It's brilliant to see you. What are you doing up here?'

'I could ask you the same thing,' I barked fondly in reply.

Boris looked up at a small youngish woman and rapped out three short barks. 'This is an old friend of mine.'

The woman smiled down at him and ruffled his ears. 'Not too long B, I've got to start my shift at the hospital in fifteen minutes.'

'Is that your owner?' I asked as Boris returned his face to meet mine.

'Yes,' barked Boris proudly, 'and she's the

best owner in the world. You were right, Percy, I landed on all four of my paws when I met Zoe. She's a nurse at Great Ormond Street Hospital.'

I looked at the Westie with affection. 'I'm so pleased, Boris, but I knew it would all work out. Were you in long after I left?'

'Just a couple of days,' Boris explained happily. 'It was love at first sight when we saw each other. She's my owner, mum and best friend all wrapped into one. But what about you? Has it worked out with Gail?'

'Everything's fine, my family is great,' I barked, 'but Jenny, my owner's little girl, is in the children's hospital now, which is why we're here.'

As my friends appeared breathless at my side, I introduced them all to Boris and explained how my owners' marriage was crumbling at the same rate as Jenny's health. Boris regarded me with sympathy as I told him how I had tried everything to get them to reunite. Revealing my idea to recreate the picnic in the park, Boris's expression changed from one of sorrow to utter delight.

'Percy, that's a brilliant idea,' he barked happily. 'I'm sure it will work.'

I turned to my friends, giving them all a grateful bark of thanks. 'I couldn't have done it without them.'

Peg licked my ear, causing me to blush. 'Or you, Peg.'

'Well, I think it's great. Can I help you? I only live around the corner, and Zoe will be off to work in a minute so I'll be able to sneak out.'

I regarded Boris with fondness. 'Are you sure it's no trouble?'

'None at all,' he barked earnestly. 'I'll see you outside the store in five minutes.'

Knowing we had reinforcements put an extra spring in our step and, as we said our goodbyes to Boris, we continued up the road to the supermarket. Reaching the shop, we gathered our breath by the entrance and I looked at each of my friends with concern. The enthusiasm in their faces that I had seen just minutes earlier now seemed to have been replaced with anxiety and even fear if Bugsy was anything to go by.

'What's wrong?' I barked.

'Well, now we're here, how are we going to do this?' Peg asked, clearly speaking for the group.

I sighed impatiently. We had been through this. 'We're going to split up and each go in, grab what we can, then run out and hide the food behind the wall by the park.'

'What if we end up with six of something? Or stuff Gail and Simon won't like? Or what

343

if we get caught?' Bugsy whined.

'Us smaller dogs will go for the low stuff, you bigger dogs can try to reach for higher up items. Gail and Simon aren't fussy eaters, so, it won't really matter what we get.'

'But there is still the worry of getting caught old thing,' Jake woofed. 'I can't imagine poor Giles coming to collect me if I'm banged to rights, as the saying goes, by a security guard. Then there's every chance I would end up at the tails of the forgotten and, believe me, I really am too old a dog to be taught those sorts of tricks.'

I knew Jake had a point, but I believed in this plan and was sure it was worth the risk. Still, I did not want to make my friends uncomfortable, they meant far too much to me for that. As Boris arrived, I looked at them all in turn before barking. 'If any of you don't want to help, then I don't want you to feel as though you have to. You've all done more than enough for me already, and I don't want you getting into trouble because of me.'

'Count me in, Percy,' Boris barked brusquely. 'I don't mind getting in trouble.'

'And me!' Peg barked loudly. 'We've come this far, Percy, I'm not backing out now. I may have little legs, but you know I can run when I want to.'

As Heather and Bugsy murmured their

assent, I turned to Jake. 'What about you, old man?'

Jake reached out his left paw and nudged me playfully. 'Course I'm happy to help, Percy. Ignore me, I'm an old fool.'

'No, you're not,' I replied. 'You're a lovely, loyal dog and the best friend a pug could hope to find. I'm still not going to encourage you to do anything you don't approve of, so how about you do something a bit different to help us out?'

'Go on, old thing.'

'Do you think you could create a distraction?' I asked in a low bark. 'You know, do something to put the security guard off looking at what's going on in the store while we're busy getting the supplies for the picnic.'

'Oh, yes, Jake, you'd be brilliant at that,' Peg barked in agreement.

'She's right, lovey,' Heather yapped. 'It'd make life easier for us as well.'

Jake sat back on his haunches and regarded us thoughtfully. 'Be delighted, chaps, delighted. I know just the thing as well.'

As Jake told us his plan, a sense of glee coursed through my fur. He really was the dog that knew what to do in every situation, and this was no different. We decided that while Jake was creating the commotion, Peg, Bugsy and I would go inside first and grab what we could. Then, Heather and Boris would seize whatever was within their reach. Once our mouths were full of goodies, we would all meet over at the park and show off our haul.

I turned to my friends with glee. 'This is it! I'm as excited as if we were at Crufts.'

Wandering towards the entrance, I saw the security guard standing at the door talking to a customer. Glancing back at the others, I jerked my head towards the uniformed officer and, sensing our luck, we rushed past him and headed inside.

The store was a brightly lit world of wonder and, as I looked up, I saw the place was swamped with people rushing around, barging into one another with baskets and trolleys. Walking past a cold aisle that should have been home to meats and cheeses, I glanced at each cabinet in despair noticing there was hardly anything left.

I was just debating what to do next when I heard two women arguing over a turkey crown. Looking over I saw one was clutching the meat as if it were a precious newborn baby, when suddenly I saw the other woman shove her in the stomach causing the turkey to fall to the floor with a loud thud.

It was then all hell appeared to break loose as the two women began slapping and punching each other while other shoppers stopped and tried to break up the fight. Seeing the aisle had disrupted into chaos, I seized an opportunity and while the bargain-hunters tried to break up the warring women I snaffled ham, sausage rolls, Stilton cheese and olives from the baskets they had left on the floor.

Racing past them and around the corner into the next aisle, I caught a glimpse of Jake, who was lying prostate on the floor in front of the security guard. I watched in amazement as he played dead, so convincingly, the officer was unable to move him, pulling his limbs this way and that. I winced, it must have been horribly painful for him with his bad hips, but my friend refused to budge no matter how much the guard tried to insist. I was still staring at Jake when I heard a loud clatter next to me and realised a women had dropped her basket right by my side.

'*Urgh!*' she screamed. 'There's a dog in the supermarket! Guard! Help!'

The woman backed away from me while continuing to wave and shout for help. I suddenly felt a lurch of fear, so I raced away, straight into the shins of the guard.

'Why, you animal!' he growled.

As he reached down to try to grab me, I nipped in between his legs and raced down the rest of the aisle towards freedom.

'Get back here now,' he called after me. 'I want a word with you.'

Hearing his steps thunder towards me, I picked up my pace and ran towards the exit where I saw Jake sitting outside. Crossing the threshold and out into the chilly afternoon air, my mouth still full of snacks, I threw myself at him gratefully. I had never been so relieved to see my old pal in all my life.

'Thank you,' I barked as I dropped the snacks to the ground. 'Where are the others?'

'Heather and Boris have just gone in, and Peg and Bugsy have gone onto the park, dear boy,' he replied. 'I suggest you do the same.'

Glancing behind Jake's shoulder, I saw the guard was still trying to make his way through the throng of shoppers towards me. I felt torn, part of me could leave and take the goods, but if I was quick I had time to do what was right.

'Where are you going?' Jake barked hurriedly, as he saw me walk back into the store.

'Don't worry, I'll just be a minute,' I replied.

Inside, I saw the bank of cashiers on my right, and made my way to the closest one. The cashier was busy with a customer, so I quickly stood on my hind legs and gingerly took the note from my mouth with my front paws. Balancing unsteadily, I made myself tall enough for my nose to meet the counter and, with the cashier and customer still engrossed, dropped the note onto the desk, turned back and ran, happy I could not add theft to my list of misdemeanours.

Glancing back, I saw the security guard was still in hot pursuit. He was getting closer to the exit, so this time I took Jake's advice. Giving my pal another bark of thanks, I gathered the snacks I had dropped on the ground, ran down the hill and around the corner to the park. Outside, the air was alive with excitement now darkness was beginning to fall. Looking around, I saw commuters and shoppers, their faces beaming as they hurried home, ready to begin their Christmas celebrations. With a pang, I thought of Jenny. She would be too weak to enjoy anything this holiday. All I could do was hope my plan would give her something special to look forward to after the festivities were over. Nearing the park, I saw Peg and Bugsy straightaway. Reaching their side, I opened my mouth and let my goodies fall to the floor while I caught my breath.

'How did you get on?' I panted.

'Brilliant, Percy. I got bread rolls, crisps, nuts, rollmops, and chocolate too,' Bugsy barked enthusiastically.

'Well done, mate, you did do well.'

'I'm afraid I only managed a small bottle of Prosecco,' Peg barked, her woof full of triumph.

'Blimey, Peg,' I woofed. 'I never thought you'd get a drink like that. Wasn't it too big for your jaw?'

'Not at all,' she replied. 'I was quite careful, and besides, you were creating such a commotion yourself it was easy to take my time angling it in the right way.'

'I'm impressed at both of you,' I yapped gratefully. Turning first to Peg, I gave her a grateful lick on her cheek, then I did exactly the same to Bugsy. 'I don't know what to say.'

'Thank you is more than enough,' Peg replied. 'We don't want you getting too worn out with the gratitude as it looks as though Jake, Boris and Heather might be needing a bit of thanks too, judging by the load they're carrying.'

I spun around and did a double-take as I saw the three of them running towards me. Heather had her mouth full of more meats and cheeses, while Boris was carrying what looked like bread-sticks and a pork pie. As for Jake, who was lagging behind, he looked as though he was dragging a large blanket along the floor.

'It occurred to me that for a true picnic, the would-be lovebirds needed something better to sit on than the cold, damp ground,' Jake barked as he approached.

As Jake set the blanket onto the ground, the others piled their goodies on top and I whined in delight. My friends had surpassed all of my expectations. I never imagined they would be able to bring so much. The food filled the blanket, and Peg's bottle of Prosecco was the icing on the cake. I looked around and saw each one of my friends looked exhausted from their efforts, but as well as the tiredness in their eyes, I saw a glimpse of joy at all they had achieved.

I had heard humans talk about crying with happiness, and for the first time in my life understood why. There was no way of expressing how thankful I was for all my friends had done. Their love and thoughtfulness touched me in a way nothing had before and I hated to admit it, but I was lost for words. Thankfully, Boris was not.

'If this doesn't bring your family back together, Percy, I don't know what will,' he barked.

I nodded. 'You're right. You all brought so much. Though I do have one question: Jake, where did you get the blanket from? I thought you were worried about stealing.'

'Ask no questions, dear boy, and I will of course tell you no lies,' Jake replied. 'All I will say is that Gail and Simon's need appeared greater at this moment than the perfectly fit and able, but rather large woman who nearly ran me over with her mobility scooter. It seemed only right I liberate her of the blanket when she refused to apologise.'

Heather gave him a gentle shove. 'Jake! You old dog! The poor dear might need it.'

'I can assure you that battleaxe has more than enough meat on her bones to keep her warm,' he replied. 'She won't miss it.'

'And anyway, you need a blanket to keep you warm in winter,' Boris added. 'I should know, that one you gave me at the tails of the forgotten still keeps me warm at night, Percy.'

I felt a surge of delight to think of Boris still sleeping on my old cashmere blanket. 'Really?'

'Really,' Boris woofed. 'It means the world to me.'

'Well, there you are,' Peg barked. 'Looks like Simon and Gail will remember the blanket more than the food, so you've done us all proud, Jake.'

'He certainly has,' I yapped. 'Now we just have to sort out phase two of the plan.'

'What's that?' Peg asked.

'It's time to get Gail and Simon.'

As the others sat around the blanket, exchanging excited glances, I heard the sounds of carol singers drift through the park. Their version of 'We Wish You a Merry Christmas' filled me with renewed hope. This plan would work, I knew it. The Merry Christmas the carol singers promised was finally within reach.

25

After we had finished admiring our haul, we hid our goodies behind the wall facing the park. Safely stowed, I threw the blanket Jake had thoughtfully liberated on top, while Boris and Bugsy kindly offered to stand guard until we returned. It was a gesture that touched me to the core. Once again, it seemed the kindness of friends old and new helped make life a little easier.

'Why don't I stay with the boys and help lay everything out when Gail and Simon are near?' Heather suggested.

I widened my eyes, astonished by her kindness. 'Are you sure?'

'Course, lovey. You can give me three barks through the dog network when you're a few minutes away.'

'What treasures you all are. If you don't mind that would be brilliant,' I replied gratefully.

Heather looked away bashfully. 'It's no bother at all. After everything we've all been through, it will be nice to set it all up properly.'

'She's right, Percy,' Boris added. 'Besides,

you did so much for me at the tails of the forgotten, it's nice to repay the favour.'

'And even though you couldn't sing for all the Winalot in the world, Percy, and made Jasper scream and scream, I don't hold it against you,' Bugsy added. 'I'd do anything for you.'

A lump formed in my throat and I was barkless. 'Thank you,' I whimpered with gratitude.

Jake turned to me and gave his hips a little wiggle. 'Actually, if you don't mind, old thing, I might stay with these chaps. All this excitement has worn me out today and I wouldn't mind the rest.'

I gave Jake a grateful lick. 'Of course, you've outdone yourself today — if anyone deserves a rest it's you.'

Turning to Peg, I rubbed her nose affectionately. 'It's just you and me then, old girl. You ready?'

'Less of the old!' she yapped. 'Time to reunite a family once and for all.'

As if to prove a point, Peg set off at full pelt, leaving me to bark goodbye to our friends. Racing after her, I weaved my way through throngs of passers-by and the odd cyclist before picking up my pace. The sky was now an inky black, illuminated only by street lamps and Christmas lights, giving everyone the perfect backdrop to start their celebrations. Passing a brightly lit pub, I saw many people had already started getting into the Christmas spirit. Stopping to peer up at the windows, I could just about see revellers sitting at the bar enjoying brightly coloured drinks while they wrapped their arms around each other and sang 'Little Donkey'.

'Come on, Percy, stop dawdling,' Peg barked cheekily.

Catching sight of Peg, I left the partygoers to it and raced towards her. 'Sorry.'

This time we ran through the streets at a more relaxed pace and, as we turned the corner into the hospital and reached the entrance together, Peg surprised me by licking my face affectionately.

'What was that for?' I asked.

'Just 'cos,' she replied quietly. 'I've never met a dog as loving or as thoughtful as you, Perce.'

Despite the cold, I felt myself colour beneath my thick black fur. 'Any dog would have done the same.'

'No, they wouldn't, Percy,' Peg barked. 'You're one in million and I'm so happy I met you. I want you to know how proud I am of you. There's no pug like you.'

I returned Peg's affectionate lick. 'Or you.'

We held each other's gaze for a moment,

locked in our own private world where it was just me and Peg. Even though there had been so much unhappiness and despair between Gail and Simon, Peg and I had managed to find our own joy over these past few weeks and I knew our special bond would last for ever. The sound of a siren brought us out of our reverie and, as I tore my eyes from Peg, I saw an ambulance whizz past us and pull up abruptly at the entrance. I looked around the hospital grounds in amazement. I had thought that because it was Christmas, things might have been quieter but far from it. The place was alive with activity as families wandered in and out, cars sped by and Santa with his elves sang even more carols as they arrived with what looked like sackfuls of presents, which I guessed were for the children.

'So now we're here, what are we going to do?' Peg asked.

I looked at her thoughtfully. 'I figured we would go back to the same spot, wait for them to emerge for some fresh air, then I would go over and get them to follow me.'

'What if they don't come out together?'

'Well, then I'll get one of them to follow me, then when they see the picnic they'll realise it's for both of them. Gail's very good at understanding what I say though, so hopefully if it's only one of them it'll be her,' I barked.

Peg nodded her head approvingly and just a few minutes later we reached the quadrant where we had seen Gail and Simon earlier. Motioning to Peg, I suggested we hide behind the tree we had used before and wait for them to come out.

'We could be here ages,' she protested.

'We could,' I agreed, 'but let's hope luck is on our side and we're not.'

'I could always create a distraction to get them out here,' Peg suggested.

I licked the top of her head warmly. 'You could, but I think Jake has given us enough of those today. Let's give it a few minutes and see what happens.'

Together we returned our eyes to the square and waited for one of my family to appear. Just as I hoped, luck was on our side as within a few moments I saw Gail walk out of the small entrance and into the cool night air, with Simon just behind her.

'Told you,' I barked triumphantly.

'Sssh,' Peg whined. 'I can't hear if you're yapping in my ear.'

Playfully nudging her, I closed my jaw and turned back to see what Gail and Simon were doing. They wrapped their arms around one another and my heart leapt as I saw Simon squeeze Gail around the middle as she rested her head on his shoulder. They stayed like that for a few minutes, before they broke away and looked into each other's eyes. Wearing great big smiles, my jaw dropped as I watched them kiss passionately for a few seconds before breaking away and smiling at each other again.

Overjoyed, I turned to Peg who looked as joyful as I felt. 'We may not need that picnic after all.'

'Well done, Percy,' she barked. 'I'm so pleased for you. Look at their faces, they look so happy.'

Turning back to watch Gail and Simon, I saw their faces were still alive with joy as they kissed once more. I was unsure how they had gone from fighting to cuddling in such a relatively short space of time, but all I could think was that Jenny's surgery had gone well.

I felt a thrill at the thought, and was just about to go over to Gail and Simon and announce myself, when the sight of a blonde woman walking towards them caught my eye. With a start, I realised it was Sally, carrying a huge bunch of flowers and she was marching determinedly towards Simon.

'What's she doing here?' I growled.

Peg shook her head. 'I don't know. She and Simon had an argument this morning before he left, and she was upset for most of the morning.'

Alarm coursed through me. 'What do you mean an argument? Why didn't you tell me?'

'It didn't seem important,' Peg protested. 'They were just rowing about Simon coming and going and treating the place like a hotel. Sally said she was sick of him leaving wet towels everywhere and his coffee cups strewn across the kitchen when he came in and out at all hours.'

'That sounds like the kind of row a couple has,' I barked worriedly.

'I know,' Peg barked quietly. 'I didn't know how to tell you.'

I turned my eyes back to my family and saw the woman who was about to ruin their special moment continue to walk towards them. There was no doubt in my mind that Simon had been seeing Sally behind Gail's back. Javier and Gabriella used to row about wet towels and coffee cups all the time, not to mention the hours they kept. People only rowed like that when they were in love.

'We have to do something,' I urged.

'Like what?' Peg asked.

I cast my eyes downwards, searching the floor for inspiration, when, suddenly Peg flew past me towards the humans.

'What are you doing?' I barked quickly.

'Something I should have done a long time ago,' Peg called. 'Sorting my man-mad owner out once and for all. I won't let her ruin this for you, Percy.'

Watching Peg become nothing more than a speeding ball of blonde fur, curiosity got the better of me and I raced closer, hiding behind a bench to get a better view of the action.

Peg threw herself at Sally's legs and I gasped as Sally almost tripped and fell as she collided with her pug before managing to steady herself.

'Peg! What are you doing here?' I heard her exclaim.

As she bent down to pick Peg up, she placed the bouquet she was carrying under her arm and planted a kiss on her pug's head.

'Get off me, woman!' Peg yapped.

'It's lovely to see you,' Sally crooned, 'however did you get here?'

'On the Tube, like you probably did, you daft mare,' Peg replied.

But her words fell on deaf ears as Sally kissed the top of her head once more and, to my horror, waved at Simon and Gail who had now seen her coming towards them.

'Well, I don't know how you got here, young lady, we'll talk about that later,' Sally said, 'but right now, there's something I want to say to Simon and Gail.'

I saw Peg wriggle in protest and bark loudly. 'No, Sally. Don't do it. Simon isn't the man for you, don't break up a family. I know you want to be happy again, but not like this.'

But Peg's barks went unnoticed and my heart was in my mouth as I watched Sally march closer to Gail and Simon who still had their arms wrapped around one another. Peg shot me a helpless look from Sally's arms, but all I could do was watch in horror. Peg had done all she could to save my family and stop Sally doing something stupid, there was nothing else left but for me to go in and break this up.

I inched out of my hiding place and was just about to race towards the humans, but something in Gail's eyes stopped me. At the sight of Sally she smiled and opened her arms wide for my friend and her owner to fall into. As the two embraced, I watched Simon look at the trio hugging and saw he too was smiling. What was going on? Surely he should be terrified? Sally was about to ruin his life.

'Oh, Sally, thank you so much for coming,' I heard Gail say. 'And you brought Peg as well.'

'Oh, no, this little madam brought herself somehow,' Sally replied. 'So how has it all gone? How's Jenny?'

My ears pricked up. This was an answer I

was desperate to hear. Inching back into my hiding place again, I listened intently, taking care not to miss a word.

'She's doing brilliantly,' Gail replied, her eyes shining with happiness. 'She came out of theatre a couple of hours ago and the doctors say everything went just as it should. All being well, if her body doesn't reject the heart, she could be home in a few weeks, leading a normal life.'

Sally leaned in to kiss Gail on the cheek. 'That's wonderful, you two. I'm so pleased.'

Simon turned to Gail and grinned, hands firmly in his pockets. 'We couldn't be more delighted, Sal, it's the best Christmas present we could ever have hoped for.'

Sally chuckled as she thrust a bunch of flowers in Simon's direction. 'You won't need these then?'

'What are these for?' Simon asked.

He sniffed the blooms, while Sally looked sheepish. 'Peace offering. I just wanted to say I'm sorry about this morning. I should never have gone on at you like that when you had so much on your plate. I'd had a bad day at work, followed by a bad night's sleep and took it out on you. It was completely the wrong time.'

I couldn't take my eyes off Gail as I watched her face crinkle with laughter at

Sally's confession. What was happening? That had been the last thing I was expecting, and judging by Peg's wide-eyed look of wonder, she felt the same.

'Don't be silly, I'm sure he deserved it.' Gail giggled.

Sally shook her head. 'He really didn't. I'm sorry, Simon.'

'If anyone should be saying sorry, it's me,' Simon replied. 'I should never have abused your hospitality by staying at yours for so long.'

'No, you have been very kind to us, Sally. You've looked after Percy, let us both confide in you and taken Simon in when we were having troubles. I think it's only human to have lost your temper with him. Goodness knows, I do it often enough,' Gail admitted.

Simon raised his eyebrows. 'That's certainly true.'

'Seriously, it should be us giving you flowers, Sally,' Gail said. 'You've been a real friend to us. I don't know how we could have coped without you.'

'It really was nothing,' Sally replied.

'It was something to me,' Simon said. 'And, Gail, I need to apologise to you as well. I've been all over the place lately, and although I think leaving home was the right thing to do, I should never have lied to you about going over to Sally's after work or staying with her. I don't know why I did that.'

Gail rolled her eyes. 'Because you're a bloke, and blokes are usually a bit stupid.'

Sally smiled warmly. 'Couldn't agree more. No, I don't know why you did that either, Simon. But knowing you've always been a bit of a plonker, I told your wife immediately what was happening and said you still loved and adored her but had lost your way, and I would do my best to set you back on the right path.'

'Which was sweet of Sally, because I told her you'd lose your way permanently if you weren't more honest with me.' Gail laughed.

'Well, it looks as though you've all turned a corner now,' Sally said as Gail and Simon looked at one another.

'We'll see,' Gail said quietly. 'Now I know Jenny's going to be okay, I think we can both start to think clearly and look at what's best for our family.'

Sally pulled Gail and Simon towards her for a group hug and I looked at Peg, her little face peeking out underneath Sally's arm. She gazed at me in surprise, before wriggling out of Sally's arms and jumping to the floor.

'Peg! Where are you going?' Sally called.

But Peg was oblivious to her owner's

shouts and scampered over to me. 'Did you hear that, Percy?'

'Yes,' I barked happily. 'Sally was just Simon and Gail's friend after all.'

'And Simon behaved like a typical bloke and was a complete idiot,' Peg barked.

I screwed up my wrinkled face in protest. 'I'm not sure that's fair. You heard him, he wasn't thinking straight. He probably thought that if he told Gail he was staying with Sally she'd think the worst.'

Peg rubbed my nose with affection. 'Like you did you mean?'

'Like I did,' I barked in agreement.

After returning Peg's nose rub, I sat back on my haunches and shook my head sadly. How could I have got it all so wrong? I had been convinced Simon was cheating on Gail and realised I had made the classic doggy mistake of thinking two bones plus two bones equalled almost an entire cow!

There was no getting away from it, I had been stupid, and if I had taken the time to find out the truth, I might have managed to get Gail and Simon back together sooner. I had failed Gail, I had failed Jenny and all because I had allowed myself to leap to conclusions. All Gail wanted was a friend when she took me in from the tails of the forgotten, and I thought I was capable of so much more. Well, this was it, I thought to myself. No more meddling, if my pug-picnic plan failed, I would step back and allow my family to work things out themselves, which was perhaps what I should have done all along.

26

Watching all three humans approach us, I realised the time had come to put my final plan into action. Remembering my signal to Heather, I let out three sharp barks and, through the dog telegraph, the sound of two sharp barks came back almost immediately. I glanced at Peg just as Gail, Simon and Sally reached our side. We were ready.

'Percy!' Gail gasped. 'I can't believe you're at the hospital again! Although seeing Peg here, I should have guessed you'd be here too.'

'Where there's one, you'll usually find the other,' Sally said, laughing.

As Gail scooped me up into her arms and squeezed me tight, I licked her face affectionately. Peering past her shoulder, I saw Simon draw near and let out a bark of welcome before he ruffled my ears and kissed Gail on the cheek.

'All right, mate? Come to check up on us?'

I said nothing, happy to revel in the fact the two appeared to be getting on better than ever. Now I knew Sally was no threat, I realised that if there was any chance of them getting back together, it was now. Giving Gail another lick, I twisted myself loose and used her leg to scamper down to the floor. Sitting at her feet, I looked up at her smiling face and barked. 'Can you follow me?'

'Oh, sweetheart, I haven't got time for your games now, I've got to get back to Jenny. In fact, I think we should work out how to get you back home,' Gail said, as she checked her watch.

'Yes, I'm sure Doreen won't mind dropping him off again,' Simon added.

I whined irritably. I had not gone through all this to be whisked away by Doreen, lovely as she was, at the eleventh hour. I glanced back up at Peg, who gave me a slight nod of the head. Turning back to my family, I saw they were still discussing the best way of getting me home. Looking out to the car park, and the inky blue sky, I seized my chance and bolted.

'Percy!' Gail shouted. 'Come back! Where are you going?'

'Yeah, come on, mate,' Simon called, 'I'm too tired to chase you.'

But I paid no intention to their pleas and, as everyone dashed after me down the road, I continued towards my final destination, determined to make this plan a success. Just as before, I weaved in and out of human legs, the cool air whipping around my face as the humans plus Peg continued to follow. The faster I raced, the more I gulped for oxygen. I had never done so much exercise before and all this running up and down was causing me to suffer breathing difficulties. I slowed down, and snuggled deeper into my warm jacket, hoping to catch my breath. Thankfully, running at a slower pace worked a treat and, as I turned into the park, my breathing became easier and I was able to easily bark hello to the others and let them know I was nearly there.

As they came into view, I stopped in my tracks, unable to believe my eyes. Under the light of one of the old, Victorian lamps, my friends had spread the tartan blanket out so it formed a perfectly straight square. On it they had arranged all the meats, cheeses and snacks in the shape of a fan while the bottle of Prosecco rested on the side, suggesting the perfect way to start the celebrations.

Feeling a large cold droplet fall on my nose, my heart sank. Was it really raining? I glanced up at the sky in despair only to discover I was not being rewarded with the usual soggy British downpour but, instead, snow had put in an appearance just as it had all those years ago. I felt truly blessed and my heart swelled with love and gratitude for all my friends as I hurried towards them.

'We suddenly realised we didn't have any plates or glasses,' Jake barked, when he saw me, 'so it's all going to be a terrible mess, not the done thing at all, old thing.'

'Lighten up, Jake,' Boris teased, 'it's romantic.'

'That's what I said,' Heather barked. 'They can use their fingers to eat and swig the fizz out of the bottle. Half the fun of being a human, I imagine, is you get the chance to use opposable thumbs, which are a lot more fun than our old paws.'

I beamed at my friends. 'It's perfect, it really is. I just hope Gail and Simon agree.'

'Thanks, lovey,' Heather barked again. 'It really was no trouble, but it looks as though the moment of truth is almost here. Look, here everyone is now.'

Spinning around, I saw them all rush through the entrance and walk towards me. With their coats flapping open, and clouds of white breath rushing from their mouths, they appeared as out of breath as me and I wanted to put them out of their misery.

'Over here,' I barked.

At the sound of my woof, Gail ran to my side and, reaching me, her face broke into a delighted grin. She picked me up and kissed me all over. 'Percy! Thank God! I thought we'd lost you.'

'Yeah, buddy, you gave us a bit of a scare,' Simon added.

'Not to mention a workout,' Sally teased, breathing heavily.

As Peg jumped out of Sally's arms, she joined the others. They were all sitting around the back of the blanket like some sort of windbreak. As for me, I could barely contain myself and jumped out of Gail's arms onto the floor below, so one of them could stop looking at me and instead see the spread.

Eventually, Gail clasped her hands to her mouth and shrieked, 'Oh, my word! What's all this?'

Taking a step towards the blanket, she looked at the fan of food, and bottle of fizz that Peg had thoughtfully provided.

'Oh, my! Simon!' she gasped. 'This is wonderful!'

Before I could answer, Simon walked towards her and bent down.

'It really is,' he breathed. 'Look at it, just like the one we had all those years ago.'

'When you asked me to marry you.' Gail smiled, tears rolling down her face as she wrapped her arms around her husband. As I watched Gail clasp Simon's face between her palms and kiss him firmly on the lips, I felt a surge of love and it was all I could do not to jump up and down in delight. The picnic was working!

'You work tirelessly for our family every day, and this,' he said, his eyes drifting back to the spread on the floor. 'This has reminded me that you are the lynchpin that holds us all together. I would be lost without you, Gail.'

'And I'd be lost without you,' she said simply, sinking onto the picnic blanket and hugging her knees with delight.

Simon sat next to his wife, and picked up one of the rollmops Boris had found.

'Remember these?' He laughed, holding one out to Gail.

'I do,' Gail said, chuckling. 'I was so touched you remembered how much I loved those all those years ago, even though you hated them. It was one of the reasons why I said yes when you asked me to marry you.'

'And what were the other reasons?' Simon asked, before kissing his wife gently on the lips as the snow continued to fall.

'Because you're good, kind, thoughtful,' she whispered. 'Because you make amazing bacon sandwiches. Because you know just how much I love *Dirty Dancing* and always watch it with me even though you think it's soppy. Because you're an incredible father, who loves our child more than life itself.'

I held my breath as Simon wrapped his arm around his wife, and kissed her properly.

'And what about you?' she asked gently as they parted. 'Do you still love me?'

Simon looked down and tilted Gail's chin up with his finger. 'I can't believe you even have to ask. The moment I saw you I knew you were my world, and when we kissed for the first time, I felt like I'd come home. My world stops and ends with you, Gail. It always has and always will. You, Jenny and Percy are everything to me. I don't want to lose any of you. I've been a fool to push you away.'

'No, I've been the fool,' Gail said. 'Instead of talking to you, I snapped at you because deep down I blamed you for Jenny's condition, and hated myself for feeling like that when I knew it wasn't your fault.'

'Gail, stop beating yourself up,' Simon said gently. 'If I'd have been in your position I would have felt just the same way. What's important now is the future.'

Hearing the word 'future', I whined and looked up at my friends. They were all gripped by what was happening. Jake's paw was resting on Heather's, while Bugsy and Boris had slumped to the floor. Boris had one paw over Bugsy's eyes and I chuckled, realising the Border collie would find it difficult to watch the scene unfold as he was easily embarrassed and hated seeing people kiss. Behind them stood Sally — she too had tears rolling down her cheeks and I immediately felt guilty for thinking she had been trying to break up a home. Just like me, all she was really guilty of was trying to put a family back together.

Out of the corner of my eye, I caught sight of Peg and saw her tongue had lolled to the side of her mouth as she stared up at Gail and Simon, her eyes filled with hope. My heart swelled with love. Watching Simon and Gail declare their love for one another made me realise that it was time to tell Peg that I wanted to be more than friends. My feelings had been growing for the pug by the day, and now I knew I was not returning to the tails of the forgotten, I felt sure we could have a future together.

I padded towards her and put my mouth to her ear. 'I love you,' I barked.

Peg turned to me, her eyes filled with surprise and longing. 'I love you too,' she replied gently. 'I've always loved you; you made me more breathless than I was already when I met you.'

I could scarcely believe my ears as I gazed into her gorgeous eyes. Peg felt the same way as me. Christmas truly was the most magical time of the year.

'For the love of Snoopy, at least rub noses with her, Perce!' Heather barked. 'You two are made for each other, any fool can see that!'

I broke my gaze and looked around at my friends to see they were all beaming with delight at me and Peg. Carefully, I took a step towards the pug and rubbed my nose against hers as my pals barked their cheers.

Pulling away, I saw Peg's eyes were filled with love. Giving her one final lick on her ear, I turned back to my friends and regarded them all fondly. We had all been on this journey together, rooting for Simon and Gail for so long. Now with Jenny safely on the mend, there was a chance of a happy ending and we all desperately wanted them to take it.

'Come home, Simon,' Gail whispered, breaking the silence. 'Come home and let's be a family again.'

'There's nothing I would like more,' Simon whispered.

Epilogue

As the fire crackles in the grate, I stretch all four of my paws out lazily on the rug and watch in delight as Jenny rips off the paper of her last present. It has been twelve months since her heart transplant and if I hadn't eaten so much bacon at breakfast I would be joining her now as she jumps up and down on the rug, admiring the new computer she has received this Christmas.

'Thanks, Mum and Dad,' she says, beaming, 'this is truly epic.'

'You're welcome.' Simon smiles. 'Just don't ask me for help using the thing, it looks like you need a degree in physics just to turn it on.'

'Daaaaad,' she moans. 'You're so uncool.'

'I know,' he says happily, sinking back onto the sofa and pulling Gail in for a hug.

I grin to myself. There was a time Simon would have tried to convince his little girl he was still a cool father but, since he moved back in last Christmas Day, a lot changed. Not only did he become more thankful of the simpler pleasures in life, but he also got rid of his man cave, which is just as well, as he and

Gail are now expecting another baby at Easter.

When Gail discovered she was pregnant, I will confess she had what could only be described as a meltdown. She ate a lot of chocolate, wept that giving birth to a baby had really hurt, but mainly worried about whether this child would have another heart defect like Jenny's.

I told her that life is something nobody has any control over and reminded her that you have to take happiness where you can find it. The wonderful thing is Jenny is now doing wonderfully well, which is a huge source of comfort to both Simon and Gail.

Naturally, Jenny had a long recovery after the surgery, but as her health improved she became just like any other teenager, something that started with the frequent reminders she gave, informing us she was almost an adult because she was thirteen. We all guessed it was something she had picked up at her new school, because although she has to be careful, her scars have naturally meant she is the coolest kid in her year and everyone wants to be her friend.

Watching her now, race up the stairs to find her mobile phone so she can swap Christmas present stories with her friends, fills my heart with gladness. There are times it seems hard to believe Jenny was ever poorly at all. It really is wonderful to only worry about whether or not she has done her homework instead of whether she might live or die.

I get up and stretch. The fire has become too hot for me and, more than anything, I want a cuddle with my family. I have already been spoiled this Christmas with so many gifts, like a new bed, bags full of treats, chew toys and squeaky rabbits, not to mention lots of tennis balls for me to play with. But all I really want is to be with my owners right now and, as I pad across the room towards the sofa, I see Gail has propped her legs up on Simon and is stroking her newly rounded bump. Seeing me sit by the corner of the settee looking upwards, her face breaks out into a massive grin.

'Come on then, Perce.' She smiles, patting her lap.

'How are you doing, Gail?' I bark softly, as I settle onto the warm space between her and Simon.

'I've never been happier, my lovely boy.' She smiles again, kissing me softly on the nose.

'Good,' I bark. 'Me neither.'

'Or me,' Simon adds.

Both Gail and I look up at him in astonishment. Simon has never been able to understand me as well as Gail, and so it is a complete surprise he has worked out what I just said.

'I've been practising my communication skills,' he says, shrugging. 'The therapist told me it would be good for our marriage.'

I nod in understanding. After the picnic, although Simon and Gail were on cloud nine when he moved back in, they were realistic enough to realise they needed to solve their problems. Sensibly, they enlisted the help of a therapist and worked through their marital issues. Now they are the envy of all their friends and family, who accuse them of acting like newlyweds, which goes some way to explaining Gail's pregnancy.

As for me, I wake up every day feeling blessed. I worked so hard to try to get Gail and Simon back together and now we really are one big happy family I know how lucky I am. I have stopped worrying about whether or not I will be sent back to the shelter. I have realised that even though life changes it does not necessarily spell disaster, and families stick together through thick and thin. Then of course there are my friends who I see every day, and I continue to be so thankful they are a huge part of my life.

The big news is that Jake has proved there really is life in the old dog yet, as he and

Heather have started dating. It happened shortly after the picnic, as apparently their eyes met while they were laying out sausage rolls and the rest as they say is history.

Bugsy still has a fair amount of growing up to do, but he is definitely getting there. As for Boris, we still keep in touch, but now I no longer have a reason to trek into London to the hospital, we are not able to see as much of one another as I would like. Still, the dog telegraph reliably informs me he too has met a lady, but sadly the same communication network is somewhat undecided as to who the lucky bitch is.

I look at Gail, see her eyes shining with happiness and rest my chin on her bump so she can stroke me with her hands. Lying on her lap is something I will never tire of, and I sometimes wonder if there is a huge price to pay for being so happy. Without warning the doorbell sounds, interrupting my thoughts. As Simon gets up to answer it, I jump down from the sofa and follow him out into the hallway, with a sneaking suspicion as to who it is. Sure enough, as Simon flings the door open, I see Sally and Peg on the doorstep.

'Happy Christmas!' Sally gushes, kissing him on the cheek.

Simon returns her embrace. 'Happy Christmas to you too, Sal. Good to see you.'

Simon shuts the door behind Sally and takes her coat and the bottle of wine she has brought around. I bark a 'Happy Christmas' to Peg, before sitting down at Sally's feet waiting for a head stroke. Since the picnic, she and I have become quite close, and I have found that she is such a lovely, warm and caring lady I am convinced it is only a matter of time before she meets Mr Right. Peg and I have thought about setting her up on a date, but after spending so long fixing Gail and Simon's problems the whole gang has decided to give relationship issues amongst our owners a miss for a while.

With Sally safely welcomed, I turn to Peg to greet her properly. 'Happy Christmas, you. Have you had a nice day?'

'So far,' she yelps. 'But now we're together, I think it's about to get a whole lot better.'

I flush with pleasure. Peg always knows just what to bark to make me blush. Gently, I propel her towards the kitchen, I want to show her the present I have got her for Christmas before we all tuck into lunch.

'What's this?' Peg asks, as I push a large package towards her wrapped in silver paper.

As she sniffs it curiously, I watch with pleasure as she tears the paper off. Naturally, I was unable to wrap it myself, but Gail and I went shopping especially for my girlfriend last week and I picked out the gift and paper.

'Oh, wow! A pink bone-shaped bed with my name on it! I love it!' Peg woofs with delight.

As she sniffs it again, she treads little circles around it before bellyflopping onto it with pleasure, paws hanging over all sides. It's wonderful to see her so contented and relaxed. Lately, I have noticed she has been really tired and that was how I came up with the idea of a new bed. I thought it might help her sleep better.

'So I imagine you're wondering where your present is?' she yelps lazily.

'Er, no,' I bark, 'I wasn't expecting anything.'

'Weren't you?' Peg protests. 'Well, in that case, I shouldn't have bothered.'

'Oh, well, if you — '

'Course, I got you a present, Percy!' she teases, cutting me off.

'Where is it?' I ask.

As I look out into the hallway trying to see a box or bag with my name on it, Sally, Gail and Simon emerge from the living room, squealing with excitement.

'Percy! My man!' Simon says, scooping me up in his arms. 'Congratulations, I never knew you had it in you!'

Puzzled, I search his eyes, wondering what

on earth he is talking about, only for Gail to smother my face in kisses.

'I can't believe it, Perce! I'm so proud of you.' She beams, before bending down to stroke Peg. 'And you, girl, just think, we're going through the same thing together! It's going to be wonderful.'

I turn to Peg, wondering if everyone has had too much festive juice, when Jenny suddenly appears at the kitchen doorway.

'What's going on?' she asks, removing her headphones and staring at me, Peg and the adults in clear bemusement.

'Percy's going to be a dad!' Gail gushes. 'Peg's pregnant.'

'OMG!' Jenny gasps, her hands flying to her mouth in shock. 'That is epic, Perce!'

'It's more than epic, it's brilliant!' Simon yells.

As he smiles down at me, I turn back to Peg, a mixture of shock and delight coursing through my little body. 'Is this true?' I bark. 'Is this my present? Are you really having my puppies?'

'Happy Christmas,' Peg woofs contentedly. 'The vet told me and Sal yesterday. Congratulations, Perce, you're going to be a brilliant daddy.'

Looking across at Peg once more, I feel a prickle of fear. What if I turn out to be a

terrible dad? What if I let Peg down? Or worse, my own pups? I feel like crying myself, suddenly overwhelmed by the sheer responsibility of it all when I feel Gail scoop me up in her arms.

Wordlessly, she carries me to the kitchen door and together we look out across at the garden where we have enjoyed so many heartfelt moments over the past year.

'You've done so much for my family,' she whispers. 'You might not think I realise just what you've done for us, but I do. Now, I want to do everything I can to help yours.'

I turn to her and rub her cold nose with my wet one. Since moving to Barksdale Way, Gail had made me realise I was very far from unlovable, and now it was time for me to prove the very same thing to my own offspring. If there was one thing I could be sure of, it was that all my pups would realise love was always more than enough.

Acknowledgements

Huge thanks must first of all go to my wonderful agent, Kate Burke at Diane Banks Associates, and my fabulous editor, Sally Williamson. Their patience, support, tireless generosity and endless supply of biscuits have made crafting this novel a great pleasure.

Special thanks must also go to Daniel Prescott and Sarah Regan at Cardiomyopathy UK. Sarah was kind enough to answer all my questions from the downright ludicrous to the plain stupid. Any mistakes contained within these pages are entirely my own.

All the pug owners who let me babysit and play with their dogs so I could understand how wonderful pugs are, thank you. I promise now to stop hounding you in supermarket car parks in a bid to find out all about your dog, so, rest assured, you can now shop safely and in peace.

I would also like to say thank-you to the lovely Jennifer Krebs and Charlotte Mursell at HarperCollins who have done their best to haul me out of the dark ages and make me more active on social media. I'm a work in progress and still trying!

And not forgetting the deep gratitude I would like to express to my very own support crew: Rebecca Irwin, Rebecca Marrion, Craig Evry, Team McLaughlin, Barbara Copperthwaite, Karen Shaw, the Wednesday Lady Butterflies, and the Lobina clan. Your patience as I talked nothing but Pug, along with all your help, funny pug pictures and stories have all been greatly appreciated, and Percy would not be alive and well without you all.

Finally, but very importantly, a massive thanks to my parents, Barry and Maureen, and my husband, Chris. You always believed I could do this, even when I was unsure — thank you!

We do hope that you have enjoyed reading this large print book.

Did you know that all of our titles are available for purchase?

We publish a wide range of high quality large print books including:
Romances, Mysteries, Classics
General Fiction
Non Fiction and Westerns

Special interest titles available in large print are:
The Little Oxford Dictionary
Music Book
Song Book
Hymn Book
Service Book

Also available from us courtesy of Oxford University Press:
Young Readers' Dictionary
(large print edition)
Young Readers' Thesaurus
(large print edition)

For further information or a free brochure, please contact us at:
Ulverscroft Large Print Books Ltd.,
The Green, Bradgate Road, Anstey,
Leicester, LE7 7FU, England.
Tel: (00 44) 0116 236 4325
Fax: (00 44) 0116 234 0205